THE TIME THAT'S GIVEN

A Novel by

DAVID LITWACK

THE TIME THAT'S GIVEN

FIRST EDITION SOFTCOVER

ISBN: 1622534425

ISBN-13: 978-1-62253-442-5

Editor: Lane Diamond

Cover Artist: Cindy Fan

Interior Designer: Lane Diamond

www.EvolvedPub.com

Evolved Publishing LLC

Butler, Wisconsin, USA

Printed in Book Antiqua font.

BOOKS BY DAVID LITWACK

Along the Watchtower

The Daughter of the Sea and the Sky

THE SEEKERS (3-Book Series)
Book 1: *The Children of Darkness*
Book 2: *The Stuff of Stars*
Book 3: *The Light of Reason*

The Time That's Given

FOREWORD

Oh, the power of a great story. Let's face it: we humans need stories. They teach us about who we are—where we came from and where we're heading. They also, when done well, make us better people by forcing us to ask ourselves if we're doing the right thing, or if we can just do a little better.

As an example, David Litwack offers us this gem from Chapter 7 (a chapter destined to be a classic lesson in great fiction):

~~~

The words of the ghost stories faded into the background, and I felt alone, just me and a universe bigger than I'd ever conceived. A single thought rang out in my mind: I am! *I realized I was no longer a child, an extension of my parents. I was a sentient being with hopes, fears, and dreams of my own. What lay ahead was* my *life, to live as I chose.*

The choice: to burn brightly for a brief time like the embers of the fire, or to never flare at all; to make a difference, or to one day vanish without leaving a trace.

~~~

This book offers so many of those kinds of moments, in which we might, as readers, say, "Yeah... exactly. Hmmm... wait a minute...." And who can't use a little prodding from time to time?

More than that, however, *The Time That's Given* felt to me like a very personal story, a glimpse inside the heart, mind, and soul of the author. As David's business partner, publisher, and editor, perhaps I have insights that you do not, but David's recent life seems to have fueled much—or most—of this story. As a result, we get an intimate view of a good man, trying to make sense of the senseless, trying to find purpose where so much of what *was* his purpose has been taken from him.

All authors pour a little of themselves into their work. It's perfectly natural; after all, how might we delve into our characters and bring them to full life, if we don't call on our own experiences, attitudes, opinions, blessings, curses, education, prejudices—the whole package. We offer little tidbits of ourselves, perhaps sprinkled sparingly here and there. Yet within the pages of *The Time That's Given*, we have something different: we have one of those rare occasions where the author's story is not only influenced in some small way by the author's life, it's truly *inspired* by that life.

I've always thought well of the man, who has repeatedly struck me as an intelligent, caring, generous man of integrity and strong character. Now comes *The Time That's Given* and, though it might not have seemed possible, I like David Litwack even more.

Even if you don't know David, you will come to know and love these characters. And if you should come to love, in that distant way we often love an actor or an author or a public figure, then all the better. You will have chosen well.

Dave Lane (aka Lane Diamond)
CEO, Managing Publisher/ Editor
Evolved Publishing LLC

DEDICATION

In loving memory of Mary Anne,
and for Amy and Lisa, and a future filled with hope.

THE TIME THAT'S GIVEN

DAVID LITWACK

PART ONE

THE CANDLE'S FLAME

"To light a candle is to cast a shadow."
Ursula K. Le Guin

Chapter 1 – The Dimming

It came upon me one late winter evening as I waited for the call that never came. I'd been anxious to hear from Betty, but when the phone rang, Helen's voice sang out instead, too cheery for the circumstance.

Of course. How could she know?

Betty had been discreet, telling no one but me. No need to upset our expectant daughter needlessly.

A nor'easter of medium proportions had blown in that morning, leaving not much snow, but whipping the landscape with such stinging sleet that it forced me to cancel my walk and stay indoors. With little left to do but cook my customary meal of chicken and rice, and worry about my dear wife, I pondered how little value I added to the world.

Since retiring nine months before, I anchored my days with a trek to the Lexington green, site of the first battle of the revolutionary war and the shot heard round the world. There, I'd circle to the front, gaze into the eyes of the minuteman statue, and pat his patina-coated musket before returning home—a trip of four and a half miles. On the way back, I'd ignore the growing pain in my left hip and envision the minuteman confronting his fate with dignity and courage, awaiting the redcoats and the chance to change the world. Though no such opportunity loomed in my future, I'd square my shoulders and jut out my chin, mimicking the statue, and quicken my pace as I conjured up heroic acts of my own.

Now, with the tree branches glazed and the driveway too slick to stand, I puttered about my kitchen, slotting dishes into the dishwasher and wiping down the tabletop with a sponge I should have replaced two weeks ago. Thanks to the storm, I spent the entire day still in my slippers and bathrobe, indulging my internet addiction. Around me, the cable TV blared, the laptop flashed, and my iPhone beeped. Every few minutes, I checked for messages, hoping for a surprise—a contact from an old friend, a text from Mark, or the much-awaited news from Betty. No such luck. Nothing but political solicitations and ads.

Yesterday, I stayed indoors as well, but not because of the weather. I'd awoken to a bulletin of another terror attack, this time at a nightclub in the wee hours of the morning. Young revelers celebrating their youth had been gunned down, with dozens killed and many more wounded. I sat glued to the story as it unfolded, positioning my computer screen so I could peer over it to the oversized TV on the wall. I poked around blogs for more details, trying to make sense of the senseless, until the sunlight dimmed and my eyelids drooped.

I'd slept fitfully last night and switched on my media first thing this morning, hoping for a glimmer of good news. A quick check, I promised myself, no more. Stories like yesterday's fed my addiction. Regardless of what I found today, I promised I'd tear myself away and escape to the fresh air for my walk, but the storm had thwarted my plan.

I'd lived alone since Betty went off to Ithaca in January. At college, she'd majored in art, and had taught the subject in middle school for twenty-five years, but always, she mused about reviving a career of her own.

When we both retired last June, we traveled the world and reveled in quiet moments together, but I was prone to darker moods and, with so much time on my hands, I began to grate on her otherwise sunny disposition.

On an unseasonably chilly day in September, she announced her intention to pursue her lifelong dream. While I preferred a less eventful retirement, my life partner of thirty-one years and mother of my children had different aspirations. How could I blame her? Despite her oncologist's assurance of an eighty-three percent survival rate at five years, her bout with breast cancer had left her mindful of her mortality. As the five years approached, and I worried about each mammogram, she grew more eager to take advantage of her remaining time on this earth. After thoughtful deliberation, she gathered her courage and a portfolio of her paintings, and applied to get her MFA. Though neither of us expected any school would accept this sixty-something former art teacher, Cornell responded that they'd love to have her.

When I grumbled about being left alone, she urged me to join her, reminding me I was retired and had nothing to tie me down. But I was in the midst of a reading of *The Lord of the Rings,* the fourth of my lifetime. The first had been as a thirteen-year-old newly addicted to fantasy, the second a marathon recitation conducted in my college dorm, and the third after my father died. Now, halfway through the Two Towers, I was not about to abandon Frodo on his trek to Mordor. Yet something more insidious was at play. In my brief retirement, I'd begun to retreat from the world, increasingly withdrawing to my study and losing myself in my backlog of books.

Betty refused to back down. The program only lasted two years, and a mere ten months per year at that, plus she could fly home for the occasional holiday weekend. She insisted time would pass quickly and I'd adapt. So, shortly after Christmas, she packed up her artwork and went off to study high above Cayuga's waters.

In the three months since she left, I failed to adapt at all. I missed sitting across the table from her at meals, as we shared the day's news and our innermost thoughts, and I slept poorly at night, unaccustomed to lying in bed alone.

Together, we'd raised Mark and Helen. Mark now resided on the west coast with his wife, the two of them busy with their careers in high tech, and with their self-absorbed decoration of their new home, a faux castle on a hillside overlooking San Francisco Bay.

Helen, our youngest, lived with her husband a mere half hour away. I adored Helen, though since Betty left, she fussed over me to no end, urging me to buy one of those bracelets to alert someone if I fell or became incapacitated. We'd developed a recurring routine. She'd nag, and I'd assure her I was healthy, fit, and not *that* old. I encouraged her to worry less, especially now that she was expecting my first grandchild.

With Helen's due date approaching, Betty decided to forego her final class before Easter and come home for the birth. She'd been scheduled to arrive today, but the storm had cancelled her flight, and with the whole east coast under a blizzard, she was unable to rebook for two more days.

I hoped Helen's baby didn't come early.

Now a new wrinkle: Betty's latest mammogram at the Cornell Medical Center had showed a cloudy mass—likely benign, the doctor had said, but he took a biopsy to be safe. As far as I knew, no results had come back.

After her flight was cancelled, why had she called Helen rather than me? Was she afraid to tell me over the phone?

A beeping from the TV interrupted my thoughts, along with a drumroll and sculpted logo heralding breaking news.

Now what?

I'd wasted yesterday watching coverage of the terror attack. How could I bear a new crisis? No crisis followed, but I winced nonetheless as a female anchor informed me that two hundred days remained until the next election.

An urge came over me, making my hands shake. If I were to remain in the dark about Betty's news, and helpless in the face of events, I could at least escape from the world, constrict my space, and be totally, utterly alone.

I silenced the talking head on the TV, shut down my computer, and powered off my iPhone. Then I double-knotted my bathrobe tie and retreated to the small study used to pay bills and read—the only room with no windows in my sprawling seven-room home.

In the past few years, I'd decorated the eight-by-eight with souvenirs from the trips Betty and I had taken abroad—after our nest had emptied and before she went off to school. A faded tapestry covered the left wall, one I bought in Carcassonne for nine-hundred and thirty-eight dollars despite Betty's objections. It depicted a castle complete with moat and drawbridge, and a knight on armored horse trotting across it. Opposite the tapestry, a glass case housed my collection of eclectic artifacts, Roman and Japanese swords, a steel breastplate, a plumed helmet, and several gypsy charms.

By the door stood the Ikea bookcase I'd assembled to store my fantasy novels. Though still half-empty, a few dozen covers blared at me with images of heroes and dragons, demons, sorceresses, and elves. I grabbed the latest, with the leather bookmark protruding midway through the pages, intending to lose myself in its prose.

After shutting the door, I cleared the clutter from the surface of the desk to make space for my elbows—and perhaps a place for my head, should I doze off—but before cracking open the book, I leaned in to admire the shelf above the desk that contained my collection of candles. I'd made a habit of buying a candle unique to every location we visited. Each had a story behind it.

Whereas Betty preferred art galleries with modern sculpture, my preference tended more to the obscure and occult. The trips became our first parting of the ways. She'd tour museums, while I'd wander off the beaten path, scavenging through cluttered alleyways in older sections of the city, searching for medieval weapons, figurines of knights, wizard's wands... and candles.

I eyed the candles one at a time: the tall one from Jerusalem with the blue and white braided wax, used to mark Sabbath's end; the elephant from Delhi with the wick sticking up from his rump; an Irish rose with the wick nestled between its petals; the tacky Stratford on Avon skull I couldn't resist buying—poor Yorick, etc.; a winged cherub from Rome bearing an urn upon its shoulder; two parakeets nuzzling; and my favorite, the one molded in the shape of a boy.

I picked up the last and fingered its surface, recalling how I'd discovered it in a dusty shop off an alley in the old city of Prague. The shopkeeper had urged me to handle it with care.

"A unique candle," he said. "It will provide light when nothing else can dispel the darkness."

I suppressed a grin. I liked the look of the candle but found the storekeeper odd. "Are you suggesting this candle is *magic*?"

The man drew closer. "Magic indeed."

"Will it grant my every wish?" I asked, playing along. The sandalwood incense pervading the shop must have dulled my skepticism.

He chortled, an unnerving sound. "Not wishes. It's not a genie in a bottle."

"Then will it provide answers to my hardest questions?"

His magnified eyes glistened through coke-bottle glasses as he whispered these words. "Not wishes, not answers, but this candle will light your way so you may find the answers you seek. Of course, its success depends on the questions you ask."

I struggled to maintain my manners, though a part of me wanted to believe—the reason I searched in these alleyways.

As I groped in my pocket to pay, he gripped my arm and squeezed until he commanded my attention. "A warning: don't light it frivolously."

I pulled out a twenty euro note and extended it to him, but he withdrew the candle.

"Not enough?" I said.

"I cannot sell this boy alone."

I smirked. These tourist shops were all the same. "How much more?"

"Nothing, but a second piece must accompany it."

"But *wait*, there's more," I mumbled under my breath, parroting a thousand commercials I'd seen on TV.

The shopkeeper released my arm and shuffled behind the counter. From beneath it, he pulled out something concealed in the palm of his hand. As he extended it to me, his fingers spread, revealing a thumb-sized vial that glowed with a purple iridescence, though it was unclear whether the color came from the glass or the liquid inside. The vial was capped by a black cork.

"Take this as well. No charge."

"Is this potion magic too?"

The shopkeeper's lip curled, a slight wrinkle, but less than a smile. "The candle will light your way, but in the moment of choosing, this will bring you peace."

I checked my watch. Betty would be waiting by now.

I reached for the vial, anxious to leave, but he pulled it back one last time. "Never open it until it's time to choose."

Now, smiling at the memory of that encounter, I fondled the candle and wondered. The wax had been sculpted with exquisite detail and dyed with subtle tones. The boy stood at attention on glistening black boots, with skin-tight gray pants tucked into them. A short red waistcoat fit tightly over slim hips, and gold epaulets made his shoulders more square. An ornamental belt girded his waist with what appeared to be a dagger hanging from it. On his head, he wore a tricorn hat like that of the minuteman, but this one had a gilded edge. A purple plume rose from its top and, although made of wax, it gave the illusion of waving in the breeze.

Most striking was the boy's face. The artisan who'd molded the piece had taken care with the features—a solid chin contrasted with a puckish nose; round cheeks displayed a flush so robust, blood might be flowing through them; and thin lips curled into a Mona Lisa smile. The figurine bore an impression of powerful innocence.

I nodded to myself, as I was wont to do when I'd made a decision. For the months since Betty left, I'd rattled about the house when not on my walk. I prepared and ate meals, showered and dressed, brushed my teeth, and kept the house clean. I watched football on weekends and read novels until my eyelids drooped.

I set up a Facebook profile, googled old colleagues and friends, and invited them to friend me. I joined groups for fantasy lovers and wikis for my favorite authors. I followed links from one to the next and bookmarked those I liked. My list grew so long that, by the time I followed them all, read their articles and scanned their comment sections, I could loop back to the top and find fresh content. The result: I spent entire mornings browsing, until my stomach growled and the clock on the screen showed noon, yet none of it made me wiser.

I fingered the candle. *'...you may find the answers you seek.'*

Now was the time

As I fumbled through the drawer for a book of matches, my hand brushed the vial, dusty from its exile in the dark. I pulled it out as well—the shopkeeper has made such a fuss about the two staying together—and placed it on the desk next to the candle.

After three breaths in and out, I struck a match and lit the wick.

The flame hissed and flickered, then settled into an even glow. A moment later, I rose on wobbly knees, shuffled to the door to switch off the light, wobbled back and plopped on the leather office chair to study the flame.

As the hat atop the boy's head began to melt, time slowed and the space narrowed—as I'd hoped—but the change continued beyond what I'd intended. A sinking feeling crept over me, as if some unseen hand was lowering me in a bucket down a deep well, and the circle of light overhead receded.

The flame flared—an event I oddly expected—and its yellow turned blood red as it rose a foot or more. Now angry and tall, it seemed more blow torch than candle. Fearing its heat, I rolled the chair back, but as I did so, I caught out of the corner of my eye a liquid shadow rolling across the floor, a dread encroaching like the onset of old age.

I turned to confront the shadow—just my imagination, nothing more. After a few seconds staring into the dark, I swiveled back to the candle, and the flame seemed to glow brighter than before. I held my breath and listened. In the silence, I imagined a muffled moan, like the sound fog might make as it dragged across the ground.

For the past months, I'd nurtured a fantasy worthy of my books, that an evil virus had infested the world and only I had discovered this, and that I would spend my latter years finding its source and destroying it. Now, dwelling on this delusion, I embellished it with details—a face conjured in the flame, a magical sword materializing in my grasp, perhaps a charmed amulet around my neck.

My reverie was interrupted by a hissing from behind, too loud to be imagined. When I searched the room for its source, I found the shadow had indeed taken substance. It flowed across the floor in waves, climbed to the foot of my chair, blackened the hem of my robe, and rose until my hands grayed as they fumbled for some means of defense. At last, the shadow reached the candle and spread from the boots of the boy to the plumed hat.

Then it touched the flame.

Poof.

The flame extinguished, and the room went dark.

I groped on the desktop for the matches, regretting I'd so casually tossed them aside, but as my fingertips swept the wooden surface, I knocked them to the floor. Over my sixty-two years, the floor had grown farther away; some mornings, I struggled to tie my shoes. Here, in total darkness, I had little chance of finding the matches, so I rose instead and hobbled to the door, my slippers slapping above the hiss of the shadow. I located the doorknob, but when I tried to turn it, it spun in my grasp, as if protected by one of those safety attachments parents use to keep toddlers in place. I patted the wall beside the door, found the jamb, and slid my fingers along it to where the light switch should be.

Nothing but polished wood.

Helen was right. I should have ordered one of those life alert buttons, though with the weirdness pervading this room, I suspect all technology would fail.

Before panic overwhelmed me, a glimmer of light flickered from behind.

I spun around.

A boy stood next to the desk, his face aglow as if illuminated by a spotlight from above. No... not quite a boy. Yes, he bore a slight stature with the slim hips and narrow shoulders of youth. Yes, his skin shone smooth as wax, with no furrow across his brow and no crow's feet about his eyes. Yet he carried himself like a more mature man, and those eyes... deep wells of brown that exuded a lifetime—or perhaps many lifetimes—of experience with a harsh world. Wisps of gray slipped out from beneath the brim of a familiar hat and tumbled about his ears.

I gasped when I recognized that hat, a tricorn with a gilded edge and a purple plume. Before me stood the boy from the candle, life-size and alive.

"Who are you?" A quiver invaded my voice, and it surprised me to be taking these events seriously. I'd slept poorly the night before, and this was surely a dream.

"I am the guide you summoned, Albert Higgins." The boy's pitch was more youthful than adult, but his tone sounded clipped and formal, like one accustomed to the ways of an Elizabethan court. His words bore a hint of an accent, Scottish perhaps, but from a highland village remote from the modern world.

Despite the situation, my lifelong aversion to my birth name sprang to the fore. "I didn't summon you, and don't call me Albert. No one has called me that since my mother died."

This so-called guide glanced at his boot tops and shuffled his feet like a grade-schooler chastised by his teacher. "Then what shall I call you?"

"Burt is what my friends call me... the few I have."

"I'm sorry. Burt it shall be from now on."

I wanted to give him a moment to collect himself, but I couldn't contain my curiosity. The two days stuck in the house had bored me, and if this were a dream, I intended to take full advantage of it. "Let's say I go along and pretend you're real. Where are you supposed to guide me to?"

"To wherever you seek."

I glanced at the floor where, in the glow cast by the boy, the murky shadow swirled around my ankles. "Where does this gloom come from?

"From the source of despair."

"Ah! And where is that?"

"A complex question with no single answer. I can bring you to a place where you may seek the answer yourself... assuming you wish to go."

I pictured the snow swirling outside. "I wish to go."

His eyes drooped at the corners, intense brown eyes that might have been a thousand years old, but still no crow's feet formed. "Are you certain?"

The question made me wary, but I determined to take the chance. It was, after all, a dream.

I nodded.

"Very well, but first, you've forgotten something—that which must accompany me on all my journeys." He gestured to the desk, where the shopkeeper's vial now throbbed purple.

I shuffled over, grasped it, and slipped it into my pocket, keeping my fingers wrapped around it. The glass felt hot to the touch.

I glanced back at my guide, and heaved my shoulders up and down. "I'm ready."

"Very well, Burt. Come with me."

"I'm still in my bathrobe and slippers. Can't I change first?"

"No need."

The boy slid one hand to his hip, where it rested on the pommel of his dagger, a clear crystal ball with a glowing spark within that mirrored the purple of the vial. He extended his other hand to me. When I demurred, he stepped closer and beckoned with such empathy that I could no longer resist.

I expected his hand to be cold and lifeless, like wax, but a pulse throbbed through his fingers as if blood rushed through the veins.

A flutter filled my stomach, and I swallowed hard. *What if this isn't a dream?*

"Come with me," he said, "if you hope to find the answers you seek." He led me toward the lone exit of the windowless room.

I hesitated, knowing the knob wouldn't turn.

Sensing my reluctance, he winked at me, and the Mona Lisa smile curled at the corners, a complex gesture beyond what the most accomplished artisan could mold from wax.

Entranced, I followed.

Then, without testing the knob, we stepped straight through the solid wooden door.

Chapter 2 – The Children's March

We emerged not into the shelter of my living room, but to the fully exposed outdoors. A light wind brushed my cheeks, making me bunch my bathrobe around my neck. With no parka or hat, or scarf or gloves to protect me from the cold, I anticipated being buffeted by sleet, but I needed no such protection. A bright sun shone overhead, and the breeze embraced me with warmth.

As my mind tried to grasp what I saw, my vision blurred, and what appeared to be heat waves rippled up from the ground. The earth undulated beneath my feet as if I stood on the deck of a ship in a storm. I stumbled and nearly fell.

My guide caught me by the elbow and gave a nod of assurance. "It's always this way for those who travel with me. Transition between worlds is hard, but the wooziness lasts only a few seconds."

I closed my eyes and counted to ten. True to his word, the unsettling sensation passed. Once the ground steadied, I glanced around to assess my new surroundings.

We stood at the edge of a dirt road on the side of a hill, up to our knees in a field of goldenrod. Far ahead, an impressive vista loomed. Mountains rose in the distance, their saw-toothed peaks jutting up to jab the sky. A ribbon of blue snaked along their base, what must have been a broad river. Downhill, to my right, nestled a shire-like village, a place that might have given birth to the heroes of my fantasy novels. Thatched-roof cottages clustered in a circle, forming a modest farming community situated by the banks of the river.

Uphill, the road rose to a craggy crest, on top of which stood a more forbidding structure, in circumference as broad as the village. A stone wall girded it with Arthurian-like battlements rising at intervals. The dirt road that wound toward it changed to cobblestones before a drawbridge, now lowered, allowing access through an arched gateway.

Behind the walls, several turrets poked the clouds, tickling my fantasies, but this structure fell short of my expectations. No chain-mailed foot soldiers manned its parapets, and no knights in armor guarded its entrance. The turrets seemed more decorative than defensive, and black soot stained their tops. Looming above them rose the source of the soot: three smokestacks dwarfing the turrets and spewing ash. The structure seemed less a medieval castle than a factory, built with a storybook façade to embellish what lay within.

On the road before me, a parade of children trundled past, climbing to the structure on the hill. The girls pushed wheelbarrows covered with canvas, and the boys trudged alongside bearing wooden yolks on their shoulders, supporting buckets on either side. A few acknowledged my presence with a begrudging glance, but most stayed focused on the hilltop.

I turned to my guide and raised a brow. "Why do they ignore us?"

He pointed to their burden. "They labor under a heavy load."

As he spoke, a girl with raven hair strode by, no more than nine-years-old, so small she struggled to keep the barrow steady on its lone wheel.

As she passed, she peeked my way. Her dark eyes widened, and she twisted around to the boy who followed. "Look, Matty, a wizard."

The momentary distraction caused her to lose her balance enough to make the barrow totter and tip. Her knuckles whitened on the handles with the strain, and she bit her lower lip. Once she'd stabilized her load, she tossed me a look of resignation and resumed her march uphill.

The boy she'd called Matty trailed behind. He appeared older by a year or two, with tangled locks colored the same as the girl. He stumbled, not an arm's length from me, and dropped to one knee, his buckets thudding to the ground.

I peered inside. Each brimmed with a translucent gray muck, as if the fog from my study had taken solid form. I reached out to grasp his elbow and help him back up.

Matty scanned me head to toe, scrunched up his button nose and scowled, but he'd fallen behind the girl. He pushed off with a grunt and hastened to catch up.

"What is it they carry?" I whispered to my guide.

"Buckets of gloom, wheelbarrows of woe."

For the next five minutes, a dozen or more children shuffled past, eyes fixed on the structure ahead, laboring beneath their load.

When the last one passed, I queried my guide. "Why did you bring me to this horrible place?"

"You asked to find the source of despair."

I looked uphill and narrowed my gaze, mimicking the minuteman confronting his fate, and viewed the structure anew. I'd spent too many years worrying about my fate and doing nothing to change it.

Time to act.

"May I go there?"

The boy from the candle turned and swept a hand across the path, urging me to lead the way.

I hesitated. "What will I find inside?"

"That's for you to discover... I'm only your guide."

We fell in line behind the last of the children as they climbed to their goal. By the time we reached the archway, the first had begun to leave. Empty wheelbarrows now clattered along the cobblestones, and the buckets were stacked, one into the other, so the boys could carry them in one hand. As they put the moat behind them, faces that minutes before had borne the weight of the world returned to the innocence of youth. With their dark deed done, they skipped down the pathway to the village. The landscape rang with their laughter.

At the drawbridge, my guide motioned me inside.

I stepped across, slippers flapping on the wood, but on the far side of the archway, I hesitated. Despite the moat and battlements, the interior appeared more modern than medieval. No knights lined the passageway, and no guards blocked the way. No massive wheel drove a pulley to lower a spiked gate, and no torches in sconces flickered on the walls. Instead, recessed lighting revealed a three-story atrium, sterile but not unpleasant, like the reception area of the many corporate headquarters I'd visited in my former career.

A young man with closely cropped hair, wearing a blue button-down shirt and maroon necktie, sat at a desk, doodling away at a notebook and trying to appear busy while avoiding the eyes of the children. He ignored us as we approached.

Behind him, a row of three steel doors marked a bank of elevators. Those who had not yet unloaded their burden waited in well-ordered queues, six to each elevator. As a door slid open, they let the others exit, and filed in without coercion or fuss, as if performing an everyday chore.

When all had boarded, and we stood alone with the receptionist, I waved a hand to take in the white, sound-deadening panels in the ceiling, the potted plants and the elevators. "How can this be the source of despair?"

My guide glanced at his boot tops and shuffled in place, a gesture I'd come to know well. "You asked a hard question. I did my best to answer. Sources of despair are complicated things."

I checked above the nearest elevator, where two lights stuck out from the wall, one dark and marked "Lobby" and the other lit up with the letters "UZ."

"What is UZ?"

My guide shrugged and pointed to the ceiling three floors above us. "Unloading Zone."

Tiny black dots swam before my eyes, as if I were experiencing another transition. A bell dinged, the UZ light went dark, and the Lobby light flashed. The doors before me slid open, and more happy children emerged, leaving an empty elevator behind.

My guide motioned me toward the gaping doors.

I spoke more insistently this time. "What will I find?"

He stepped inside and waited for me to join him. "My role is to show you where to look. The answers are yours to find, as much as they might exist."

I stared at the gap between the floor and the elevator, which suddenly seemed a chasm. "Is it safe to go? I push no wheelbarrow and carry no bucket, and I'm certainly not a child."

"Safety is a relative term. Have you been safe in your life so far?"

I glared at him, recalling the old shopkeeper's words:

"Your questions will be well answered, but only if well asked."

I fumbled to phrase the question well. "Shouldn't I... have armor... or a weapon? I'm a bit exposed in my slippers and bathrobe."

He rolled his eyes as if questioning how he'd been saddled with such a fool, and shook his head.

I sighed and stepped inside. On the right panel, a single 'up' button protruded. I reached for it, a habit from a thousand elevators past, but my finger wavered in midair. "Should I press it?"

"It's your quest, not mine."

The shopkeeper in Prague had warned me. The guide from the candle possessed powerful magic, but would provide no answers without a struggle.

I drew in two breaths, buying time to formulate my next question. "Is there a reason... why I would *not* want to go?"

"Yes."

"Why?" My voice echoed off the metallic walls and faded to silence.

My guide squinted up to the topmost turrets where the smoke billowed, and his words billowed as well, no clearer than the smoke. "Because the source of despair may be different than what you seek."

Chapter 3 – The Factory

I extended a finger and pressed.

The button lit up, the doors slid shut, and a motor hummed.

As the elevator lurched upward, I brushed my fingertips against my reflection on the polished metal wall. An aging man in a bathrobe stared back at me, but with a spark in his eyes and his legs spread wide, adopting the posture of the minuteman.

When the humming stopped, the doors opened, and I exited to a narrow corridor, the end of which opened up into a high-ceilinged chamber. Metal cauldrons filled the far side, each taller than a grown man and three times as broad, with a ramp leading up to them. Vents above them sucked up steam from their boiling contents, driven by pumps and gears that ground away with a dull drone—the source of the soot from the smokestacks. A fetid odor permeated the air like rotten eggs. The children who had not yet deposited their load waited in queues before a wooden desk.

I scanned the chamber, searching for a demonic figure, some winged creature or dark lord who directed this morality play, but found only a man who appeared more clerk than demon. Tufts of hair leaked out from the edges of a green visor, and a frayed tweed jacket with patches at the elbows cloaked a too small frame. He sat on a stool behind the desk, his feet not reaching the floor.

On the desktop lay a leather-bound ledger. As each child approached, the clerk asked their name and ordered them to place their load on an adjacent scale. Then he hopped off the stool to peer at the numbers on the scale through thick glasses, which emphasized his bug-like eyes. Once satisfied with the weight, he settled back down to record their delivery, scratching with a quill pen on the pages of the ledger before waving the child past.

Each boy or girl trundled up the ramp and dumped their load into the vat. As the gray liquid oozed from the barrows and buckets, the bearer's mood lightened as well. Once they'd emptied their containers, their grimaces curled into smiles. Childlike again, they skipped off to await their turn at the elevator.

I lingered in the shadows until only a half-dozen children remained, and then snuck in for a closer look, hoping to avoid notice. The flapping of my slippers on the tile floor alerted one child to my presence, the boy next in line. He turned, and I recognized him at once, the ten-year-old with the raven locks whom I'd tried to help on the road.

He took a step toward me and opened his mouth, but before he could speak, the clerk cleared his throat. The child's turn had come, so he hefted his yoke and set his buckets on the scale.

"And you name is...?" the clerk said.

"Matthias."

The clerk recorded the boy's name and the weight of his cargo, and motioned him past.

After discharging his load, Matthias headed toward the elevators with a lighter heart. As he passed me, he paused, set down his now empty buckets, and approached. With his tiny hand, he fingered the hem of my bathrobe and gaped up at me. "*Are* you a wizard?"

I ruffled the tuft of his hair. "Why would you think I'm a wizard?"

"Because you're wearing a wizard's robe."

"This? You think this is a wizard's robe?" I chuckled, but my attempt at humor became lost in the grinding of the gears.

The girl who had accompanied him came to his side. "Well," she whispered. "Is he?"

"I don't think so, Hannah."

"He might be, Matty. He *might* be. Sometimes the magic hides."

The boy stared up at me, unable to face her, his eyes glistening. "My sister hoped you could help."

I determined to hedge my reply. After all, my presence here defied reason, and I had a magical guide accompanying me. Perhaps I *could* help. "If I *were* a wizard, what would you ask of me?"

"Candy, for a start," the little girl said.

"Candy?"

"Yes. Sweet jelly beans in fruity colors, made with a wizard's touch."

A bell behind me rang, and the elevator doors slid open. She and her brother joined the others, leaving me alone with my guide.

When all had departed, I stepped up to the desk as I'd seen the children do, though I bore no burden.

The clerk glanced up from his ledger, took me in, and raised a brow, unimpressed by my wizard's robe. "What may I do for you?"

I rose as tall as my old bones allowed and rocked back and forth on the balls of my feet. "What is it you do to these children?"

"Oh, that tired old question." He went back to his accounting, drawing a solid line beneath the column, and began tallying up the numbers.

I leaned on the desk to regain his attention. "Why do you force them to come here with such a burden?"

He raised a finger, motioning for me to wait as he double-checked his figures. When satisfied all balanced, he met my gaze. "My job is to sum up the input and total the output, but I don't force them to come. I'd be happy to have them stop, but I don't know how."

When I refused to budge, he set down his quill, took off his glasses and wiped his brow. No longer magnified, his eyes narrowed. "If you believe you can stop them, please try. I'll go off into a peaceful retirement and be forever in your debt. Now if you'll excuse me, if I take time to chat, I fall behind. They keep coming, you know."

I hovered over him for a minute or more to no avail. The conversation had ended.

I glanced at my guide, whose bemused expression implied I'd made a fool of myself.

He whispered to be certain no one but me could hear. "Time to go."

I trudged back to the elevator, beginning to wish I'd never lit the candle. Once inside, I refused to push the button, staring instead at my image in the polished brass doors. An old man stared back, disillusioned—no sign of the minuteman now.

Outside, where the cobblestones met the dirt, I found the two children, Matthias and Hannah, sitting cross-legged on a flat rock at the side of the road. Matthias's empty buckets lay on the ground before him, next to Hannah's wheelbarrow.

The little girl spotted me first and scrambled to her feet. "I knew you'd come. I told Matty you were a wizard, but he laughed at me."

Matthias stood to join her, and placed his hands on his hips. "Well, are you?"

Time to change my approach. In this world, I had no idea what role I played, so I mimicked my guide. "Being a wizard is a complicated thing. I may or may not be able to help, but first you must answer my questions. Why do you come here?"

The boy shrugged. "The gloom needs to go somewhere."

"But why can't you just play and be happy?"

Hannah's hands fidgeted, and she kept turning to me and back to the boy. At last she poked him on the arm. "Tell him, Matty."

The boy's back straightened, and he tried to appear older than his years. "They say a war rages, and so the gloom lies over the land. The say—"

"And the boatman," the girl interrupted. "Tell him."

Mathias whirled on her. "Hush, Hannah." Then back to me. "My sister's little and speaks of things she doesn't understand." He lowered his chin to his chest and stared at his boot tops. His voice lowered as well. "Whispers fill the air. They say we'll all die someday, that our mum will die like my dad, and when she does, we'll be alone. She told us no, she'd always be with us, but I think she lies to make us feel better." He gazed back up at me with pleading eyes. "Wizards are supposed to be wise. Can *you* tell us the truth?"

I settled down on the flat rock and urged the children to sit beside me, Matthias on my left and Hannah on my right, as I used to do with Mark and Helen in a time so long ago.

I wrapped an arm around each. "Life is complicated as well, and no one—not even a wizard—knows the truth. But wizards have ways to dispel the gloom, if you're open to listen and learn."

Hannah nestled into the crook of my arm and gazed up at me with dark eyes. "Will you teach us?"

What could I say? I'd dug myself a hole, so I stood and loomed over the two, trying to appear wizard-like. "Go home to your mother. I'll consult with my fellow wizards, and if they deem the task worthwhile, I'll join you later."

My words seemed to lighten their load even more than dumping their burdens of gloom had. Both popped up and, after a hurried bow, raced off with a spring to their step.

Once they'd moved out of earshot, I confronted my guide. "Is this how you give me answers?"

"Would you prefer I return you to the small room in your home? I can bring you back with a wave of my hand. I can leave you with the candle lit, and you can watch it burn down."

My eyes narrowed as the children settled to specks in the distance, so easy to abandon and forget. I shook my head. I'd abandoned enough in my life.

"You thought such a quest would be simple?" my guide said.

I sighed. "What will I learn in the village? Will I find answers to my questions?"

He raised and released his slim shoulders in what passed as a shrug. "I can't say for sure."

Far downhill, Matthias and his sister Hannah disappeared into a cluster of cottages. I pursed my lips and blew out a stream of air. "Then I'm bound to follow them to find the source of their gloom."

Chapter 4 – Graymoor on Nox

I set one foot on the path, and then another, with no hint of where my steps might lead. The road descended from the castle's hilltop through scrub and rock, until it settled into a less steep grassy glen, and from there tracked the river downstream. The water of the river, devoid of vegetation or algae, sparkled in the sunlight.

Despite the strange circumstance of my arrival, I found a village similar to farming communities everywhere. Thatched cottages were fronted by picket fences protecting kitchen gardens from critters. Nearby fields had been tilled in rows, with sprouts of various shapes and colors peeking up through recently turned furrows. And the villagers I passed bore that permanent squint from studying the sky too often, searching for rain.

At the heart of the village, a few shops bordered the kind of square I'd visited on my travels to the older sections of European towns. At its center lay a stone fountain, with a statue of a fish in the middle spewing water from its mouth. A manicured lawn surrounded the fountain, forming a common, its grass freshly mowed with not a single weed marring its surface. The lawn was enclosed by a display of day lilies, except for a crushed stone path leading to the water.

If this was the gathering spot for its people, the village seemed to have no care in the world.

As I approached, I caught the annoyed chatter of children. At the far side, behind the statue of the fish, I found Matthias and his sister with their yoke, buckets, and wheelbarrow strewn on the ground before them. As soon as they spotted me, they stopped their bickering.

Hannah poked her brother in the arm. "See! I told you he'd come."

Matthias slid off the stone wall surrounding the fountain and made a small bow. "Welcome to Graymoor on Nox, master wizard. Have you come to help, as my sister claims?"

"Well, that depends."

I heard a snicker behind me and, out of the corner of my eye, caught my guide concealing a smirk with his hand. Undeterred, the children approached with a mix of apprehension and awe.

Hannah scrunched her nose at me. "Depends on what?"

"On where the gloom comes from. As we stand in this delightful square, I find it hard to understand what problem you need me to solve."

Matthias stepped forward, blocking his sister from view. "If you're really a wizard, you would already understand."

I knelt as far as my creaky knees allowed, low enough to confront my questioner eye to eye. "Understanding does not come from wisdom alone. It requires knowledge. So, for a start, why don't you show me around your village, and we'll see what I can learn?"

I reached out a hand, but before he could grasp it, his sister shoved in front and took it instead.

She looked up at me with eyes too big for her head. "Forgive Matty. He's grown too old to believe. *I'll* show you the village, and *he* can follow."

The children circled the square with me, pointing out their favorite shops: the bakery where their mother sent them each morning to fetch fresh bread, and where the baker slipped them fragments of cookies that had crumbled in the baking; the market where they took ripe vegetables from their mother's garden and warm milk from their goat, and bartered them for ham and cheese; and the blacksmith's shop where they went when their chores were done, because they liked to watch the sparks fly and the metal glow, and listen to the hiss when it cooled in the water trough.

"But is there a special spot," I said, "a place where you go to play?"

The children glanced at each other, exchanging unspoken thoughts of the kind passed only between a brother and sister close in age. I caught a trace of fear, but then Matthias bit his lip and nodded. Hannah led me to the river with Matthias trailing behind.

We stopped at a spot where a gnarled tree's roots clutched at the bank, leaving the tree leaning forward at a sharp angle toward the water. This tree—or perhaps two trees that had long ago intertwined—had a split trunk that formed a hole in its center, providing a gateway to the river.

Matthias slipped through the hole, clutching a branch to ease his descent, and drew a wide arc with his free arm from north to south, as broadly as his small frame allowed.

"The River Nox," he announced.

I took in the water's flow and admired its surface, dappled with stars from the afternoon sun. "A pleasant spot with no hint of gloom. Do you come here to fish?"

"Not fish. We're not permitted."

He searched the ground for a flat rock and skidded down to the edge of the muddy embankment.

Hannah clung to my side with one hand, while she stretched out the other to her brother. "Not too far, Matty!"

He cast her a ten-year-old's look of defiance, took one last halting step, and flung the rock with such force he nearly lost his balance.

"One, two three... seven skips, a new record."

I shuffled in my slippers down to the water, and reached out to grasp his hand. "Wonderful. Now come back here where you'll be safe."

He rumpled his brow. "What's the matter, wizard? You worried?"

"I was afraid you'd tumble into the torrent. Why do you need to wander so close to the edge?"

"I'm not allowed to come this close when grownups are around, but I like to go as near the edge as I can without going over. Out on the edge you discover things you can never see from the bank." His eyes shifted to the corners, and he shivered. "And the river should be safe this far from sunset."

At these words, the three of us glanced up to the sky. The sun lingered, but no more than a thumb's width above the trees. Matthias scrambled up the bank, and led us away from the river at a brisk pace.

We walked for only a few minutes, pausing at the fountain to retrieve their burdens, and then wandered down the main road to a narrow path with only five cottages, two on either side and one at the end. This last, the most modest of the five, appeared to be their home.

The children asked me to wait by the gate, so as not to surprise their mother. As they set down their load at the base of the porch, a handsome woman of perhaps thirty-five emerged from the cottage to light the candle in a brass lantern by the door.

As the lantern flared, warding off the impending twilight, she glared at her tardy children. "Where have you been? You know better than to stay out so late."

I lay back in the shadows, watching from a distance as mother and offspring exchanged tense words. The dusk was deepening, and a cluster of moths had gathered to circle the lantern.

At last, Hannah turned and pointed back at me, so excited she bounced on her toes, causing the floorboards of the porch to creak.

Her mother's expression, which had hardened as she scolded her children, now softened, making her appear younger.

Matthias called out to me. "What are you waiting for? My mother says to come in."

As I drew nearer the cottage, the lantern light revealed a dark-eyed woman who, like her children, possessed long locks of hair the color of crow's wings. When she caught sight of me emerging from the shadows with my bathrobe and slippers, she crumpled her brow, causing a crease to form above the bridge of her nose. Our eyes met, and something akin to recognition flickered between us, leaving me confused and mute, but she had no such hesitation.

She tilted her head to one side and studied me top to bottom. "Hannah claims you're a wizard, but how are we to know for sure? Strange garb alone does not make magic."

I reached into my trousers pocket, searching for an answer, and found a pair of quarters left over from a cup of coffee at Starbucks.

"An unbeliever?" I said with a wink of my eye. "Then watch this."

I held up one coin so it glinted in the dying rays of the sun, making sure all beheld it. Then I closed my fist and waved my other hand with a flourish. When I opened the fist, the treasure had vanished. I grinned at the children, now wide-eyed, reached behind Hannah's ear, and out popped the lost quarter.

The children clapped their hands in glee, but their mother glared at me, on to my deception, though making her offspring smile felt like magic of sorts.

I extended a hand to her and decided to use my full name, thinking it a better choice in this setting. "My name is Albert, and yours is...?"

She made a small curtsy. "Elizabeth. A wizard, eh? But can you do more than coin tricks?"

I fumbled in the pocket of my robe, and my fingers brushed the candle's companion vial. On impulse, I pulled it out. As if on cue, the purple liquid inside performed beyond my expectations, pulsing and glowing with an intensity that overwhelmed the lantern.

Elizabeth's eyes widened, and she fell back a step. "Very well, master wizard, perhaps you *do* possess some power. Will you join us for dinner? We don't have much, but enough for a fourth."

I spun around to a laugh from behind—my guide stood on the porch steps, his face highlighted by the setting sun. From the family's lack of response, it seemed that only I could see him.

Elizabeth opened the door for me, but the children rushed through instead.

She called after them. "Matthias and Hannah, you stop right now! No dinner until you put away your burdens. After that, you may fetch an extra plate for our guest, and pour him a glass of ale."

The chastised children abandoned the porch and gathered up the yoke, buckets, and wheelbarrow. Only after they'd vanished inside the nearby shed did she re-open the door and invite me in.

We ate a modest meal of peas and carrots from the garden, and cheese and bread bartered from the shop in the village square.

After Elizabeth put the children to bed with a hug and a goodnight kiss, the two of us retreated to the kitchen, where she placed a kettle on the stove.

While she waited for the water to boil, she checked back on the children, hovering by their bedroom doorway and listening.

When convinced their breathing had settled into its nightly rhythm, she steeped tea in two mugs, and sat opposite me at the kitchen table. Both of us wrapped our hands around the mugs and stared into the steam, allowing a proper interval between the fantasies of children and the more sober affairs of adults.

She broke the silence first. "Why have you come to our village, master wizard? To perform cheap tricks and give my son and daughter false hope? For despite your magic potion, I suspect you lack the power to change our lives."

I took a sip and winced, more from the sting of her words than the bitter taste of the tea. I fumbled for a response. "I... came here... to search for wisdom."

She set her cup down and raised a brow. "Wisdom, is it? Are we some curiosity for you to study?"

"I didn't mean to—"

"A war still rages to the south, the very war that took the children's father, and I find no wisdom in that. The fighting affects us even here in our small village, like living at the edge of a storm. Evil humors flit about, permeating the air like a damp fog and seeping into our bones. We spend our time glancing about with shoulders slumped, expecting each day to bring bad news. The children sense our fear and pay the price. Do you have a magic cure for that?"

I fidgeted in my seat, twisting to the left and right in search of guidance. The boy from the candle squatted in the corner, cleaning his fingernails with his knife, unconcerned with the predicament he'd placed me in. No guidance there.

I drew in a long breath. "I don't know if I can help or not, though I'd like to try. First I need to better understand. Why do the children bear these barrows and buckets up the hill? Is the war the source of their gloom?"

Her lips tightened into a thin and bloodless line. Instead of answering, she shuffled to the window and stared out in silence for a minute or more, though it seemed like an hour. As she waited, slowing her breathing as people do to calm themselves when frightened, the moon rose fat and full, filling the upper pane and bathing her in its pale light. As the night deepened, the evening star appeared alongside the moon.

Her shoulders shuddered in a sigh, and she turned back to me. "The children sleep, and the time for the joining has come." She returned to the table and took a last sip of tea. "I need to go. You may come with me if you wish."

As we passed out the door and down the side path, other adults emerged, forming a somber parade. No one spoke a word of greeting.

No words were uttered at all. The villagers trudged ahead with blank stares, their footsteps crunching on the gravel until we reached the village square, where they formed a half-circle before the fountain.

My heart quickened.

Now my reward for lighting the candle. At last I'll discover the source of gloom – a villain or demon who visits the people at night and spreads despair across the land.

I circled the crowd, searching behind the statue of the fish, but encountered only my guide with a whimsical smile. I opened my mouth to demand an answer:

Where is the demon that cursed this town? And how might I defeat him?

My guide placed a finger to his waxy lips and shook his head to stop me speaking.

No villain was to be found.

When all the adults had taken their place in the circle, they joined hands and bowed their heads, a ritual apparently practiced many times before. The moon had achieved its apex now, an orb so bright that it made the lilies glow.

A wizened man who appeared to be the village elder, raised his voice in a solid baritone and chanted these words:

Deliver us from evil.

Other voices joined in the prayer, a plaintive plea repeated sixteen times, gaining strength with every utterance until it peaked and faded away, lost in the rush of the fountain.

When they finished, each turned and hugged the person on either side. Following along, I accepted a bony squeeze from a man to my left and turned to face Elizabeth. After a brief hesitation, she drew closer, and we embraced.

She held on not in the way of casual strangers, or of old friends meeting after a time apart. She held on for longer than the ceremony required, and her muscles relaxed as she shared her burden with me.

As we embraced, the moon grew dim, and the evening star separated from it and stood alone against the black of night, shining brighter than before. Whether this woman believed me a wizard on not, I'd brought a glimmer of hope to her, much like the glowing star. In turn, she had stirred something in me, a warmth I'd missed so much these past months.

We strolled back to her cottage, and when we moved away from the others, I grasped her by the arms and forced her to face me. "I'll help, Elizabeth. I don't know how, but I'll help if I can. If only I could discover the source of this gloom."

She stared back at me with glistening eyes. "Stay with us for two weeks more, helping with the chores and earning your keep. Stay until the moon wanes, and then, in that darkest of nights, you'll see why we pray."

Chapter 5 - Rhythms and Rumblings

Elizabeth exiled me for the night to sleep on a bed of straw in the shed adjoining the cottage, with my only companion the family's goat. The shed housed rows of jars containing preserved vegetables, a few slabs of smoked meat, and other stores of food too scant for a family of three. A knee-high stack of firewood lay alongside—enough to warm their lodging for two days—accompanied by a hatchet stuck in one of the logs, a tool too small for splitting wood.

On one wall hung a rack with rakes, spades, and hoes to maintain the garden, as well as a hammer, rusty saw, and other implements for home repair. On the opposite side, cradled in a waist-high shelf, lay the children's burden, the buckets, yoke and barrow, emptied now and newly washed. Yet this was no mere storage shelf. Three boards of lacquered wood bracketed it, decorated by flowers picked from the garden—an odd place for embellishment, since no one but the goat would view them... and now a phony wizard as well. Some artisan had carved a symbol on each board, an ornate circle framing what appeared to be a wolf's head. Mounted on the wall above it was a simple long knife of the kind used by medieval footmen, and a round leather shield, marred with slash marks across its center—the scars of combat.

I lay awake at first, my mind churning too much to sleep. Every time I closed my eyes, I pictured the faces of the children trudging up the hill, and recalled the tremor in their mother's arms as we embraced.

When my eyes popped open for the fifth time, I noticed my guide slouched in the doorway watching me. An ascendant moon highlighted his usual inscrutable expression.

"Are you here to gloat?" I said.

"Not gloat. I'm here to help."

"Some help you are. You plop me into this place where odd things happen, and leave me to my own devices with no explanation."

"I'm your guide, not your parent. I can lead you to your quest, but it's yours to pursue."

My pained reaction must have impressed him, because he took a step toward me, and the corners of his brows drooped as if the wax had begun to melt. "Might I do something to ease your way?"

I shifted to my side to take the weight off my aching back, and grunted. "Can you at least help me fall sleep?"

His half-smile settled into a frown, and he waved his hand. A moment later, I faded off.

Elizabeth woke me from my dreamless slumber early the next morning, before the rays of first light had penetrated the shed. She greeted me as a full member of the family... complete with a list of chores.

I rolled onto my stomach, staggered to all fours, and scrambled to my feet, shaking off the effects of the hard floor on my hips and back. While she prepared breakfast, she tasked me with chopping one day's firewood, with a more ambitious goal of augmenting the stack in the shed. I hacked away with the little hatchet until my arms ached, but fell short of the goal.

After a meal of ham and bread less fresh than the night before, she asked me to help Matthias and Hannah fetch water from the fountain in the village square. "We only own three buckets, but need five for our daily needs, two to cook and three to bathe. The children have grown strong enough to handle one each, but Matthias insists on carrying two to save the third trip. He never complains, but the load weighs on him. An additional bearer would ease the task."

I eyed the buckets by the kitchen door, receptacles smaller than those used for the gloom. "What if we added the ones in the shed? Then I'll carry two, and we can complete the chore in a single trip."

Her eyes shifted to the corners, and she glanced away. "We're not permitted."

So the children and I trundled off to the fountain, bearing a bucket apiece.

We filled them with water as clear as a mountain stream, each as full as we dared without risking some sloshing away as we staggered home. I discovered a bucket of water weighed more than I recalled. Matthias did fine with his reduced load, but my arthritic knuckles throbbed, and poor Hannah had to lug hers with two hands between her knees, forcing her to walk with a waddle.

Halfway back, I spotted a stone bench at the entrance to a side path, and suggested we set down our burdens and take a moment to rest. The children quickly agreed.

Each of us sat with hands folded in our laps, peering into the buckets as if seeking a secret at the bottom.

When the silence became bothersome, I drew in a pained breath. The subject was sure to be sore, but I needed to know. "What happened to your father?"

The children exchanged thoughts, as they were wont to do, and silent words passed between their eyes.

Matthias accepted the obligation to answer. "Gone."

"Gone where?"

"To the war."

"How long ago?"

"Two years this coming summer."

Hannah bounced in her seat. Despite their agreement, she was determined to tell the rest of the story. "They came from the south, gruff men. Took him and two others from the village." Her eyes glistened, and she needed to swallow her tears before continuing. "He never came back."

Matthias stood and paced in little circles, glaring at the ground as if trying to burn a pattern in the weeds. "No body. No nothing. Just that rusty old sword and the shield in the shed."

Hannah slid closer to me on the bench. "I tried to stop them."

Her brother glared at her. "You tried all right, as I did. I banged on their breastplates until my knuckles bled, and Hannah kicked them in the shins, but we were too little. They swatted us away like flies."

Hannah's eyes grew wide. "Some say more bad things are on the way. You're a wizard. Can't you do something to stop it?"

I extended an arm to her, and she snuggled in as I struggled to muster enough air to reply. "I'll try."

Matthias glanced up at the sun to gauge how much time remained to complete our chore. "We have to go," he said, his voice deepening—a boy pretending to be a man. "There's one more load to do."

Hannah slipped out from under my arm. "Thank you for helping us."

"I haven't done anything yet."

"Helping with the water, I mean."

When we started up again, I held my bucket in one hand, and urged Hannah to let me use the other to share hers. Her tiny hand grasped the handle next to mine, and the burden seemed less heavy this time.

Minutes later, we arrived back at the cottage, dumped our load into a basin in the kitchen, and went back for more. No further discussion ensued of their father or of the other "bad things."

After breakfast, I gathered the wood not needed by the stove that day, and carried it to the shed. After adding the few logs to the pile and stacking them crisscross to allow for a flow of air, I caught the children's burden out of the corner of my eye.

With my hands still smarting from carrying the water, I shuffled over to the buckets to check them out, and gasped when I looked inside. In the dim light of the shed, I could see a gray muck shadowing their bottoms. The barrow and buckets had accumulated an inch of fresh gloom.

Soon, I settled into the rhythm of this lovely family's routine. We weeded the garden and picked the ripe vegetables, tended the chickens, milked the goat and made butter from its milk, and bartered with neighbors for other necessities. Each night, Elizabeth and I went to the fountain to participate in the curious ritual, though no sign of evil appeared.

While Graymoor on Nox was too small to have a schoolhouse, a tutor arrived every Tuesday to review the children's lesson and assign new work for the coming week. Once he left, however, their studies lagged.

The adults in the village provided little assistance. They had too much to do and, despite their congenial manner, a pall hung over them from worries unseen. Besides, they themselves possessed a limited education, having learned not much more than basic arithmetic... with single digit factors only. The children's assignments were more complex—three-digit multiplication, long division and, heaven forbid, fractions.

Like mothers everywhere, Elizabeth wished more for her children and prodded them to practice their lessons each night, but lacking the skill herself, she couldn't help them. So, I sat at the kitchen table by the light of a flickering candle and drilled Matthias and Hannah on their numbers.

In our few free hours, I showed them how to carve toys, much as I used to do during Michael's Cub Scout days. One year, father and son transformed a block of wood into a sleek car that won the pinewood derby. This world lacked the necessary power tools, of course—no sabre saw or sander to craft such an elegant vehicle. Instead, we fashioned rough-hewn toys carved with a kitchen knife and smoothed with an awl.

All these mundane talents reinforced the children's view of me as a wizard. In addition to my bathrobe and slippers, a rudimentary skill at woodcraft, and a fourth-grade proficiency with ciphers, sealed the deal.

Unaccustomed to physical labor, my left hip nagged more than usual, and periodic spasms plagued my lower back—sleeping on the hard ground added to the pain. Between my assigned chores and the children's lessons, I hobbled around the village to keep my muscles loose—but also to learn more about the cloud hovering over the land. I discovered not a single harsh soul resided in Graymoor on Nox. Every man, woman and child, young or old, relaxed the thin line of their lips into a smile as I passed and nodded a good day. Some even interrupted their labors to comment on the weather or ask after my wellbeing.

Oddly, no one seemed surprised at my sudden appearance, garbed in slippers and robe, and they refused to acknowledge the dark factory looming at the top of the hill. If not for the buckets in the shed filling with woe, I would have doubted I'd witnessed it myself.

My guide viewed my confusion with bemusement, as if he'd experienced something similar a thousand times before, albeit with different cynical old men. Whenever I tried to query him, he brushed my concerns aside. When I pestered him further, he berated me: "You picked the quest."

On the ninth day, after finishing my morning chores, I stepped onto the front porch to rest and reflect.

Elizabeth emerged from the cottage bearing her wash, and began hanging them on a clothesline to dry.

Despite my sore back, I rose to help with the chore.

As she finished the last of the children's laundry, I observed her in profile. The arc of her neck showed smooth and perfect as she raised on tiptoes to hang one of Hannah's shirts on the line.

The sight reminded me of a day long ago, after Betty and I had married, but before our children were born. It had also been a spring day....

In New England, spring meant the first day after the snow melted, when the sun at last beamed strong enough to let the tips of crocuses peek up from the muddy ground.

The prior September, we'd bought our first house, a modest three-bedroom cape. With the autumn waning, Betty had barely enough time to plant a few bulbs in the yard before the hard frost. Now, on the first warm Sunday in March, she rushed inside to fetch me, and dragged me outdoors to check out the buds in her garden. The two of us sat on the front stoop, for the first time in months without jackets, and admired the flowers.

We sat like that for an hour, speaking little but snuggling together for warmth. Only when a cloud covered the sun and a wind kicked up did we rise to leave, but before retreating inside, she knelt down and plucked a single purple petal from a bud. Cradling it in her hand, she led me up the stairs to our spare bedroom, which remained unfurnished, so bare our footsteps echoed off the walls. There she placed the petal on the window sill, laying it like an offering on an altar.

When she turned back to me, her eyes were aglow. "The first growth of spring, a sign of renewal."

Her excitement spread to me, and a stirring welled in my chest. No need to explain; I knew what she meant, for that room one day would be the bedroom of our first-born child.

Now, the same excitement stirred in me, despite Elizabeth being so much younger, and her husband gone less than two years. Yet no discomfort settled between us, as if we'd known each other before.

I stared up at a cloudless sky and sucked in a breath of air. Then, as she turned to go back in the cottage, I grasped her by the wrist and spun her around. "Such a pleasant day. Will you take a few moments and go for a walk with me?"

She started to shake her head.

"Surely you can spare the time."

She dried her hands on her apron, and glanced through the open door as if seeking permission from the children. At last, she nodded.

I tried to lead her to the river, to the spot the children had brought me that first day, but she refused, shaking her head so hard her raven locks swished across her face. Instead, she led me in the opposite direction, to where a stand of birches clustered like a border at the back of the village.

As we stood beneath the canopy of green, she pressed a finger to her lips and pointed to a bough overhead. A moment later, in reward for our patience, a high-pitched, wavering whistle greeted us, the first note long, followed by three short ones. Her eyes took on a sparkle thus far unseen, and she pointed again, more insistently this time. Overhead, I spotted a brown bird with a downy white throat and a yellow stripe between eyes and bill. It perched on a reed-thin branch, singing away with a voice too strong for its size.

A tenderness overwhelmed me, so powerful it astonished me. I stretched out my hand to her, but she backed away.

"You've been so kind, master wizard, so helpful to my family. The children love having you around. Two years have passed since they had a man in the cottage. I only wish...."

She glanced up again, searching for the bird.

"Wish what?" I said.

"Nothing you can provide." The light in her eyes dimmed as though the last illusion had been stolen from her. "It's best we go."

At once, the white-throated bird sang anew, but now from a higher branch, and as we turned to go, it flapped its wings and flew off deeper into the woods.

The morning of the fourteenth day dawned. I'd watched these past days with trepidation as the full moon waned, first to a half and then to a quarter, and at last to a sliver that hardly gave light at all. Now, as I anticipated the moonless night, I paused my weeding and scanned the surrounding trees, listening for the chittering of sparrows heralding the dusk.

All had gone silent.

I set down my hoe and checked the horizon. Dark clouds scudded across the setting sun, casting shadows that slogged across the ground.

Time slowed, as in a dream, suspended like a balloon floating in midair, and I wondered why my guide had brought me here. To witness some cataclysm, perhaps, some once-in-a-lifetime event that would change how I viewed the world, that would alter forever the person I'd become.

Whatever was to come, I hoped it would happen soon. Like the minuteman, I awaited my moment, my shot heard round the world. I longed for the threads of this make-believe world to converge—this village, the factory on the hill, Elizabeth, Matthias and Hannah, the war to the south—to weave together and form a tapestry, a flash of insight that would cause my prior life to make sense. Yet in this dream, like in my fantasy books, I'd have to wait.

I missed my home. I wondered if Helen had tried to call. When she received no answer, had she come to the house and, finding me missing, called the police? Had the worry caused her to go into labor? Had my first grandchild arrived early because of my foolhardy jaunt into this fantasy world?

What of Betty? Had she waited until the nor'easter subsided or, anxious to share her news in person, had she attempted the perilous drive in the snow? Had she been rewarded by an empty house, her husband missing and an ache in her heart, pondering why her best friend would run off at such a time without so much as leaving a note?

When I glanced around, I caught my guide standing at the edge of the garden whittling a twig with his knife. I rushed over and grabbed him by the arms. "My home. I arrived here two weeks ago. Has that much time passed in my home as well?"

He whittled away for two more strokes, then slipped the knife into its scabbard. "It's difficult to explain."

"Try me."

"The question is not whether time passes the same, but rather whether what you call your home continues to exist while you're here."

A panic fluttered in my stomach. "My home is gone?"

"I didn't say that. It's more like.... Have you ever awoken early in the morning from the midst of a vivid dream?"

I hesitated to answer, fearful of where the thought might lead.

"And did you ever wonder, upon awakening, which side of waking was real?"

I nodded and, feeling suddenly lightheaded, slumped down on the chopping block, unwilling to face him.

He came closer and rested a hand on my shoulder. "Why did you pick such a difficult quest? What did you hope to find?"

I waited, breathing in and breathing out as I dug small furrows on the ground with my hoe.

At last I narrowed my eyes and confronted him. "I longed to find the demon who'd caused so much pain. I longed to fight him, like the heroes in my novels, to defeat him once and for all, and in so doing, to end despair forever."

He tightened his hand and squeezed, a rare show of concern.

I waited for his response.

"A noble goal," he said at last, "but one beyond my powers to provide."

Chapter 6 – Wolf's Head

Once the orb of the sun disappeared below the rim of the horizon, a change came over the village. Everyone emerged from their cottages, stone-faced and silent. As they shuffled toward the square, the shadows deepened and dark clouds gathered to the north, from whence the river Nox flowed.

The people of Graymoor ignored the approaching storm, assembling at the fountain as the adults had done for their nightly prayer, but this time the children came too. Then, as if someone had given a signal, they formed a line, one family to each row, and headed off to the river. No laughter filled the air, and no shouts of delight lightened their mood. Young faces that had beamed with joy hours before took on a glazed expression. The children trudged along with the same stupor as when they'd climbed the hill to deposit their gloom.

We stopped where the gnarled tree provided access to the river, the gap in its trunk now a black hole.

The children left their parents, shifted nearer the tree, and stood motionless with hands to their sides. The flow of the river slowed, resembling more a milk pond than a stream, and with no moon or stars, the water turned dark, and the wind itself stilled.

All eyes turned upstream.

Out of the darkness, a speck of light emerged and grew in size, until the outline of a boat appeared, made visible only due to a flaming torch affixed to its bow. The boat had neither sail nor oars, but drifted on the current. As it came closer, the torchlight reflected off its lone occupant, making me shudder. A man, it seemed, but one whose head was either that of a wolf, or who wore a wolf-like mask crafted so well as to obscure the difference.

As the boat settled onto the muddy bank where Matthias had earlier skipped stones, the boatman bent down to the hull and picked up a leather pouch. He raised it high above his head and, as everyone watched, he shook it three times, making a rattling sound, and offered it to the crowd.

The village elder—the one with the baritone who had led the nightly prayer—reached into the hole in the tree and accepted the pouch. With bowed head, he passed the pouch around to the children.

One by one, they closed their eyes and pulled out something small enough to be concealed in their hands.

The boatman waited until everyone had chosen, and shouted a single command: "Show!" The word echoed with a sound not of this world.

Young arms rose, and innocent fists uncurled, exposing their content.

I squinted to see what they grasped. Most appeared no more than a simple stone—all but one, which pulsed with a purple glow like an amethyst set on fire, made brighter by the surrounding darkness.

The boatman stuck out a hand, and with a bony finger swept back and forth across the children before lighting in the direction of the boy with the glowing stone. The crowd fell back a step, leaving the child exposed—a boy with raven hair.

Matthias.

A gasp sounded from behind me, and I turned to catch Elizabeth bringing a hand to her mouth to suppress a cry as Hannah rushed back and buried her face in her mother's side.

The wolf-headed boatman beckoned to Matthias.

The boy's face, which had so recently borne a look of wonder as he skipped rocks from that very spot, showed pale in the stone's light.

The elder placed an arm around the boy's shoulders, led him to the gnarled tree, and lifted him through the hole in the trunk.

Matthias turned and scanned his neighbors, searching for his mother, his moistened cheeks reflecting a purple glow. For a brief moment, he caught my eye, a hint of hope flashing, but then he glanced away and turned toward the river.

Without a word of protest from the crowd, he slipped down the bank to the water's edge. Only when he came within grasp of the boatman did he fight back, clawing and scratching at his captor to no avail.

I rushed forward, dove through the gap in the tree with surprising speed, and swung wildly at the wolfman, but my fists passed right through him. I fought until I lost my balance and fell to one knee in the mud.

Unperturbed by my assault, the creature bound Matthias with a hemp cord and laid him on the boat's bottom like a sack of flour. Then, without the aid of sail or oar, the craft slipped from the shore and continued riding the current to the south.

A hand rested on my shoulder. I tensed and turned to fight—only to find my guide shaking his head.

"Why?" I said.

"Because you are not of this world."

As the boat with Matthias drifted downriver, the flickering light from the torch vanished as if doused by the boatman, and the stars reappeared. The somber villagers turned from the scene and shuffled back to their homes, with only a slump in their shoulders to suggest anything unusual had happened.

I rushed after the elder, grabbed him by the elbow, and spun him around. "Why do the children go?"

"They go, because they've always gone." His boot pawed at the river bank as he spoke, leaving a scar in the ground.

When I stuttered, unable to respond, he unfastened my fingers from his arm and continued his trudge home.

Hannah rushed toward me, a primal plea on her face. "You said you'd help!"

When I stood statue-like with nothing to say, she burst into tears and began pounding on my chest with her tiny fists.

Her mother came closer and eased her remaining child away, half covering her eyes to dampen the memory. "Forgive her. She's young, and doesn't accept the way of the world."

"I'm old, and neither do I." I gazed to the north, from whence the boat had come, and to the south, where the unknown lay. When I turned back to Elizabeth, I found the deepest well of sorrow in her eyes. "I'd do anything to bring the boy back to you."

"I know."

A gash opened in my heart, and I embraced both the grieving mother and her sobbing child.

When we separated, the weary lines around her mouth fanned out as she flexed her facial muscles, but no smile came—only resignation. "I believed you were a good man when I met you, but even then, I understood that some things cannot be changed."

She cast one last longing glance downriver and spoke, forcing each word over the knot in her throat. "It's over. No sense lingering here." She wrapped a loving arm around her daughter and led her away.

Once they were far enough down the path, I turned on my guide. "Why did you bring me to this place of such sadness, when I can make no difference?"

"I brought you because you asked."

"Where is he taking the boy?"

"To the source."

I shook my head. He'd misunderstood my question. "The source of the river lies to the north. He's taking the boy south."

"Not that source. The source you asked to find." When I stared at him, puzzled, he added. "The source of despair."

I surveyed the river to the south, seeing it anew. "Then if I'm to fulfill my quest, I need to follow the boy?"

He nodded.

"But when I get there, will I be able to rescue him?"

"No."

"Why?" My voice was rising.

"Because, as I explained, you are not of this world."

I stepped closer, until we were nose to nose—so close I hoped his waxen smile would melt from the heat of my eyes. "Then, dammit, make me part of this world!"

He never flinched. "If your aim is to end all despair, why do you need to risk so much to save a single child?"

I pondered his question, searching for reason in the scrim of stars that once again lit the sky, and in the slosh of waves that once again lapped the shore, but I discovered the answer in a daughter's plea and a mother's sorrowful eyes. "Because both here and in my own world, I've found an ocean of sadness, and though the boy may be but one drop in that ocean, he means so much to me."

"You are without doubt one of my more challenging seekers."

"You've brought me this far. Now add this new goal to my quest. Help me rescue the boy." I waited three labored breaths. "Is that in the realm of your magic?"

He nodded, but his hint of a smile faded. "Yes, but before you make such a choice, consider this. The more you become part of this world, the harder it will be to return."

Chapter 7 – A Hike in the Woods

That night, I lay on the bed of straw with hands behind my neck, glaring up at the rafters. Through the open doorway of the shed, starlight filtered through as the evening's haze gave way to a clear sky.

While my guide had obscured in riddles what awaited me, I understood the import of the choice before me, one of those crossroads that occurs but a few times in your life, moments that change not only your circumstance but who you are.

I recalled my first such crossroad many years before, in the summer of my thirteenth year. My parents had shipped me off to camp, a pleasant place by a pond in the New Hampshire woods. I enjoyed my time there, making friends, learning how to swim and paddle a canoe, playing baseball, and ogling the girls.

On a clear evening, similar to this one, our bunk gathered around a bonfire to sing songs, toast marshmallows, and tell ghost stories. As I gazed at the fire, the top log collapsed onto the pile, sending a stream of sparks floating up into the air. I craned my neck and followed them until each had spent its glow and vanished like a shooting star in the night. When the smoke dissipated, a blanket of jewels sparkled in the sky.

The words of the ghost stories faded into the background, and I felt alone, just me and a universe bigger than I'd ever conceived. A single thought rang out in my mind: *I am*! I realized I was no longer a child, an extension of my parents. I was a sentient being with hopes, fears, and dreams of my own. What lay ahead was *my* life, to live as I chose.

The choice: to burn brightly for a brief time like the embers of the fire, or to never flare at all; to make a difference, or to one day vanish without leaving a trace.

When at last I dozed off, I was visited by one of the few benefits of age—the vast reservoir of memories that often graced my dreams. Many a night, these dreams would intrude on my sleep—the good and the bad. I'd take those unearthed memories and stitch them together through the night, until the images flowed and the voices whispered, growing in substance and volume like a breeze turning into a wind.

This night, I dreamed of a time twenty-five years before.

Betty had gone shopping on a sunny Saturday in July and left me alone with the kids, five-year-old Helen and seven-year-old Michael. After struggling to keep them entertained at home, I decided an outing was in order, a chance to let them burn off some energy.

I took them for a hike to Fiske Hill, site of one of the minor skirmishes following the battle of Lexington.

As we strolled through fields of milkweed, with pods floating through the air like snow, I made up an adventure story to keep them engaged.

The three of us had been whisked away into a Narnia-like fantasy, where an evil demon ruled, with the arched gateway to the park replacing the magic wardrobe. Our quest demanded a trek to the top of the hill. On the way up, each of us would select a fallen branch to serve as a walking stick, and if we encountered the demon, the sticks would transform into enchanted swords.

Of course, no demon appeared, and we returned without incident to the parking lot, leaving our sticks by the side of the trail for other hikers to use.

Later that night, as Betty and I dozed in bed, we heard the pad of bare feet stopping outside our door, followed by a muffled sob. I rolled onto one elbow and squinted to focus my eyes. In the glow of a hallway night light, Helen stood trembling.

"What's wrong?" I said.

"The demon from the story you told us about. I dreamed he was chasing me through the woods."

Betty glared at me. "I told you your silly stories would scare the children."

Without answering, I slipped out of bed, wrapped an arm around Helen's shoulders, and led her back to her room.

Once she settled under her covers, I remained by her side. "There's nothing to be afraid of. It was only a dream."

"But it seemed so real, just like your story."

"Demons live only in the realm of made-up fantasies, not in the world we live in. Now relax. I'll stay with you until you fall back asleep."

"But what if he comes again? What if I get trapped in the fantasy world and can't return home?"

I took a deep breath, buying time to consider my answer. "Then you'll have nothing to fear, because in the fantasy world, you'll have magic of your own. You'll be the hero who defeats the demon."

She sat up and squeezed my arm so hard that I felt the urgency of her question in her touch. "How can you be sure?"

"Because I know you." I brushed away a lock of hair that had drifted across her face, and wiped a tear from her eye. "Because inside that head of yours, you're too smart for that demon, and because there's goodness in your heart."

I awoke to a crunch of dried leaves at the entrance to the shed, and glanced up to find Hannah standing there as Helen had so many years before, but in place of the glow of a night light, her face was bathed in starlight. In that pale light, a single tear trembled on her cheek like a dewdrop on a flower, before rolling down to her lips.

I beckoned her to come closer.

Without hesitation, she rushed in and snuggled by my side. Her breath came in short bursts, warming my arm as she sobbed, and the tears on her cheeks mingled with mine.

"Matty's gone. We've always been together, and I want him back."

"Me too." I whispered the next words, unsure I wanted them heard. "I may... have found a way to help."

She glanced up at me, her face full of the hope only a wizard could arouse. "How?"

The word hung in the air until the last echo of her voice died away. I stumbled with my answer. "I have a choice to make... but it's difficult ... complex wizard stuff. Your visiting here may have helped me decide."

She rested a hand on my arm and gazed at me with eyes too big for her head. "Then I pray you choose well."

After she left, my guide shuffled in from the yard and stopped where the child had knelt. "Have you decided?"

I squeezed my eyes shut, not to block out this world, but to believe in it even more.

Do I dare take the chance?

When I was young, strapping and eager to take on the world, my father would tease me, claiming my head was stuffed with dreams. Though the years had dampened those dreams, some still smoldered, and I'd had dreamer enough left in me to light the candle.

I nodded. "Yes."

"Then come with me."

We wandered some distance outside the village to a clearing in the woods. There, under the ghostly canopy of an ancient beech, my guide gathered leaves and pine needles for my bedding.

"You expect me to sleep here?"

"This ground's no less comfortable than the shed."

"Why here?"

"Your role is to set the goal. Mine is to guide you."

When I refused to settle on the makeshift bed, he relented.

"It's hard for flesh and blood to understand." He gestured up to the sprawling branches of the tree, which seemed to embrace the clearing and protect it. "This place is imbued with magic and enhances my ability to provide the enchantment you need—no easy task. Now get some sleep. For this transition, you'll need all the strength you can muster."

Realizing I'd learn nothing more, I followed his advice and lay down. But every time my eyes closed, I pictured the wolf-headed boatman carrying Matthias away. The vision haunted me until my eyes popped open again, searching out the cottage that housed what was left of the family.

My guide recognized my struggles, and waved his hand as he'd done before. The ground beneath me swayed, and my mind clouded. My head became too heavy to raise. My arms and legs numbed, and my vision blurred. Only my heartbeat remained, a steady rhythm like a metronome.

In this state, I discovered reality was a choice, a blank canvas on which I could paint whatever I wished, and on my whim, I could create a new world. Content in this knowledge, my concerns faded away.

I sighed, and the trees sighed with me. The night breathed softly, and I fell into a deep sleep.

In the middle of the night, I awoke to an ache in my right arm, a throbbing like I experienced after letting Michael pitch to me during his little league days. On summer evenings after work, I'd dig out the worn catcher's mitt from my childhood, and follow his pitches as they smacked into the glove with a thud. Though I never told Michael, I had to ice my arm after each of those sessions, and the pain caused me many a restless night.

Now, as I rested on the hard ground, pressing my eyes closed and trying to fall back to sleep, a foreboding overwhelmed me, a sense I was no longer alone, that another being lay beside me. I held my breath and listened.

The distinct breathing of another sounded inches from my ear. When I turned ever so slightly, I felt the whisper of warmth on my cheek.

My guide? Unlikely. He never sleeps, and I've never caught him breathing.

I opened one eye a slit and glanced to the far end of the clearing. He stood where I'd seen him last, leaning against the sprawling beech, visible in the darkness only thanks to the faint glow that followed him everywhere.

Still troubled by the unnamed dread, I rolled to my other side, and my eyes sprung wide. A man lay beside me. I tried to speak with him in that way we have when we speak in dreams, but my voice emerged more like a moan.

I turned back to my guide and rose to one elbow. A question formed on my lips, but I hesitated to speak it, unsure if this was a dream within a dream.

He nodded with a hint of a smirk, and mouthed the words:

Trust me.

What choice do I have?

I slumped back to the ground, more confused than before, but of one thing I was certain: in the morning, I'd awaken to a new reality.

Chapter 8 – Lumberjack

I startled to the poke of a boot to my ribs, a jarring sensation interrupting a pleasant dream, but the pain from the poke was no dream. I opened my eyes to a gruff stranger with a thick red beard.

"Up lad," he said. "There's work to do. The lumber won't wait."

His words grabbed my attention. No one had called me lad in years.

As the mist of sleep dissipated, I took in the face of a man with broad shoulders and bulging forearms. Despite his stern expression, his eyes displayed a kinder disposition.

"Up lad," he said again. "First day's always the hardest."

Lad?

I glanced past him. At the edge of the clearing, my guide slouched against a tree, picking at his teeth with a twig sharpened with his blade. I opened my mouth to speak, but he raised a finger to his lips and let out a loud *shhhh.*

The man with the red beard never flinched, apparently deaf to the sound. As he turned to walk away, he called back. "And don't forget your axe."

An axe lay in the grass beside me where he pointed. It sported a stout handle longer than my arm, and its steel head glistened in the morning sun.

I groaned, mustering my courage to move. Even in my soft bed back home, I'd arise in the morning with a stiff back and a sore left hip. How much worse would I feel after a night on the ground? But on this morning, I scrambled to my feet with no pain at all.

As I bent to retrieve the axe, I gaped at my hands. The swelling in my knuckles had eased, the brown liver spots had vanished, and the purple veins had cleared.

I hefted the axe and hustled after the red-bearded man, having no problem keeping up with his long stride. He led me to the river, a short distance upstream from the village, where a half-dozen men sat on freshly cut logs, eating breakfast.

When I arrived, the others grunted a greeting between bites, and their leader told me to wash up in the river. I shuffled to the bank, hoping the cool water might drive the cobwebs from my head.

As I knelt to splash my face, an unfamiliar reflection stared back. The markings of a lifetime had disappeared, the worry lines had faded, and my eyes sparkled with the anticipation of youth.

On impulse, I tugged at the sleeve of my tunic—leather boots and a tunic had somehow replaced my bathrobe and slippers. A thick forearm appeared, tanned as burnished maple and covered with black hair. As I flexed my fists, the cords of my muscles rippled, as defined as the arms of my youth.

While not displeased with shedding my bed clothes and aging body, I had one concern. I fumbled around the tunic pocket and sighed with relief as my fingers caressed the vial, as always warm to the touch.

After we finished an ample breakfast, the red-bearded man set us to work, assigning each of us a section of forest to chop down trees, strip off their branches, and trim them to logs of manageable size.

For a couple of winters, during the oil crisis of the seventies, Betty and I had committed to heat our home with wood. We bought a stove and had seven cords of firewood delivered to the end of our driveway. On crisp fall days, I went out with my splitting wedge, split the logs, and stacked them at the back of the yard to dry for the season, but I hadn't chopped a whole tree since Boy Scout camp.

Now I exercised the skills I learned that summer when I earned my totin' chip badge. My shoulder muscles expanded and contracted as I hefted the axe on high and drove the blade into the trunk at alternating angles, making the chips fly.

Once every hour, we took a break, and the foreman passed around water skins. As I quenched my thirst, I checked with my guide, who waited on a flat rock by the river. He'd smile, wink, and go back to picking his teeth.

We chopped all morning, until the sun reached its zenith, and the foreman rang a bell three times. Then we broke for lunch, with each workman heading home to his family. With nowhere else to go, I sought out Elizabeth and the children, wondering if they'd recognize me.

My concern was unwarranted.

Hannah spotted my approach, and despite my metamorphosis, skipped out to meet me shouting, "The wizard is back!"

Upon hearing her daughter, Elizabeth burst through the cottage door, but paused to take the measure of me. After a moment, her red-rimmed eyes brightened, and a hopeful spark ignited within them.

She stopped an arm's length away and nodded approval. "Well, wizard, it appears you possess real magic after all."

Hannah wandered over to the lilac bush and picked a cluster of purple droplets, still moist from the morning's dew. A surge of affection welled up in my chest as she handed the gift to me, beat down at once by the recognition that I'd done nothing thus far but raise their expectations. For now, the child saw only the good in me and none of the bad. I prayed not to disappoint.

I shared a quiet meal with them, leaving much unsaid. Matthias's absence hung over us, yet the mood remained upbeat. The power of my newfound youth had brought renewed hope to mother and child.

Following the lunch, I returned to work. My axe whistled through the air and landed with a thud on the trees. I swung it a hundred times or more, but my muscles never complained, and my arms never tired.

Magic indeed.

Once we felled a tree, several of us would bind it with ropes and drag it to the river. As the current sent it drifting south to its destination, the foreman scribbled a record of its passage in a ledger. When the sun sunk nearer the horizon, he handed three of us a long pole with a grappling hook at its end and led us to the bank. Following the lead of the others, I waded knee-deep into the water and gazed upstream. In the distance, I caught a round wooden basin bobbing toward us.

Unlike the wolfman's boat, this was a crude craft, more tub than boat, and contained no passengers. As it approached, we hooked the vessel with our poles and tugged it to shore.

The foreman reached inside and withdrew a waterproof pouch.

"What's that?" I said.

"Reports. The lords of the south love reports. This here's the ledger from the clerk at the top of the hill. Tonight, I'll add my report to the pouch, and in the morning, I'll send it downriver with the logs."

At day's end, when all had departed, I lingered alone by the river bank. My guide slunk up from behind and pointed to the vessel. "Your chariot to the source."

I eyed the tub, float-worthy enough for a passenger or two, but far from a comfortable ride. "Is this the best you can do?"

He shrugged. "You choose the quest and I the way, but the magic chooses the means."

What choice do I have?

The wolfman rode with the boy on the current, and so would I, but with no idea of the length of the voyage, I needed to first gather supplies.

I returned to the cottage to share what might be my last meal with my adopted family.

We ate in silence, with both mother and child sensing something unspoken.

When we finished, I turned to them. "I need to go away on a wizard's journey, and I can't say when I'll return, but you'll always be in my thoughts, and my goal remains the same—to bring you hope. Now, if you'll excuse me, I have a long day ahead and will need to rest."

With that, I retreated to the shed, lay down on the straw, and pretended to sleep. When the candles in the cottage had burnt low, I rose and, with some guilt, stole enough food for a day and a half, and stuffed the provisions into a sack.

As I slipped through the soft sod of the garden, past the next day's store of wood, I spotted the tarp used to keep it dry. The tub, never intended to hold passengers, offered no shelter and would leave me exposed to the weather, so I pulled the tarp off the pile and added it to the sack.

When I turned to go, I found Hannah blocking my way.

"Where are you going?"

"I told you, on a wizard's journey."

"Are you going to find Matty?"

I rested a hand on her cheek, and my lips parted, but no words emerged.

What can I say?

She gazed up at me, waiting for an answer with eyes wide, bathing me in the kind of hope only a child possesses.

"I'll... do my best. Now go to sleep and pray I succeed."

She turned and shuffled up the steps to the porch, dragging her feet, but after she retreated inside, I caught her spying on me from behind the kitchen curtain.

Time to go.

I twisted the neck of my sack, tied a knot, and raced off before I lost my nerve.

At the river's edge, I tossed the sack into the tub, but hesitated to board. Instead, I gazed up the hill to the castle, where I'd first arrived in this world, and back toward the cottage, where the dear family slept. I pressed my eyes shut and pictured my own family. The years of my life played through in my mind; my children grew from infant to adult in a slow-motion dream.

What am I about to do?

As I prepared to board, I caught the patter of running feet on the mossy path down to the river—a girl approaching clutching a sack of her own.

"I'm going with you," Hannah said.

"No, you're not. I forbid it."

Before I could stop her, she dumped her sack into the tub next to mine, and clutched my wrist with both hands. "Matty and I have never been apart until now. I won't let you go without me."

"It's far too dangerous for a child."

"Not if I'm with a powerful wizard."

As I attempted to move her aside by force if need be, her mother appeared from the shadows, bearing her own supplies.

"You too, Elizabeth? I assumed you had more sense."

"She insisted on going." When I glared at her open-mouthed, she added, "I lost one child. I'll not lose another."

As her mother and I debated, Hannah let go her grasp and hopped into the tub.

As I turned to remove her, Elizabeth jumped in as well.

"Well," she said when both were settled inside. "What are we waiting for?"

Afraid they might slip from the bank and float away without me, I joined them, but now, with so much weight, the bottom stuck on the bank.

The vessel was bigger than I suspected, broad enough to stretch out our legs, and tall enough to hide our heads from prying eyes on the shore. I rose up on one knee and peered over the front. The river ahead loomed black, a winding path to the unknown.

I assessed the determination in the faces of my passengers—they would not be deterred. After three breaths in and out, and a longing look back at the village, I reached over the side with my axe handle and shoved us away.

The three of us huddled on the moist planks and grasped hands, as our vessel drifted from the shore.

Then, in a blink we broke free, seized by the current and swept away into the night.

Chapter 9 – River Run

As our humble vessel bobbed around the bend, leaving the village behind, Elizabeth gazed up at the stars.

Hannah curled up in her lap, humming a tune too cheerful for the circumstance. Whenever the vessel swayed, a wisp of raven hair fell across her eyes, and her mother brushed it away.

The calm lasted a short time.

As we slipped into open water, the current picked up, sending us on a wild ride. One moment, we careened downstream at breakneck speed, with waves sloshing over the side and soaking us with spray. The next, we were caught up in an eddy and spun around like an amusement park ride.

Thankfully, as the moon rose overhead, we settled into calmer waters, and a gentler rocking lulled our exhausted party to sleep—all except me. Such a starry night, floating in a magical world, should have filled my mind with dreams, but instead I lay awake listening to the water lapping the hull and wondering what had brought me to this place.

The rocking stirred memories of a day more than thirty years before, when I was riding the railroad for work.

I started my career as a system engineer, supporting clients in the field. With my territory in the northeast, a typical week consisted of leaving home on a Tuesday morning, and traveling for the next three days on the Amtrak from Boston to Philly. While many called this route the Acela corridor, I never rode that sleek express, which flew past the cities where I needed to go. Instead, I spent long hours on the lumbering northeast regional, with frequent stops along the way.

My schedule involved an early start each day and visits to two or three customers, where I'd answer questions, fix technical glitches, and tune performance. At close of business, I'd drag my suitcase down the hall of some budget hotel, order junk food room service, and collapse for the night.

On one such trip, I dozed off on the train. When a crusty conductor nudged me awake to demand my ticket, I realized I'd missed my stop. No choice but to get off at the next station, twenty-five minutes away, and backtrack.

When I boarded the return train, half-awake and frustrated, I found the car full but for a single seat. I lurched down the aisle as the train started up, and flopped into that seat. It took me a moment to realize I'd landed next to a young lady I couldn't stop staring at, someone I swore I'd met before.

She ignored me at first, concentrating on drawing on her sketch pad, no mean feat with the rocking of the train and the bouncing of the tray in front of her. I followed her delicate fingers, stained with pencil dust, as they transformed a blank page into an image of a young man who looked remarkably like me, sitting beneath an apple tree in bloom.

She caught me staring and glanced up, squinting to determine friend from foe.

"Do I know you?" she said.

"Not yet. I'm Burt."

"I'm Betty." She extended a hand, but drew it back shyly. "Excuse the pencil stains... an artist's hazard."

"You draw well." I gazed out the window, studying the houses speeding by, trying to slow the train with my eyes. "Where are you headed?"

"The city. I'm a student at NYU. I was visiting a friend in Philly. And you?"

I flushed. "I was headed to MetroPark from New York, but dozed off and ended up in Trenton. Now I'm late and mad at myself, so I hope I don't seem rude. I'm usually not like this."

We chatted for the rest of my brief ride, comfortable with each other in a way unusual for people who'd just met. She checked the time every few minutes to make sure I didn't miss my stop again.

When the conductor announced MetroPark, she smiled and said, "Are you sure you won't keep me company until Penn station? Then you could repeat the trip one more time. Jersey's so lovely this time of year."

I smiled back and shook my head.

As I rose to leave, she tore off a corner of her drawing, scribbled something, and pressed the scrap into my hand. "Give me a call the next time you're in the city."

That scene, which had played out like a movie on the darkened sky, transformed into a different memory.

Betty and I had debated whether to take two-year-old Michael on his first trip to the zoo, concerned he was too young, but a fine April day enticed us outdoors. If nothing else, he could race around the open spaces before exhausting himself and settling in his stroller.

He had little interest in the zoo, unable to distinguish between live beasts and those viewed on TV, but when we passed through the gift shop on the way to the exit, Michael came alive. He jumped free of his carriage and headed straight to the display of stuffed animals.

He sat on the floor for fifteen minutes or more, fondling one after another—an alligator, a lion, a panda too cute for words, and an all-too-traditional teddy bear—before settling on a little brown otter.

As we drove home, I glanced into the rear-view mirror and caught him asleep in his car seat, embracing his new-found friend. I tilted my head toward Betty, urging her to look. She struggled around with her belly seven months pregnant with Helen, and stared at him for what seemed like half the ride. When she turned back at last, she brushed my shoulder with her fingertips without saying a word. For all my cynicism, that moment was one when I forgave the world its iniquities and believed all was right.

A few years later, Michael broke his arm in a fall from a jungle gym and required surgery. While we waited for the doctor to emerge with news, I struggled to console a distraught Helen, telling her again and again her brother would be fine. At last, she fell asleep in my arms. I bent down and kissed her freckled nose, hiding how worried I was and thinking I would never love my wife and children more than I did at that moment.

As I started to doze off, a nearby splash startled me, and I opened my eyes to a massive silver fish circling our tub.

"Are you comfortable in there?" the fish said.

From the familiar glow surrounding the creature, I recognized him at once as my guide.

"How did you get like that?"

"I couldn't fit in the boat, so I adopted this form, because I liked the fish in the fountain. Do you approve?"

"Very nice," I said, trying to be polite. "So you can take any form you want?"

"Of course," the fish said, and took a lap around us, dove underwater, and came up squirting a spray above me, missing my head by inches.

"Then why do you appear as the boy?"

"Looking like the candle is less jarring. Imagine how you'd react if a talking fish appeared in your study."

A fish in my study? I'd have called 911 and never gone on this quest.

The fish leapt from the water, did a pirouette, and landed with splash. "Besides...." He squirted more water. "I like the hat with the plume."

"I don't suppose you could shed some light on our destination."

"And spoil the surprise?"

I coughed out a thin laugh, but my grin settled into a frown. "Will I find the boy?"

"That's the goal, isn't it? But it's your story. I'm merely the scribe. Whether you'll succeed or not is up to you."

The next day dawned with an angry sun that sent sparks skimming across the surface of the water. As we drifted farther south, it blazed hot overhead, forcing me to spread out the tarp for shade.

The vegetation along the bank changed as well, no longer the shire-like shrubs near the village of Graymoor on Nox. Instead, serpentine mangroves lined the shore, their tangled roots wriggling in the brackish shallows—a sign the river was nearing the sea, and our journey its end.

A half-hour later, fishing shacks appeared, with half-rotting docks jutting out into the water and nets strung out along them to dry. Next came cottages fronting tilled land, which increased in density as we floated by.

Ignoring the heat, Elizabeth slapped aside the tarp and leaned forward to check out the view. As she scanned the horizon, Hannah rose to her knees as well, but ahead the river bent hard to the east, obscuring what lay ahead.

At the bend, the channel narrowed, and we became stuck on a shoal. This messenger tub, intended to carry little weight but with so many passengers on board, had run aground.

I leaned over the side with my axe to push off, but the tub refused to budge. As I pondered a way to free us, the silver fish swam by, leapt out of the water and, much to Hannah's delight, landed with a splash, casting a wave and setting us afloat again.

Moments later, we rounded the bend, and my eyes widened. On a plain to the east lay a sprawling city with dozens of shops and hundreds of homes—a settlement like many others but for the dark cloud hanging over it, hiding the sun. At the mouth of the river, a sheer cliff climbed five hundred feet or more, protecting the city from the sea. I scanned the cliff's face but spotted no obvious ascent, no switchback cut into the rock, no path of any kind. Nothing short of ropes and a harness, bolts and carabiners—tools unavailable in this world—would allow us access to the top.

What truly set my mouth agape lay at the top of the cliff, a structure like the one uphill from Graymoor on Nox but much larger. A stone battlement surrounded it, from this distance appearing impossible to scale, with no visible gate or entrance. Not three but seven smokestacks loomed above it, belching forth soot and fouling the air.

"Is that where they're keeping Matty?" Hannah whispered.

"And if so," her mother said, "is your magic strong enough to find him?"

I glanced at my two companions, and then to the top of the cliff. "The answer to your questions—I don't know. But first, we best leave our little craft behind."

As we drifted near a jut-out, I swung my ax, hooked the root of a mangrove, and tugged us to shore. Once the three of us stood on dry land, I sent the tub floating on its way again.

"Let the lords of the south receive their reports on time, while we approach the city on foot, posing as a family of three come to shop in the marketplace. There, we'll meet with the locals, engage in the news of the day, and see what we can learn."

Chapter 10 – Grim Harbor

For the first fifty paces, I hacked my way through the mangroves with my axe, carving out a passage for the others to follow. Thereafter, the vegetation thinned and travel became easier. Eventually, we stumbled on a more well-worn path leading to a dirt road, broad enough for a mid-sized wagon, or three strays walking abreast.

With little shade on either side, our pace slowed as the sun blazed overhead. Each of us trudged along soaked in sweat—that is, until we neared the city and came under cover of the castle's cloud. Moisture that had made our clothing cling to our skin now raised goosebumps whenever the least wind blew.

After a half-hour's walk, past cottages not so different from those in Graymoor on Nox, we came to a stone arch that heralded the entrance to the market, with the words "Grim Harbor" engraved across its top. Inside, we discovered a meaner place than the village we left behind.

A dozen or more beggars crouched in the dust at the far side of the gate, and as our little party passed through, all rose to follow us. Unshaven men with sunken eyes dogged our steps and begged for handouts.

A one-armed man hopped up and extended a crutch to block our way. "Entry into Grim Harbor is not for free, especially for strangers."

A second joined him and gawked at us with a toothless smile. "Two coins are due, the toll for passing through the gate."

A gaunt man missing one eye jumped in, and pawed at Hannah with a three-fingered hand. "Pretty girl, have some food in that sack for a hungry man?"

Hannah turned to me, unsure of how to respond.

I rose up to my full height, brandishing my axe, and knocked the crutch aside.

The beggars gave way.

Once past them, a throng engulfed us, sweeping us through the winding alleyways and forcing us to lock arms to keep from being separated. I would have lost all sense of direction but for a bell tower carved into the cliff looming above the market. At its top, a clock peered over the people bustling below, with a face blaring out the time like an all-seeing eye. At each quarter hour, its bell struck with such force that my teeth chattered.

Hannah spun in circles, glancing to her left and right, at more people than she'd met in her life, but her mother stayed focused on the objective ahead. She craned her neck and fixed on the cliff, assessing how to scale it and locate her son.

I took a different approach, studying the faces of the villagers passing by. All gazed at their boot tops with a joyless cast to their features. At one point, an old man brushed past me, wobbling a bit, so we bumped shoulders. When he glanced up to mumble an apology, his bloodless cheeks and blue lips seemed frozen. As he ambled off, his gait seemed frozen as well.

In one alleyway specializing in fresh produce, a woman meandered through the stalls with a baby boy attached to her hip. At each stall, she tested the fruit, squeezing an orange, sniffing a pear, and checking the price hanging over each bin. A clever choice might net her three pieces instead of two. A selection with hidden rot meant she and her child might go hungry that day.

All the while, the baby took in the faces of the crowd, focusing on those with the brightest colored smocks. From time to time, he'd check out the clouds overhead, or turn to follow a sparrow flapping its way to the top of the cliff. Different from the others, his eyes shone, with no trace of hopelessness or despair, a child too young to have encountered the follies of man. Only later would he learn.

I stopped to watch the woman haggle, hoping to understand their ways. She pointed to each orange she'd selected, passed the vendor a coin and held open a cloth sack. The vendor dropped one into the sack and then a second, but as he reached for a third, I caught him palming the fruit and switching it for another—a rotten one the woman had rejected.

I grabbed his hand. "Not that one."

"An honest mistake." He pressed his hands together in front of his chest and made a small bow, no more than a tip of his head, and tossed the fresh orange into the sack.

As I headed off trying to catch up to Elizabeth and Hannah, the woman with the baby grasped my elbow and gaped at me.

She licked her dry lips and, with some effort, forced the corners of her mouth upward. "Such kindness, sir. A trait so rarely found."

I mumbled, "You're welcome," while glancing past her, afraid of losing the others in the crowd, and hustled off to catch them.

After a time, we came to an older section of the market, featuring a maze of alleys reminiscent of the spot in Prague where I'd purchased my guide's candle. Pushcarts with various merchandise crowded both sides, and shoppers stopping to browse further narrowed the passageway.

Displays of pots and pans, and knives with blades that flashed in the torchlight, gave way to collections of headscarves waving in the breeze created by passersby. The next set of wares heralded its presence with scents wafting our way. Soon we were surrounded by barrels of spice—cinnamon and nutmeg, and sprigs of freshly picked rosemary. Stalls with cakes and pies followed, and loaves of braided bread still hot from the oven. These spices and baked goods intermingled with sweets, apples dipped in caramel, or strings soaked in boiling sugar until the confection crystalized around them.

All through the market, Hannah pranced from one display to the next, stopping at each and badgering her mother to wait, but Elizabeth trudged forward, intent on the cliff. As it drew nearer, her eyes grew big as moons.

At the corner of a narrow alley, my guide reappeared, no longer a fish. Now returned to his boyish form, he signaled for me to follow with more than his usual smirk. He stopped before a shop with candles.

A merchant stood in front, arranging his display on a pushcart. Though the thought defied reason, he looked familiar. I glanced at my guide, who winked back and mouthed the words: *all things have a purpose*.

The merchant caught me staring. "Do I know you?"

"We met in Prague?"

"What is Prague?"

"I'm sorry. I mistook you for someone else. May I check out your wares?"

He nodded, stepped aside, and waved me through the doorway.

His collection of candles appeared drab and uninspiring, most made to provide light and nothing more, but behind the counter, I spotted a smattering of more exotic candles crafted for display. As I scanned them, much as I had when shopping for souvenirs on my travels, I gasped. On the top shelf, half-hidden behind the others, stood my candle—the boy with the tri-cornered hat.

"May I see that one?" I said, struggling to hide the tremor in my voice.

The shopkeeper dragged a three-step ladder to the spot below the shelf, and fetched the candle for me.

As I pretended to inspect it, marveling at how similar it seemed to the one I found in Prague, he eyed me and shook his head. "Not a practical piece. So much effort for a candle that can only melt once."

I met his gaze. If I added a pair of coke-bottle glasses, he might pass for my Prague merchant. "Perhaps... this candle possesses magic?"

The shopkeeper chortled, an annoying laugh that degraded into a cough. "Magic? I assure you, you'll find no magic in Grim Harbor. This is not some fantasy world. Here we struggle to survive. If you take this useless candle off my hands, I'll give you half-off."

"I'll take the candle and give you full price, if you tell me how to reach the castle at the top of the cliff."

He huffed and snatched the candle back. "Not worth the cost. Now be on your way with your strange outlander ways."

As I turned to go, my guide stepped aside from the entry way, revealing a customer newly arrived at the store—the woman with the baby. In such a crowded market, her presence could be no coincidence. She had followed me here.

She tossed me a nod to leave the shop and meet her outside. Alone in the alley, she pulled me close and lowered her voice. "There's no magic for those who've given up hope, but every now and then, I gaze at my child and dream." When the baby began to fuss, she shifted him to her other hip. "Your request is a strange one, but *I* can show you the way—a favor in return for your kindness. Before the birth of my child, I worked at a stall by the cliff. Sometimes, I'd sneak off and follow the boatmen as they dragged their recruits up top to be trained for war. I'll show you if you still insist...." She glanced at Hannah, and pointed up high. "...though the castle is no place for a family with a little girl."

Elizabeth came up from behind and rested a hand on the woman's arm. "I have another child, a boy, who was once a babe like yours. The boatman took him, and I long to get him back."

The woman shook her head. "A perilous proposition. I pray you change your mind."

Elizabeth reached into her sack and withdrew a leather pouch with a few coins. "I can pay you."

"No payment required for a fool's errand... though you appear no fool." She faced Elizabeth, whose eyes had begun to glisten, and after a moment's reflection, she nodded. "Perhaps you *will* find magic. I'll do as you ask."

As the woman led us through the market, a wind kicked up, strong enough to penetrate the fabric of my tunic and make me shiver. When we passed a kiosk selling firewood, she stopped and eyed the stacks. "Tonight will bring a chill, and I'd dearly love some wood for my stove, if only I had a third hand to carry."

Elizabeth reached out both arms. "Let me hold the child."

"Are you sure?" the woman said.

"More than sure. It's years since I've borne a babe, and I'd relish his touch."

The woman handed over the child, who snuggled in, sensing another mother's warmth. After the exchange, the woman bought three stout logs—all she could afford.

Before she could take them, I stepped in front and hoisted the load along with my axe, marveling how light they felt in my now youthful arms. "Lead the way. I'll bring these home for you."

"But your task to the cliff...."

"Our task can wait."

The three of us followed the woman to the edge of the city, where a one-room hovel lay, with a dirt floor and walls made of not much more than pine boughs, too flimsy to stand up to a strong wind.

She set down her sack, placed the child in a frayed wicker basket, and told me to leave the logs by the stove

The shadows had lengthened, and as she predicted, the chill that pervaded the town deepened. She grabbed a log, like the others too thick to fit in her stove, and began chopping with the sharpened edge of a rusty shovel, managing to hack off but a few splinters.

I stayed her hand. "My axe and I would be happy to help, if you let us."

She set down the shovel and turned to me, her eyes misting. "Forgive me. I'm unused to such kindness and have shown bad manners. I am Marta, and this is my son, Jethro."

"And we are Albert, Elizabeth and Hannah."

She wiped her hand on her smock and extended it to me. "I'm pleased to meet you. Will you share my modest meal?"

I clutched her hand in both of mine. "We'd be most grateful, but first, allow me."

I lugged all three logs outside, hefted my axe, and swung it with such force that I split each one in a single stroke.

With only a lone stool in the hovel, we sat in a circle on the ground to eat our meal. Marta offered to split an orange with us, but we declined, passing her instead two slices of bread and smoked ham from our sacks. She refused at first, but when Hannah begged to feed the child, she relented.

Hannah slid over next to the boy, and at her mother's urging broke off bites small enough for him to chew. The child clapped his hands and squealed with delight at his first taste of ham, making Hannah smile for the first time since her brother was taken.

When we finished our meal, Marta hoisted the baby on her hip and led the three of us to the base of the clock tower, with my guide trailing behind. With dusk settling onto the town, the shops had closed, the shoppers had gone home, and we stood alone.

In silence, she gazed up at the cliff, and her lips parted, but she spoke not a word.

I waited, imagining I could hear the clock in the tower ticking.

"It's here," she said at last, "where you'll find your way."

I ran my fingertips over the surface of the tower, searching for some switch or tripwire to open a hidden door.

Elizabeth came to my side and searched as well, with one hand on the sheer stone and the other over her heart.

I turned back to Marta and shrugged. "There's no opening here."

She appeared to wake from a trance, and her eyes moistened. "Pardon me, sir, but as I stand by the tower, I regret bringing you here. I owe you a debt, but this is no way to repay it. Best the entrance stay secret, and what remains of your family go on your way."

Her words ignited a spark in Elizabeth's eyes, and her face flushed. "That decision is for us to make." She wrapped an arm around her daughter. "This girl had never known a day without her brother before the boatman came. We will not stop until our family is whole again."

Hannah bit down on her lower lip and reached out a quivering hand. "Please, mistress, help us find Matty."

The woman scanned the cliff as if to gauge the distance to the castle above. At last, she accepted Hannah's outstretched hand, pulled her close, and gave her a kiss on the cheek.

"Very well." She passed the infant to Elizabeth and shuffled to the left edge of the tower, where gnarly vines obscured the base of the cliff. As she poked and prodded, the baby began to cry.

The woman interrupted her search and went to calm the child, but Elizabeth needed no help. She rocked from side to side and chanted soothing words, until the baby's eyelids fluttered, and he fell asleep. Despite the moment, Elizabeth smiled at me. "A good omen. Nothing is so peaceful as a baby asleep in your arms."

At last, the woman found what she searched for: a section of vine that was not vine at all, but vine-like branches crafted of stone and attached to a wire mesh behind.

"Lend a hand," she said.

I set down my axe, grasped two sections of the vine, and pulled. The entire mesh swung wide, revealing an archway large enough for the tallest man to pass through. Beyond the opening, partially hidden in shadow, lay the start of a spiral stairway.

The woman retrieved her infant from Elizabeth and made a small bow. "Such a blessing to find those so kind. I hope I've done you more good than harm, and I'll pray for your success."

Once she turned the corner, I queried my guide. "What will become of her and the child?"

"Who's to say? I'm a guide, not a soothsayer."

"But you lived a thousand lives and visited this world before. You must have a hint."

He waved a hand, much as if causing me to sleep, but this time I experienced a waking dream. Scenes flashed in my mind. The baby became older and the mother as well. Her skin blotched and thinned as the boy grew tall and broad. Then he was whisked away, pressed into service as a soldier to fight in the war.

I scowled at my guide. "You claimed to be a scribe to whom I could dictate the story. This is not how I wish her tale to end."

The scene flickered and more of the future showed. The mother became older and then younger. A man appeared in her life, kind and caring, and another angry and harsh. The boy grew sickly. The boy grew strong.

"Enough," I said. "Stop toying with me."

"But this is the way of the future, brimming with possibilities. Why don't you focus on your own story, the one you've yet to write?"

I went back to the gaping archway, blew out two breaths, and crept inside, at once inhaling the stench of refuse and human waste. I shuffled forward until my boots pressed against the face of the first step, but could see no more than a dozen stairs winding up into the distance.

From far ahead, a keening sounded, like wind whistling though cracks in the cliff, or the cries of souls in pain. Behind me, a muffled footstep dragged across the stone floor—Hannah leading her mother through the archway, her form half-hidden in the shadow cast by the dimming light of dusk.

"Where do you think *you're* going?" I said.

"To find my brother."

Elizabeth closed the gap between us. "And I to find my son."

"It's too dangerous. This wizard goes alone."

She pressed a hand to my chest and waited as if counting my heartbeats. When she spoke at last, a tremor marred her voice. "You're strong, wizard, and your magic may be strong as well, but the pleas of a mother and daughter can melt stone. We stay by your side."

I spun around and gaped up into the darkness. If Michael had been kidnapped, I'd have done anything to save him, and Betty would have stayed by my side.

I sighed and nodded.

My right boot hovered over the first step and settled gingerly, as if testing for solid ground. My left boot followed. As I gazed up, I realized my guide had pranced ahead, light as air. The corona that always accompanied him lit my way.

He paused before the stairway disappeared around a bend and beckoned for me to catch up. Afraid of getting too far ahead of the others, I turned to wait for mother and daughter. With my guide's glow invisible to them, they'd made little progress. Elizabeth bore a brave face, but Hannah's whimpering exposed her fear.

What if the source of despair is more forbidding than I imagined?

I leapt the stairs two at a time to reach my guide, and hissed through clenched teeth, too softly for the others to hear. "Before I lead them to who-knows-where, I need a weapon more powerful than this axe, something I can rely on to protect them."

"Like what?"

"Like an enchanted sword." When he gaped at me, I added, "In my fantasy novels, the hero always carries a special weapon to fight evil—a wizard's staff, a magic ring, a charmed bow."

"You're a silly man, Burt Higgins."

I made to poke him in the chest, but the keening rose to a shriek, and my finger froze in mid-air. "Silly or not, I won't take another step without it."

My guide sighed. "If you insist, I'll play along with your game. Follow me."

He skipped down the stairs past the others, making neither sound nor breeze, and raced out the archway, leaving me to scamper after him, with my two open-mouthed companions straggling behind.

Chapter 11 – The Jetty

I followed my guide to the end of the cliff, where the sheer rock stopped and the sea began. There, an impressive jetty jutted out into the water, protecting Grim Harbor from storms. Boulders of various shapes and sizes lay slotted together like pieces of a puzzle assembled by the children of giants. These extended so far out that, in the fading light, the final boulder remained shrouded in fog.

Before the others caught up, I confronted my guide. "Why did you bring me here?"

He gestured to where the boulders stretched out into the distance. "The weapon you desire."

I gazed out over the jetty. To the harbor side, the river Nox lapped against the rocks, but to seaward, angry waves pounded them, each proclaiming its arrival with a roar. While many of the boulders bore flat tops, others slanted at odd angles, with a coating of moss making them slick with spray. The farther out the jetty extended, the angrier the sea, with the wind whipping whitecaps across the stones.

Even from the shore, gaps between the rocks showed, some broad enough to require timing the trough between waves before taking a leap of faith—a trek far more treacherous than my stroll to the Lexington green.

"You couldn't pick an easier path?"

He made a mocking bow. "For a wizard's quest, the magic requires a proper venue."

My two companions arrived at the shore but made no move to intervene. No hint of doubt showed in their faces. They trusted not old Burt Higgins, but the great wizard my guide had conjured.

I stared across the jetty, assessing the path, and checked with my guide, knowing he answered questions only if well phrased. "At the end... where the boulders stop... will I find my sword?"

He nodded.

I took a deep breath and scrambled onto the first rock.

I hadn't climbed a jetty in years but had lots of experience. For several summers, while the children were young, we vacationed at a cottage on the beach in Kennebunk, Maine. Michael and Helen spent their days making castles in the sand, but dared the chilly water for no more than a few minutes. Yet every day, they'd interrupt their castle building to climb the jetty with me and fish at its end. They caught few fish but never ceased to relish the adventure—the trek across the rocks and the thrill of achieving the final boulder jutting into the sea.

The trek across this jetty differed in several ways. On vacation, I would never attempt to negotiate the rocks with waves so high. Moreover, these boulders presented more of a challenge than those back home, offering too many opportunities for a broken leg, or worse, a tumble into the sea. And this adventure took place with no 911 to call, and no copter to medivac an injured wizard to safety.

Yet something more insidious bothered me. As I crept from rock to rock, the wind stiffened, and the fury of the waves increased, as if the elements intended to keep me from my goal.

I began counting rocks. After each ten, I paused to rest and gauge how far I'd come before trudging forward into the mist. At last, I reached the point of no return, with the shore behind me hidden in the dusk, and the path ahead veiled in the fog.

No choice but to go on.

After several precarious steps and more than one near miss, I mounted the penultimate boulder, a stable platform from which to launch my final leap. At the far side lay a white rock slick with seawater, and with a pitch so sharp it appeared to point to the sky. A gap of a yard or more separated me from this rock, a reasonable distance for my youthful legs to vault if not for the slant and the spray.

Through the dusk and the fog, I caught a glow behind me

I turned to my guide. "Is that where—"

"You insisted on an adventure."

I counted the seconds between waves as they surged. At last, a broader trough appeared. I waited for the lead wave to crash, flexed my knees, and jumped.

As I landed, my front foot slipped on the wet moss and slid out from under me, knocking me to all fours. Before the next wave dragged me into the sea, I cast my axe forward so that its blade grabbed a notch in the rock, tugged with all my might, and scrambled to my feet.

At last, I stood at the end of the jetty. With an icy mist swirling around my head and a raging wind in my ears, I half expected a monster to rise up and swallow me whole.

"What's next?" I shouted to my guide, hoping he'd hear over the crash of the waves.

"Toss your axe into the water."

"And then?"

"You'll see."

I shook my head, for the moment wishing I'd never lit the candle. Then I pictured mother and child waiting at the head of the jetty, unable to see me through the fog yet believing in the power of my magic.

What the hell! I've come this far.

I hurled my axe into the maelstrom. The water frothed and seethed as my sole weapon sank into the sea, and then....

Nothing.

I turned to question my guide, but he'd vanished.

As I gazed out, unsure how to proceed, a silver fish burst forth on the crest of a wave, almost indistinguishable from the froth. It circled to show off its swimming prowess, leapt into the air, and spewed a stream of seawater onto the jetty. As the liquid landed, it hardened and took shape, and at my feet lay a scabbard. A leather-wrapped hilt protruded from its top, with a pommel riveted with amethyst studs, as brilliantly purple as the vial in my pocket.

I grasped the hilt and pulled, exposing a shimmering bronze sword with a double-edged blade. As I lifted it high overhead, the fog swirled around it and glowed.

I sheathed the weapon, buckled the scabbard around my waist, and headed back to the shore with a renewed spring to my step.

At last, the quest I'd dreamed of: A youthful body, a worthwhile goal....

And on my hip, an enchanted sword.

PART TWO

THE SOURCE OF DESPAIR

"In oneself lies the world and if you know how to look and learn,
the door is there and the key is in your hand."
Jiddu Krishnamurti

Chapter 12 – The Hall of the Mountain King

Despite the new weapon at my side, I hesitated at the stone archway, wary of the unknown.

Hannah and Elizabeth held no such doubts. When I'd emerged from the mist waving my enchanted sword overhead, all their doubts vanished. To them, I'd become the wizard of legend, certain to save Matthias.

With the way forward uncertain, I insisted the others wait at the base of the cliff while I scouted ahead. As they squatted on the ground partaking of food and drink, I stepped through the entrance into the darkened passageway. After pausing a moment to steel my courage, I headed off with my guide's glow showing the way. I curled around two bends of the spiral staircase until the light from below dimmed, and twenty steps more before stopping. Other than walls reeking with the fear of those who'd passed before, the stairway yielded none of its secrets.

As my eyes strained to pierce the darkness, an unwelcome dread crept into my mind. I turned to my guide. "If I die in this world, will I die at home as well?"

He stared at me for too long without answering, and then glanced away.

I grabbed him by the arm and forced him to face me.

His magical flesh shuddered, too human a response. "I warned you interfering in this world could be dangerous, yet you made the choice."

"But will I?"

His lips curled into that infuriating smile. "That depends on what you mean by death." He settled on a step, drew out his dagger, and commenced to clean his fingernails.

What do I mean by death?

Some claim you never die in a dream because such a terrifying vision would wake you first, but failing to wake, you'd die in reality too. Now, as I stood on the threshold of a perilous quest, I questioned which felt more like a dream: the world of Grim Harbor or my life back home.

As I grew older, my night dreams became more fanciful. Memories merged with scenes I read in my novels. Each morning, as the light of pre-dawn filtered through the curtains, I'd squeeze my eyes shut and cling to sleep, unwilling to abandon some elfin princess or knightly quest. What if, as we age, reality becomes too burdensome, forcing the mind to seek refuge in fantasy? What if reality lapses into dreams, and dreams become our new reality?

Is that what death means, embracing a dream so completely we wake no more?

I turned to a call from below, from Hannah at the foot of the stairway. "Where are you, wizard? Can we go now?"

I rushed back down and found her and Elizabeth perched on the third step. I squeezed her shoulder with one hand while clutching the hilt of my sword with the other. "You're right. The time for contemplation has passed. Follow me."

Since my guide's corona remained invisible to my companions, I unsheathed my blade to light the way, and set off, plodding up the stairs this time to let mother and child stay close behind.

We climbed in near silence. Beyond the scrape of boots on stone, the only other noise was a thin whine from wind whistling through cracks in the wall. As we progressed, a murmur from above overwhelmed the whine, droning on like a thousand intermingled voices with words so muffled, I could only imagine their meaning.

What are they trying to tell me? That my enchanted sword is no match for the lord of despair? That this hasty ascent will endanger my charges? That my quest will fail?

After a time, the murmurs turned to groans, indistinguishable between the trials of men and the travails of machines. As the pulsing grew more rhythmic, the machine-like quality prevailed—a distinct grinding of gears.

I prayed to whatever god might listen.

Let me choose well for mother and child. Let me not lead them into danger, and grant me this above all: let me find and rescue the boy.

I lost count of the stairs, but after what seemed like several hundred, the spiral straightened, and the passage widened into the final ascent. At its top, a greater archway beckoned. Dim light flickered through the opening, more like a murky gloom, but after so long in the darkness, my eyes narrowed.

The grinding became familiar, a noise I'd heard before, but this noise so much louder that it echoed in my ears.

With ten steps to go, I ordered mother and child to lag behind while I snuck on ahead. I took one step, then two, but the archway's base remained above eye level.

A fourth step, a fifth... I rose on my toes and peered inside.

Beyond the archway stood a grand hall, big enough to contain the Graymoor on Nox structure, moat and all. From my vantage, I marveled at the flying buttresses supporting a vaulted dome so high, its peak lay hidden in shadow.

Two more steps.

No surprise. The circular chamber hosted a dozen boiling cauldrons, each with gears alongside pumping bellows that drove the steam up through the stacks, spewing out gloom. Their size matched the scale of the imposing hall, but something other than the machinery made me tighten my grip on the hilt of my sword.

At the rear of the chamber, on a raised throne, sat a larger-than-life man garbed in what I could only describe as a shroud, a hooded garment that concealed his form and partially obscured his face. He leaned to one side, massaging his forehead with the palm of his right hand, while his left lay cupped over a wolf's head carving capping the throne's arm. His entire bearing slumped, weighed down by an excess of sorrow. At once, I understood why: here sat the aggregator of despair from all the castles in the land.

I twisted around to the scuffle of steps behind me, as Elizabeth chased her impetuous daughter into the chamber. The two skidded to a stop in the archway, stunned by what they saw.

With my free hand, I motioned them back, while I crept forward with my enchanted sword extended, ignoring how its blade had begun to shake. With every step, the demon grew larger.

He swiveled his head in my direction, eying me with little more interest than I'd eye an ant crawling across the floor.

I glared at him over my outstretched weapon, though its tip reached well below his knee, and stopped one pace beyond a sword's length away.

Foolish wizard. Still within reach of the giant's arm. He could swat me like a fly if he wished.

He made no aggressive move, though. Instead, he removed his hand from his forehead, and crinkles formed at the corners of his eyes. A voice grated through the chamber like gravel on rock. "Well, what have we here?"

My mouth went dry, and I swallowed to bring moisture before speaking. "Are you... the source of despair?"

Instead of responding, his shoulders heaved, and he let out a sigh so strong its wind nearly knocked me over.

Before my knees buckled, my guide sauntered out from behind me and tossed the demon a wave.

"Ah, my old friend," the demon said. "Now I understand."

I fell back a step and assessed the situation anew. Behind the throne loomed a clock in a varnished wood case, with an oversized face that mirrored the one on the village watchtower. As the brass pendulum in the case swung back and forth, each tick and tock echoed off the rafters of the dome. To its left, marring the plain back wall of the chamber, there loomed a massive iron door, all black but for two vertical rows of silver rivets, and with no visible knob or handle.

My gaze drifted from the door to the clock face, and from the demon to my guide.

Old friend?

The demon shifted in his throne with the pained expression of someone with chronic back ache. His lips twitched, betraying no more than a hint of a smile, as if any greater motion might crack open his face.

After studying me from head to toe, he winked at my guide, whom I'd assumed invisible to all but me. "Is there no end to such fools?"

My guide dipped his chin in what for him passed as a sign of respect. "You were once such a fool yourself."

"You're right, I suppose, but a long time ago."

The demon struggled to his feet and shuffled toward me, until he came within striking distance of my sword. With one hand, he reached out to swipe the weapon aside, but his fingers passed through the blade as if made of the sooty steam rising up from the smokestacks.

"Sheath your sword," he said, with neither threat nor malice in his tone. "Your weapon cannot harm me, and your arm will grow tired if you keep waving it about."

I did as he said, and dropped to one knee, for the air through which this demon moved filled me with dread. For the first time, I dared to meet those ghostly eyes, and withered under his gaze. My lungs struggled to force out enough air to make a sound. "Am I... in the presence... of the lord of despair?"

"Not its lord, merely its chronicler—a dreadful job." He glanced up and checked with my guide, who nodded. "You see, like you, I lit an enchanted candle, eager to end sadness in the world—a noble but futile quest. But where others gave up and returned to their world, I remained too stubborn. Realizing that finding the source of despair was a fool's errand, I begged my guide to alter my quest, choosing instead to better understand its causes. But with so much despair in the world, I stayed longer than intended, identifying and logging its sources."

I realized the crinkles around his eyes had been etched not from an excess of laughter but from the incessant squint of someone in perpetual communion with despair. He settled back on his throne and resumed massaging his forehead, though the crinkles remained.

It thrilled me with an uncertain horror to know that beneath the dusty shroud, those eyes had once viewed my old world, perhaps been a friend or neighbor who'd been seized by a longing not so different from mine. His words, however, threw me into turmoil.

What do I do next?

I cast a puzzled glance at my guide.

He shrugged. "You asked me to show you evil as perpetrated by dark lords in your fantasy novels, but no such lord exists in this world or the other. What did you expect me to do?"

"I wanted the truth, the real cause of despair."

"Yes, and unable to satisfy your simpleminded request, I brought you here, the next closest thing, for, more than anyone through all eternity, this man understands the sources of despair." He nudged me forward with a hand to the small of my back, and the man-spirit motioned me to approach the throne.

When I stopped three paces away, afraid to come closer, he gestured to the clock. "Our lives pass like the ticking of this clock—tick tock, back and forth—but with only the illusion of progress, until the hours and days wind down. And what is it worth?"

"And yet you continued to search. Can you share with me what you found?"

"If I told you, you'd refuse to believe me. No. That which I learned, you must experience for yourself." He stood up, unfolding himself a limb at a time, ankles and knees, hips and back, and hobbled toward me, wearing a look on his face that would have sucked the hope from poets and lovers alike. He stopped an arm's length away and motioned to the door behind him. "If you still insist on learning, your search must begin behind this portal."

I took a step toward the door, but halted, unsure of whether to accept his offer, until I recalled the goal I'd added to my quest: *help me rescue the boy.*

I turned to movement from behind.

Mother and daughter had emerged from the archway and were inching closer, a palpable hope on their faces.

I can't disappoint them now.

I turned to my guide and motioned for him to lead us through, but his feet stayed rooted to the floor.

"What are you waiting for?" I said.

"You're a foolish man, Burt Higgins, but a fascinating companion. I shall miss you."

"Miss me?"

"I can't help you with this part of the quest. What you seek lies beyond my realm."

"But—"

"I provide fantasy adventures, but none satisfied you. I tried to meet your requests, but my magic has limits, so I leave you now in this spirit's hands—a different approach. It's more what you're searching for, more... real."

The demon-spirit waved a hoary hand, and the portal swung wide. Through the opening lay a blurry scene obscured in fog, all of which stayed on the far side of the threshold, as if held at bay by an invisible barrier. I squinted, but made out no detail save shadowy shapes. He urged me to enter.

"Are you now to be my guide?"

"A guide of sorts."

I cast a glance back at mother and child. "And what of them?"

"Despair may be found in all worlds, but more than anything, it dwells in our hearts. To understand, you must travel the path alone." He beckoned again, more insistent this time.

I pictured Matthias, lost and afraid, then exhaled a stream of air and stepped inside.

Chapter 13 – Ships by the Shore

The fog swirled about my ankles but quickly cleared, leaving me standing at the edge of a body of water. Not a river or an ocean, more like a channel, for through the haze, I made out the outline of an island on the far side.

Behind me lay a secluded valley bracketed on three sides by craggy cliffs plunging down into the sea. Other than an approach by boat, no access appeared save a treacherous notch half way up the rear headwall. At the base of this barrier nestled a fishing village of the sort that might have graced the New England seashore in colonial times. Its villagers clustered around me on the shore, standing so still I hardly noticed them. All gazed out to sea, gaping like an audience viewing a Greek tragedy. Given the number of cottages in the village, the entire town must have turned out.

I scanned the faces in the crowd, hoping to understand why they'd come. None gave me a second glance.

My clothing fit well with theirs, handmade leggings tucked into leather boots, with loose fitting smocks on their backs, but without any visible weapons. To them, I might appear a soldier of fortune passing through their town, with my bronzed arms and enchanted sword—useless until now—still at my side.

I sensed an air of gloom beside me, and turned to catch my spirit-guide visible only as an outline in ripples of heat rising from the ground. A translucent arm stretched out toward the sea, and a bony finger pointed.

In the middle of the channel, less than a mile offshore, I saw what entranced the villagers. Two ships emerged from the fog, sailing toward each other from opposite directions. The larger one appeared to be a man-of-war with three towering masts and two rows of cannon dotting its side, while the other seemed a merchant schooner, less than half the size, and with fewer guns to defend it.

As the phantoms glided closer to each other, the crowd leaned in on the balls of their feet and held their collective breath. When the ships drew alongside, a series of flashes flared from the hull of the man-of-war. Two seconds later, the boom hit the shore, making my teeth rattle. Then, in slow motion, the mainsail of the schooner cracked, teetered, and drifted overboard into the sea.

Once the smaller ship had become disabled, a breeze swept away remnants of the fog, so the sights and sounds of the battle sharpened, as if a camera had zoomed in on the scene. The crews of both ships crowded the gunwales, facing each other and cursing. Grappling hooks, tossed from the man-of-war, seized the smaller ship in their grasp. Sabers swung in the air, sharp and menacing as the attacking crew boarded. Flintlocks fired, and more smoke filled the space between the two. After no more than ten minutes, the scene silenced but for the whisper of a woman's wail carried on the breeze.

I glanced around. No shouts of outrage, no cries of despair. The crowd waited glassy-eyed, but for what?

I turned to the faint ripple that was my spirit guide and mouthed one word without sound: "Why?"

The ripple firmed, and the gravelly voice spoke, though no one else appeared to hear. "That channel marks a passage between countries often at war. This is not the first battle these villagers have witnessed."

As I gaped, the man-of-war's crew retreated to their ship and steered it away. When they reached a safe distance, their cannons erupted once more. The schooner's remaining mast fell, and flames leapt from its deck. Moments later, the crippled craft tilted bow up and slipped beneath the waves. Seawater hissed and boiled, sending steam into the air until nothing remained but what looked like fog on a calm day.

The sea turned to glass, and out of the fog, a tiny vessel emerged. As it floated toward the shore on the tide, leaving slender v-shaped lines in the water, its blunt form clarified—a wicker cradle.

Inside lay an infant, swaddled in the charred remains of a sail.

Now the villagers pointed and cried out. A middle-aged woman separated from the crowd and rushed to the edge of the water, glancing up to the heavens and down at the infant with hands clasped across her heart. A man with one arm followed and, together, they waded knee-deep into the waves and dragged the baby to shore.

I spun about, searching for my spirit guide, chronicler of despair, but he was gone.

The woman grasped the child in her arms and faced her neighbors, who had gathered round her and the man in a half-circle. As if led by a chorus conductor, they began to sing:

As the peace follows the battle,
As the calm follows the storm,
As the day follows the night,
The morning will dawn,
the sun will rise,
And goodness will flow.
Give thanks, give thanks,
For goodness will flow.

The song died down in the lapping of the waves, and the villagers backed away to return to their homes, all except the couple with the baby.

The woman, still clutching the child to her breast, gestured to the cradle. "Don't let it slip away in the undertow. We'll need a cradle now that we've been blessed with a son."

The man rushed in to bring the crib to the shore, but when he tried to pull with his one arm, the waterlogged vessel proved too heavy. He proceeded to drag it through the wet sand.

"Not like that," the woman said. "The wicker will shred."

When the man struggled once more to no avail, I stepped forward and grabbed one end.

He smiled at me. "Give thanks, stranger. Give thanks."

The woman sang the rest. "And goodness will flow."

The two of us bore our load, following the woman with the crying baby to a cottage at the edge of the village. There, the man warmed blankets by the stove and lined the crib with them, while the woman rocked the boy and hummed a lullaby.

The child's crying ceased, and the terror eased from his eyes, until at last his tiny eyelids fluttered and closed.

When certain he slept, the woman laid him down, swaddled in warmth.

The three of us retreated to the kitchen, where the woman placed a kettle on the stove while the man set out three mugs.

Once the water came to a boil, she poured us all some tea. "Thank you for your help. I am Liza, and this dear man is my husband, Efrem."

I beheld the two of them, so happy together, and wondered why the spirit had brought me here. After a moment, my manners took over, and I shook myself from my stupor. "I'm pleased to meet you. I'm Albert."

"Welcome to Crix Haven."

"Crix Haven? An interesting name. Where does it come from?"

The man called Efrem took a sip from his mug, judged the tea too hot, and set it aside. "As I'm sure you noticed, this valley is difficult to access except from the sea. Many generations ago, one of the king's sailors named Crix became shipwrecked here following a battle. Having no interest in returning to war, he found this valley's soil fertile for farming, with plenty of fresh water, and the nearby shallows teamed with fish. Survival came easy, yet he lived alone. A year later, another of the battles took place in the channel, and this time a woman floated to shore on a charred plank from her ruined ship. Finding her injured but alive, Crix nursed her back to health, and together they raised a family. It was he who composed the song we sing. Through their example of kindness and generosity, future survivors have been able to recover and settle here."

Liza rested a hand on his and glowed. "That's how I met my Efrem, after he'd lost his arm in a battle. And now, that's how we can raise this child as our own."

I gazed into the steam from the tea, still unsettled from this flitting from world to world, and refocused on the reason I came. "A sad tale. How do you cope with such sadness?"

The woman arched a brow. "Sadness? Crix Haven has been a blessing to many, and because of these battles, our village thrives. All of us are survivors, those who arrived after a battle or, like me, descendants of those who washed ashore."

Efrem eyed my sword. "I see you're a warrior, but not one who came by boat." He twisted in his seat and pointed toward the mountains. "Few before you have tried to cross the pass. Fewer have succeeded. Why did *you* come?"

"A warrior perhaps, though a reluctant one. More a seeker. I came to explore, to learn from those like you who have faced hardship. Crix Haven is one brief stop on my journey."

"Then you're most welcome, but since the violence of your craft always follows, we pray you won't stay long. Now the light is fading, and we'd be ungrateful hosts to urge you to attempt the pass in the dark. Please accept our hospitality in exchange for your kindness. Be our guest and rest here for the night."

I glanced out the window to the mountains. The notch through the cliffs gaped back at me in shadow, starting halfway up, and with no obvious access.

I turned back to my host. "Crossing the pass exhausted me, and I stumbled through in a daze. I have little memory of the trail down to the village, and even in daylight, I'd struggle to find my way."

He reached out his one hand and rested it on mine. "In the morning, I'll guide you to the trailhead, but no farther. Mysterious forces dwell in that pass, beyond my desire to know. I'll take you to the entrance and wish you well, and then retreat to the safety of this cottage and the loving arms of my family."

Chapter 14 – Guns and Drums

The notch in the mountains lay a thousand feet high, accessible only by a series of switchbacks littered with scree. I trudged along with my head down, too focused on my footing to speculate on what loomed ahead.

After an hour or so, the slope leveled, and I stood at the entrance, but this notch was no ordinary passage. Whirling mists foreshadowed a portal like the one in my spirit-guide's castle. As I braced my back, letting my lungs fill with air, I narrowed my gaze and tried to peer across to the far side. I poked a hand into the haze to test the air but felt only a burning cold.

Another leap of faith.

I sighed and stepped through.

At once, a headwind howled and pellets of sleet stung my face, forcing me to shield my eyes. Half-blinded, I froze in place, worried my next stride might send me tumbling over a cliff, until I caught the outline of a larger-than-life man, visible only as a gap in the storm.

My spirit-guide.

He urged me on, his words coming to me as little more than undulations in the wind. "Follow... the... cairns."

From my treks in the White Mountains with Michael and Helen, I was accustomed to these stone markers, large rock piles set to keep hikers on the trail. The harsher the climate, the taller and closer together the cairns.

Now knowing what to look for, I narrowed my search and made out a cairn as high as my chin and no more than three paces away. I shuffled forward, testing the ground with each step until my fingertips brushed the stones. Satisfied they were real, I traversed from cairn to cairn until a second portal showed, a light filtering through the fog.

I paused to catch my breath before entering.

"Despair lurks in all worlds," the spirit-guide had said.

Was the refuge of Crix Haven from the history of my home or, like Graymoor on Nox, a village in the fantasy realm? Or was despair more like my night dreams, an amalgam of the two, a vision cobbled together from both worlds? What if each of these painful events had damaged the fabric of space and time, and these portals between them represented the scars?

I drew in three shallow breaths, reluctant to suck in too much of the freezing air. I'd come here to learn, and harsh lessons are never learned without pain.

Time for the next lesson!

On the far side of the portal, a welcoming warmth enveloped me, but accompanied by the wooziness I'd come to expect through these transitions. I grabbed the nearest solid object, a wooden post, and closed my eyes.

The sensation passed in seconds, but before opening my eyes, I exercised my other senses, inhaling the scents and listening to the surrounding sounds.

Indoors for sure. A crowded room filled with sweaty men. Lots of banter, but subdued. The air thick with the smoke from a wood fire and the stale smell of warm ale.

I opened my eyes and blinked twice at the scene—a colonial tavern, lit by a single candle at each of eight tables and the flicker of flames from a stone fireplace. I glanced through the haze at my fellow travelers. To my surprise, all were dressed as minutemen.

On either side of the door, muskets had been stacked by the wall. I shuffled to the window and slipped the curtain aside. Sheets of mist rippled across a village common in the light of pre-dawn.

My comrades nursed mugs of grog, and many appeared to have been drinking through the night, a potion to steady their courage. A grim expectancy filled the room.

A young man with sand-colored hair tied in a tail approached me with a mug in his hand. Despite a forced bravado, his smooth face revealed his age. No razor had ever touched his skin.

"You're late to our party," he said, "but you haven't missed much. The action is yet to come. You still have time to down a pint."

I mumbled a thank you and gulped half the mug in three swallows, only now realizing how thirsty I'd become.

As I wiped my mouth with my shirtsleeve, I eyed the boy. "And what action might that be?"

A naïve grin curled across his lips, different from the more serious demeanor of those around us, but before he answered, hoofbeats sounded outside.

A shout rose, and a cry at the door. "The British are coming!"

My fellows raced about, buttoning coats, donning tricornered hats, and grabbing muskets before dashing out to the common.

The boy brushed past me, one of the last to leave, but paused to hold the door. "Well, lad, our moment's come. No time to tarry." He motioned toward the wall. "Don't forget your musket."

We mustered in three ragged lines at the far end of the common. No one spoke. We hardly breathed. After a minute, the muffled sound of drums drifted through the fog on the breeze.

A man who appeared to be our captain paced before us, shouting orders. "Hold your ground, lads. Hold your ground."

A light flashed behind me and several more, like bits of lightning without the thunder. I snuck a peek. Around the perimeter of the green clustered a crowd in modern-day dress, taking pictures, the flashes on their cameras blinking on and off like fireflies. They stood three deep with many in the back row balancing on stools or ladders for a better view, much as I'd done for so many springs when Michael and Helen were small.

I'd been transported to Lexington's customary Patriot's Day celebration, April 19th, 6:00 AM, the annual reenactment of the battle, to be followed by the traditional pancake breakfast and parade.

But what year?

The drumming ahead grew louder, and out of the mist a spectral column of redcoats emerged. They spread out, with muskets and bayonets pointed toward our lines. Their mounted leader pranced back and forth in the no man's land between us, waving his sword and shouting for our ragtag militia to disperse. "Lay down your arms, you damned rebels!"

The men around me fidgeted in place, and a few fell back.

Our captain drew his sword as well and called out, "Stand your ground. Don't fire unless fired upon, but if they mean to have a war, let it begin here."

Those famous words uttered at every reenactment sent a chill up my spine. I gripped my musket tighter, struck the pose of the minuteman, and gazed past the British to the front of the green.

Where is the statue?

Despite the mist, I should have seen the familiar monument perched high on its pedestal, but no statue appeared.

Out of nowhere, a shot rang out, and pandemonium ensued. Muskets on both sides fired, filling the common with smoke, and the boy beside me—the one who had offered me the drink and ushered me out from the tavern—stumbled and fell.

I reached out to help him up, but upon touching his coat, drew back my hand in horror. My fingers dripped with blood.

I spun around to the sound of the spectators cheering as if watching a staged battle in a summer action movie. Several hundred cameras captured the scene.

Just a reenactment. Not real.

I lay my musket on the ground and cradled the boy's head in my hands.

He stared up at me glassy-eyed, but with the same innocent smile, and whispered words unintelligible in the tumult around me.

I leaned closer, my ear an inch from his lips.

One word resounded: "Avenge!"

Hot blood rose in my cheeks, and I drew my sword.

Time to find out how strong its enchantment might be.

Before I could charge my enemy, I caught the cries of children running toward me. "Papa, papa."

From amongst the crowd, nine-year-old Michael and seven-year-old Helen rushed out. "Papa, papa," they cried again, and as they neared the line of minutemen, they're clothing morphed to match mine, now dressed in colonial garb.

"Go back," I yelled to them.

At the front of the common, the British resumed their march, bayonets at the ready. I fingered the hilt of my sword and faced the enemy. Several of the redcoats had reloaded and knelt in a disciplined row, prepared to fire again.

I sheathed my sword and ran back to my son and daughter. As the muskets fired, I dove upon them, knocking them down and shielding their bodies with mine.

At once, the ground spun, and the children beneath me dissolved like phantoms into the grass. Moments later, the minutemen and redcoats disappeared as well, and everything turned to black.

I awoke to a man jogging me awake as I lay with my head slumped on a wooden table.

"Countdown's about to begin," he said.

I nodded and tried to shake off my daze.

Countdown to what?

I recognized a scene from my past, a memory too benign for a scar.

I sat at a military-issue field desk inside a canvas tent, with a half dozen comrades who tapped away at typewriters and primitive computing machines. Beneath the glow of a half dozen naked bulbs strung overhead, my tunic had transformed to olive drab fatigues, my calfskin footwear to black combat boots. The only hint of a weapon lay on my shoulder—the image of a bent arm clutching a sword, the insignia of my old unit. All the others in the tent wore the same.

A patch above my shirt pocket read Higgins, and the pin clipped to my collar showed a rank of specialist fifth class.

After college, I drew a low number in the draft lottery and enlisted in the army, but by the time I completed my training, the Vietnam War was winding down. I was relieved but mildly disappointed, a young man with a naive desire for adventure. Instead, I spent my tour of duty as a clerk typist in the command center of the 101st Artillery.

My job was mundane and boring, except when we went into the field. Under cover of a field tent, I typed orders resulting in real shells being fired. The most exciting exercise was time-on-target. In this drill, batteries of 8mm howitzers would be positioned at locations several miles apart. Our headquarters computed the trajectories so the rounds from each would arrive on the target at the same time.

Now, the captain in charge checked his data sheet one last time and raised his hand. "On my mark. Three... two... one... mark."

The soldier next to me fiddled with the equipment before him and announced, "Time on target, sixty seconds."

I relaxed. Compared to a sinking ship, drowning all its passengers except for an orphaned boy, or the muddled reenactment of a colonial battle, complete with a bloodied young man, this exercise felt little more than a game.

"Time on target, thirty seconds."

I searched in the folds of the tent for a hint of my spirit-guide, a shadowy silhouette on the canvas perhaps, cast by the naked bulbs. No sign of him. An uneasiness filled my stomach—a scene too benign for the chronicler of despair.

"Time on target, ten seconds... nine... eight...."

From somewhere to the right, a howitzer boomed.

"Seven... six... five...."

Another from the left.

"Three...."

One straight behind and so close the shell whistled overhead.

"Two... one...."

A dull thud sounded a few miles in front of us as the shells hit the target at once. I experienced the same thrill as in my youth, when the coffee in a paper cup shuddered and the ground beneath me trembled. Back then, after a half hour of analyzing results and documenting our performance for our superiors, we'd adjourn for the day, change into civvies and go off base for a beer.

This time was different.

The grim-faced captain ordered me and two others to accompany him. We slapped aside the tent flap and piled into a waiting Jeep.

"Where are we going?" I said.

"To assess the damage."

We rumbled down a dirt road under a tunnel-like canopy of trees, but as we sped on, the twilight fog thickened, obscuring the path ahead, and the queasiness of transition engulfed me. As the fog cleared, a bleaker landscape replaced the scrub pine of Cape Cod. Our Vietnam-era Jeep transformed into a sand-colored Humvee, and our fatigues turned to desert brown.

Ahead lay a village no bigger than Graymoor on Nox, but with a more forbidding feel. Streams of smoke arose not from cottage fireplaces but from the ruins of sandstone huts.

"Lock and load," the captain ordered, and behind me, two magazines slammed into place, and two bolts chambered a round. The captain glared at me. "You too, Higgins."

By my side lay an M-16. Though I hadn't done so in years, I inserted the clip and released the bolt.

As we slowed to enter the village, an eerie silence enveloped us, broken only by the wail of a mother kneeling over the body of her son.

The source of despair!

We dismounted from our Humvee and spread out to survey the result of our barrage. I wandered alone down the narrow streets littered with debris, my desert boots kicking up dust that merged with the smoke.

How random the destruction—here the charred leg of a kitchen table, there a child's doll with its hair singed and one arm melted. Over everything hung the shock of the villagers and the stench of death.

I fingered the safety on my weapon, sensing neither fear nor grief but confusion.

What does this have to do with me?

Then, amidst the smoke in a dead-end alleyway, my spirit-guide emerged and waved a hand across the calamity, expecting me to learn from what I'd wrought.

Sunken ships and an orphaned child; a holiday reenactment of an historic battle turned bloody; my own children in harm's way; and now, a mundane scene from my youth transformed into a nightmare from cable news—a mix of memories and late-night novels, so much like my troubled dreams.

The blood rushed to my face, and I confronted my spirit-guide. "What do you expect me to learn from this? None of these events happened. You're nothing but a charlatan, a conjurer of misery."

"Oh, but they have, after a fashion, some in your prior life and some elsewhere in the real world. Others *you* conjured, stimulated by the novels you read or your quest in the fantasy realm. Nevertheless, I've chronicled them all. All meet the standard as sources of despair."

I poked my head though the doorway of a half-destroyed hovel, with two walls shattered and its roof gone. Inside, a wicker cradle still rocked from the explosion, so similar to the one salvaged from the sea by Efram. I stared down at the empty cradle and up through the smoky haze to the sky.

What if my spirit-guide spoke truly, that despair is a blend of what has happened and what our minds fear might come to pass?

I whirled back to him. "No more concocting a mix of fantasy and reality. Show me only what's real."

Chapter 15 – The Evil That Men Do

The disgruntled spirit scowled and without warning transported me to a barren hilltop, where brambles sprouted among ragged clumps of grass. On three sides, a swamp surrounded us, with stagnant water spread slick as black glass and giving off a fetid odor. Behind us, the setting sun sent an angry streak of red across the water, and from somewhere ahead, incongruous with the scene, a festive tune wafted in whenever the breeze blew.

"What place is this?" I said.

A bony finger pointed to a two-lane paved road, a deserted pathway through the swamp. At its end loomed a single structure, a castle of sorts, but unlike those I encountered in the fantasy realm, this one announced itself as fake, a contrivance of the modern world. Its walls were made of stucco, not stone, and in place of torches lining its parapets, strings of colored lights blinked on and off. From the topmost tower hung not a pennant but a neon sign blaring the castle's purpose: Port Ferry Palace & Concert Hall.

I raised a brow at my spirit-guide, who urged me toward the structure.

As I trod down the road with steam rising from the water on both sides, the strains of music steadied and merged with the sound of revelers singing—an odd venue for a source of despair.

I crossed the faux moat and eyed the imposing portcullis, unsure of how to pass through, until I spotted a revolving glass door embedded at its base, a nondescript portal too small and modern for the structure.

As soon as I entered, smoke stung my eyes, making them tear, and the thump of an electric bass throbbed in my ears. Amidst the darkness, blinding lights flared for an instant so bright as to make the subsequent darkness deepen, a scene suggesting a magical transition, but no magic caused these flares.

Strobes.

As they flashed again, I took in a domed chamber with musicians in garish makeup playing in front on a stage. The next burst revealed an audience of revelers, young men and women closer to my children's age than my own, gyrating to the beat of impossibly loud music.

Suddenly a series of bangs rang out. A brief cheer ensued, as some assumed the noise part of the show. Then a startling silence fell over the place as the band stopped playing. Someone screamed. People fell. Gloom hung from the walls like funeral crepe.

The crowd retreated to the sides, exposing a gunman in the center firing an automatic weapon—*pop, pop, pop*—before pausing to insert a fresh magazine. A nightmare from the cable news.

I need to stop this.

I drew my enchanted sword, which blazed in the darkness. No dark lord here, but still evil incarnate. With one stroke, I'd end this madness, but when I rushed the gunman, he never flinched. My blade passed right through him, as my hand had passed through the wolf man at the river's edge.

The words of my candle guide echoed in my mind: *You are not of this world!*

In Graymoor on Nox, old Burt Higgins was unable to stop the wolfman in the fantasy realm. Now, as a wizard of that realm, I'd become like a character in my novels, well-intentioned but unable to change anything in the real world.

I hissed at my spirit-guide. "Why did you bring me here?"

"You demanded to see only what's real." His ember-like eyes flared, daring me to contradict him.

"I've seen enough. Take me away from here."

Next, I stood at the center of a city, in a roundabout bordered by dusty three-story buildings. A crowd had gathered—men dressed in loose-fitting jeans and grey shirts, and women covered from head to toe. Wide-eyed children formed the front row, placed there for a better view. Their parents rested hands on their shoulders, bracing them for the sorrow to come.

Bearded gunmen strutted about in the center, each dressed in black. Two of them dragged a straight-backed kitchen chair and wooden table to the middle of the roundabout, a setup suitable for enjoying a cup of tea... except for what lay on its surface. Someone had drilled two holes through the table top and threaded a hemp rope through them, forming a loop. Beside the rope rested a sharpened, twelve-inch knife.

The blank-faced crowd fixed its collective gaze on the table as two gunmen dragged in a smooth-cheeked boy who appeared no more than fourteen. One of them thrust the boy's right hand through the loop and tightened the knot. Another unfurled a scroll and read its contents through a bullhorn—the crime: stealing a loaf of bread.

The cowed people waited, their only response a shake of the head or an uncontrolled tear that made their cheeks glisten.

When the spokesmen finished, he set down the scroll and grasped the knife.

I scanned the crowd.

Unblinking eyes shifted to the boy bound to the table. Gunmen paced along the line, ensuring everyone watched. One stopped at a young girl who had buried her head in her mother's hip. He grabbed her ear and twisted until she winced and faced the front.

The spokesman raised the knife.

The boy screamed.

I strained to look away, but the muscles of my neck refused to respond, as if the chronicler of despair had cast a spell on them. I'd demanded reality, and reality it would be, a scene I'd read about in the online news but now would witness myself. Like the bearded gunmen, the spirit had forced me to watch, and like the whimpering children in the crowd, my eyes stayed riveted to the tabletop.

At last I fathomed this man from my own world, a man like me who had stumbled upon an enchanted candle and asked the guide to seek the source of despair. I also understood why, after a thousand such scenes, he'd grown opaque, like a wraith wrapped in shrouds.

He gave me no quarter. Before the turmoil in my heart had settled, the scene rippled and changed again, like a channel switching from one news story to the next.

This time, a different reality played, but one I'd visited often before. I stood on the sidewalk outside the concrete and glass walls of an airport terminal. Behind me, cars honked as they weaved their way through traffic. Overhead TV monitors displayed gates and schedules, with the occasional delay flashing in red. Men and woman with too much luggage or too many children in tow waited in line at the skycap station, hoping to check their bags and avoid dragging them through the terminal. None acknowledged me and my sword, or my out-of-place medieval garb.

On the far side of the sliding glass doors, weary travelers clustered around a carousel, waiting for their belongings as the occasional suitcase tumbled onto the conveyer belt.

An unremarkable scene... until a baggage handler came racing through, waving his arms and shouting. From where I stood beyond the glass doors, his word was muffled, but I read his lips: *"Run!"*

The travelers scattered, abandoning suitcases and leaving luggage behind. The occasional shoe or handbag littered the floor.

What transpired next unfolded before me like a silent movie, as a lone gunman strolled into the baggage claim area, pistol in one hand and assault rife in the other. A derisive sneer darkened his face.

At the far end, a young couple descended the escalator, arm in arm, weary travelers too distracted to recognize the danger. The gunmen glanced up, took aim, and fired. They tumbled down, their ragdoll bodies bouncing on the moving metal stairs until they thumped to a rest at the bottom.

The gunman resumed his march, glancing left and right, seeking other victims with the look of a hunter stalking his prey.

Though the baggage area had emptied, from my vantage I spotted a mother behind a column, hidden from the gunmen's view, crouched on the floor with two children. The youngest, no more than three-years-old, must have tripped as they fled and hurt his leg. The mother clutched a hand over the child's mouth to force his silence, but the softest of whimpers emerged.

The gunman heard. The corners of his lips curled upward as he strode toward the young family in no rush, knowing they had no way to escape.

I whirled on my spirit-guide. "Is there nothing I can do?"

He shook his hoary head so hard, I expected dust to fly from the shroud. "The universe has rules. You and I may be part of only one world at a time. With the proper spell, we can visit the other, but only as observers. Like me, you chose to play a role in the fantasy realm. You may not use magic found there to interfere in the real world."

On the far side of the doors, the gunman neared his prey.

"The magic transformed me to the fantasy world. Can it transform me back now?"

The spirt-guide stepped closer and rested a hand on my shoulder, though it bore neither weight nor warmth. "Do you understand what you ask? To be part of the real world is to become mortal there. I can no longer protect you."

My heart pounded, and I struggled to find air to spit out the words. "I can't stand by helpless again. Make me... real."

He nodded.

I grasped the hilt of my sword and dashed through the glass doors, but as I entered the baggage claim area, a wave of nausea struck me. The room whirled about like a merry-go-round, but only for a moment. When it stopped, everything had changed. Instead of the enchanted sword, I held a gnarled walking stick, and when I squeezed where the hilt should be, my knuckles ached. When I glanced back at the glass doorway, my reflection gaped back at me, a fool in slippers and bathrobe, no different than the one who had left his den to embark on this quest at a time so long ago.

With one exception: the vial in my pocket had taken on life, its purple glow pulsing through the terrycloth fabric of my robe.

A few steps away, the gunmen caught me out of the corner of his eye, but deemed me unthreatening, not worth diverting himself from his target—the mother and her children huddled on the floor.

He raised his weapon.

Before he pulled the trigger, I forced my aching joints to dash in front and dove upon the family, shielding them with my body. The woman trembled beneath me, and my sleeve grew moist with the children's tears.

The gunmen glowered at me. "Out of the way, old man."

I spread my arms to cover as much of the others as possible, and whispered words of comfort, as I once whispered to my own children when they awoke in the night with a bad dream. "I'm here. I will protect you."

An anger welled up within me—at my two guides, at the fantasy realm, at the real world.... At the universe and its rules.

Rules be damned!

I rose to my knees and confronted the gunmen, brandishing the walking stick like the minuteman confronting the redcoats more than two centuries before, knowing the futility of their plight. I was no minuteman, and I wielded neither musket nor sword, but now I cried out with a voice that had lay dormant for too long. "No more."

The gunman laughed, raised his rifle and aimed at my chest, but before he could fire, a ruckus from behind distracted him. The abandoned baggage claim area had been silent except for the whir of the empty carousel and the whimpering of the child. Now a new sound replaced the silence—the thud of running boots.

The first member of a SWAT team rounded the corner, his body armor and helmet making him appear like a modern version of the knights of old. Overhead lights flashed off his face plate, giving his face a surreal glow.

The gunman turned and fled, with a dozen or more police in pursuit. An agonizing minute later, shots rang out.

A SWAT team member trudged back to the baggage area at a more somber pace, and approached us with face plate raised.

"You're safe now," he said. "We got him."

I helped the young mother up, and she buried her sobs in the fabric of my robe.

When the tumult in the terminal settled, I slunk outdoors and collapsed on the curb, chin in hands and more confused than before.

I'd asked the boy from the candle to help me seek the source of despair. He'd led me to a shire-like village, where I became attached to a dear family. Now I understood why. Despair deepens when you have more to lose. I'd refused to give in, choosing instead to commit to this fantasy world and rescue Matthias. That journey led me to this broken spirit, a man who'd pursued despair so long that it had rotted his flesh. Yet in each of his darkest visions, I'd found a glimmer of light.

I felt a chill on the back of my neck, and out of the corner of my eye, I caught the spirit-guide standing over me. I refused to face him, instead fixing on the tops of my slippers as I uttered my challenge. "What lesson do you expect me to learn from this? In Crix Haven, a ship was sunk, but two loving people saved a child. I protected my own children in a fantasy reenactment of an historic battle, fought long before I was born. Now, through a stroke of luck, I delayed a tragedy until real heroes arrived." I spun around and glared at his ruined face. "I'd say your chronicle of despair is flawed."

He heaved his shoulders in a sigh. "We are nothing but observers who bring our own biases to how we perceive the world. The images we see are influenced by who we are. Apparently, you and I *are* different. When I viewed the clash at Crix Haven, no one survived. When I visited the battle on the green, only the dead and wounded remained. And never would I have risked resuming my real-world form to save a stranger. Perhaps the goal you seek may be other than what you claim."

"You're right. I *am* different. I have no interest in chronicling despair. I want to find the demon who caused it, to use magic like the heroes in my novels to defeat him, and by so doing, to end despair forever."

"Ah. A noble quest, but in my eons of searching, I've found no such demon. Yet despair pervades, woven into the fabric of the universe."

Dark images swirled through my brain, blaring like banners on websites or videos on cable TV. I pictured Betty during chemo, head shorn, pale and weak from the poison pumped into her veins. I imagined her alone in a car or a train, perhaps stalled by the snow, trying to get home to tell me the latest news. What if her cancer had returned?

I blocked out the thought, afraid the spirit would read my mind, and focused on more benign images. I pictured Helen, not as she was now, full grown and swollen with child, but younger, like Hannah. No. Younger still, when her sense of wonder remained. When I could bring her the simplest present, purchased in haste at an airport gift shop—a spinning top, a stuffed koala bear, or a blue beret for her hair—and no matter what, she'd rip open the wrapping paper, fling her arms around me and squeeze.

And younger still. When Michael was born, I traveled a lot, the curse of too much expertise. I was the wizard from headquarters who flew in to solve the problems that befuddled the local staff. By the time Helen arrived, the company had matured, and each office employed wizards of their own. I spent more time at home, helping Betty with the kids. At night, after Helen fell asleep, I'd hover over her crib and marvel at this child, watching the soft movement of her eyelids as she dreamed, conjuring up adventures yet to come. Now another marvel: she was about to give birth to a child of her own.

I glanced back into the airport terminal, where the SWAT team clustered, and yellow crime tape circled the scene. Outside the circle, the young mother sat on a bench with a blanket wrapped about her shoulders, telling her story to a reporter while a camera crew broadcast her every word. From time to time, she scanned the area for the man who'd saved her family, but perhaps due to the spirit's magic, I stayed hidden from view.

Despair woven into the fabric of the universe?

I rose to my full height, as much as my creaky joints allowed, but still reached no higher than the spirit-guide's waist. For the first time, I fixed on his dead eyes. "What if hope is woven in as well, an equal force, and a different path we might choose?"

The spirit's eyes narrowed and his back stiffened. "You don't understand. I've shown you but a fraction of my vast chronicle. Let me show you something more, and we'll see if you find hope there."

Chapter 16 – Tremors

The queasiness of transition hit worse than before, forcing me to one knee and then to the ground, lest I totter and crash to the pavement. After a moment, the light-headedness receded, but this time gave way to a deep sleep. I dreamed my head rested not on the concrete sidewalk but on the desk in my study back home. There, surrounded by my fantasy novels, a sense of serenity pervaded. Soon, Helen would burst through the locked door with Betty in tow, and the three of us would hug and cry. I'd apologize for the worry I caused them, and Betty would forgive me and tell me all was well. The confusion ignited by the lighting of the candle would fade, becoming nothing more than a muddled memory swaddled in scrim.

Alas, serenity was not to be.

I awoke to a rumbling and to the ground quaking beneath me. As I staggered to my feet, brushing off the concrete dust from my bathrobe, I noted with disappointment how the stiffness in my hands remained.

Concrete dust?

The haze surrounding me was no longer the fog of transition but concrete dust raining down from cracks in the ceiling above. A grand chandelier rattled overhead, and its bulbs flickered and went dark.

A bellman in uniform raced past me toward the door, screaming, "Get out!"

I followed him outside to find people running through the street as fragments of walls rained down around them. Rebar twisted and groaned, and buildings crumbled. Behind me, the sign above the doorway—apparently a boutique hotel—swung wildly. Seconds later, the wall supporting it thudded to the ground, the debris missing me by a few feet.

The rumbling lasted an agonizing minute, followed by an eerie silence.

Amidst the crumbling buildings and dust so thick it coated my tongue, people shuffled around with the thousand-yard stare, searching for loved ones.

I flowed with the crowd in a daze, wondering why I'd been brought here. I'd come to realize that both of my guides only nudged events in a chosen direction, but the ultimate purpose was dictated by a greater force.

Two blocks ahead, barely visible behind a collapsed wall, two children who might have been Michael and Helen scavenged. Together, they dragged out a metal container and laid it on its side. The boy grabbed a chunk of cement block and smashed open the mangled latch. From inside, he pulled out a picture album, photographs of family members perhaps deceased. As they flipped through them, the two embraced and fought back tears.

I moved on, following the procession of the dazed. As I wandered the streets, coughing and spitting out dust, I came upon a crowd gathered around the ruins of a two-story tenement. Its roof and three of its walls had collapsed, but the front had stayed intact, though leaning precariously, supported by nothing more than a wooden doorframe. Several young men knelt in the rubble, digging with their bare hands to reach what must have been an open pocket beyond.

I stopped next to a woman who'd wrapped her hands around herself in a hug. She caught my eye and lowered her voice in that way people speak at funerals. "A neighbor boy, father's gone, mother passed last week. Now he's buried under the rubble."

The men worked without tools, afraid to disrupt the unstable structure. Who were they, these would-be rescuers? Relatives or friends? First responders? Or well-intentioned passersby wanting to help?

I glanced down at my hands, with their bulging veins and liver spots—the markings of age. These hands no longer grasped an axe or a musket or an enchanted sword, nor did some evil demon challenge them, but they might still do some good.

I strode forward and joined the rescuers.

As the hushed crowd watched, we sifted through shards of glass and fragments of bricks as small as my fist. We lugged away granite blocks so heavy they required two of us to carry. I dug for an hour or more until the tips of my fingers bled. The only sound beyond our breathing was the crash of stone on stone as we tossed debris onto a nearby pile. Every few minutes, the leader would hold up his hand for us to pause and listen.

Everyone froze, men and women, old and young, until the softest whimper pierced the air. We'd pivot toward the sound and resume our toil.

At last, a patch of torn red cloth stuck out from the pile, and a single shoe, and then a child's bare leg, so covered in muck it appeared more building debris than human limb. I and two others waded in and removed a dozen more stones, exposing a young boy, perhaps Matthias's age. He gaped at us, eyes pleading though he made no sound. As we cleared the last of the rubble to set him free, I noted his chest rose and fell in a normal rhythm.

For an instant, we froze, stunned at what we'd found. Then I leaned in, lifted the boy and cradled him in my arms. As I carried him to safety, he wrapped one arm around my neck and rested his head on my shoulder, letting go only when I reached an ambulance and handed him to a waiting paramedic.

Is this a dream or reality, or bits of both?

I had no time to ponder, no way to tell, but of one thing I was certain: the boy was alive.

The paramedic laid him on a stretcher, and two others clustered around, one measuring his blood pressure, the other probing the crook of his elbow to insert an IV.

Now useless, I hovered nearby, a fool in a bathrobe, his mind too stunned to ask the condition of the boy.

At last, as they lifted the stretcher into the ambulance, my voice returned. "Will he... live?"

A weary responder rested a hand on my arm. "We'll have to wait for the doctors."

He shut one door, but before closing the other, he gestured to me. "Would you like to ride with the boy?"

I twisted around to see if he'd spoken to someone else. No one there. "I... don't know this boy. I'm not a relative."

"So? You cared enough to save him. We have no rules at a time like this. Hop in."

I stared at the vehicle with the blue bar on its roof and the words "Children's Hospital" painted across its back. Then I scrambled in and squatted by the child as the siren wailed and the ambulance whisked us away.

Chapter 17 – Riverway

The ambulance skidded to a stop at the Children's Hospital, and the rear doors swung wide, revealing a bright blue sky that seemed so inappropriate for the day. Rapid response vehicles jammed the parking lot—police cars for those able to walk, and ambulances for the more severely injured. Medical staff dashed from one to the next, diagnosing wounds and barking orders. Before I could utter a question, two of them carried the boy away.

I stumbled out and let my eyes adjust to the sunlight. Above the entrance where they'd taken the child, a sign in red letters proclaimed: "Emergency Room." High overhead, a tower rose seven stories, housing operating and diagnostic facilities, and patient rooms for longer term care. A granite portico capped the topmost floor, bearing the engraved words: "Until Every Child Is Well."

As the paramedic who'd taken the boy from me stowed his equipment and prepared to go back to help others, he caught me standing by the entrance looking lost and forlorn.

He pointed to the double doors. "Down the corridor to the left. At its end, you'll find a waiting room. Ask the receptionist to record your name, and they'll notify you with any news."

I mumbled a thank you and stumbled inside.

Over the years, I spent too many days in hospitals, first with my elderly mother and then with Betty's breast cancer. This hospital seemed not much different from the others. The entrance led to a sterile corridor with fluorescent lights overhead and steel handrails lining the walls. Several malfunctioning bulbs flickered on and off at intervals, and all around me, men and women bustled about in white jackets or green scrubs.

I passed the many victims of the quake, at this hospital all children. The lucky ones lay stretched out on gurneys with a pillow for their heads, but with so many needing care, some had to settle for the hard floor. A few moaned or cried out in pain, but most suffered in silence as doctors and nurses triaged the wounded. All stared at me as I passed, eyes pleading for the kind of help I had no skill to provide.

In the waiting room, I registered with a kindly receptionist and described the nameless boy, before settling into a padded blue chair. I leaned my head back and stared at the white ceiling tiles, pondering the lessons of my spirit-guide.

Why was he nowhere to be found? Was this place where so many labored to help others insufficient misery for the chronicler of despair? Or had he concluded my journey differed so much from his that I must now travel alone?

Time crawled. I followed the second hand creeping around the clock on the opposite wall, counting fifteen seconds before tearing my eyes away. Instead, I studied the faces around me—old faces waiting for news of their loved ones, and young facing getting older. When I'd surveyed them all, guessing at each of their stories, I glanced back at the clock. Only two minutes had passed.

Every now and then, a doctor in surgical scrubs would come through the doors, confer with the receptionist in hushed tones and call out a name. Some mother, father, or grandparent, or aunt or uncle, would shuffle forward, extend a hand in greeting, and follow the doctor to the privacy of a small conference room.

None came for me.

Waiting, waiting....

A hospital waiting room brings your darkest memories to the fore. My mind now wandered to a place I'd blocked out for years.

I recalled the day Betty received the news. Her annual mammogram had turned out abnormal, so the doctor ordered a biopsy. For some reason, the results took four days to come back. During that time, the two of us started whenever the phone rang.

When the call finally came, Betty's eyes narrowed, and her lips stretched taut and pale. As she listened, a look passed between us—a look between lovers and friends who had long since let down the walls guarding the inner self.

And I knew.

After forever, she covered the phone with her hand and whispered in words without tone, "It's cancer."

The following weeks were filled with research on the internet and conferences with doctors. The medical and radiation oncologists, and the surgeon rallied us as they laid out the plan. They were our team, dedicated to making her well. Together, we would beat this disease, though until after the surgery, her prognosis remained uncertain.

"If we find clear margins," they said, "and the lymph nodes are negative, she should be fine."

At last, the time came for her lumpectomy. Betty and I kissed and professed our love, and they wheeled her away, leaving me standing in pre-op, arms dangling at my side like a scarecrow. My eyes stayed fixed on the doors marked "Authorized Personnel Only" until a kind nurse grasped me by the elbow and led me away.

The hospital where they performed Betty's surgery lay in the heart of the Longwood Medical Center, boasting some of the best care in the world, with state-of-the-art technology. The waiting room was high-tech as well. A sixty-inch flat screen on the wall displayed a list of all the patients with a colored rectangle next to each name.

I checked in with the receptionist, who explained the color coding—blue for pre-op, orange for operating room, purple for post-op ICU, and green for recovery. Sensing my unease, she wiggled her mouse to verify Betty's status on her computer.

While I waited, I pressed both hands flat on her desk, leaning so hard the blood drained from my fingers.

After what seemed too long, she looked up and frowned. "I'm afraid the operating room is a bit backed up today, and she may not go into surgery for a while. You won't hear from the surgeon for at least a couple of hours. Why don't you go get some coffee instead of waiting here? There's a small café at the end of the hall."

I had no use for coffee—I was jumpy enough—so as was my custom in times of stress, I went for a walk.

My footsteps took me away from the ambulance sirens on Brookline Avenue, to a quieter place, one I hadn't visited in years.

I'd gone to high school nearby, and every afternoon I'd head home down Longwood Avenue, past the columned façade of Harvard Medical and the world-renowned hospitals, across the riverway, and down the old stone bridge to the Muddy River. This treed pathway made up one segment of the Emerald Necklace, Frederick Olmsted's dream of creating a chain of parks that would hang like a green necklace around the peninsula of Boston. The paved path along the river provided a popular playground for walkers, joggers, and cyclists, though it remained unused compared to the bustle a few hundred yards away.

Many an afternoon, after a bad day at school, or when still fuming from that morning's quarrel with my parents, I'd take respite there before boarding the T to go home. I'd divert from the path, and seek out a secluded bench from which I could watch the Muddy River make its way to the sea.

Now, while waiting for Betty to come out of surgery, I sought this refuge again. I descended the stone bridge, its steps so worn by time that each sloped downward, and rediscovered my favorite spot near the water, shaded from the sun by the sprawling branches of a willow. Before me, the Muddy River lay calm, except for the wake of a duck paddling past and the circular ripples made by fish popping up to snatch bugs skimming across the surface.

I peered into the murky water, searching for answers to my questions. Why is there such pain in the world? What cosmic sin caused the ones we love to suffer? Would the woman I cared for the most return safely to me?

I needed all my will not to race back to the waiting room, to check if the color on the screen had changed. More than once, I popped up and paced about before returning to the bench. Finally, I settled down—it would be a long couple of hours—and with elbows in my lap and chin in my hands, I let my life play out on the water.

On the first anniversary of our meeting on the train in Jersey, Betty and I went out to dinner at a fine restaurant overlooking the Charles in Cambridge. She was finishing up her studies at NYU, and I lived in Boston. Though we found time to be together on most weekends, and a few weekdays when my business took me her way, our partings became increasingly hard.

As we sat over candlelight, leaning close and staring into each other's eyes, I asked the question I'd been waiting to ask for months. "So what are we going to do about us?"

She reached across and rested a hand on mine. "I don't want to be away from you anymore."

"Neither do I."

Betty had never been much of a singer. When she tried, her head would tilt to one side, and her voice would take on a little girl lilt as she sang off-key. This time, she offered a line from a Simon and Garfunkel song:

Let us be lovers and marry our fortunes together....

And so we did. For the next thirty-one years, she lifted me up through my darker moods. Together, we raised Michael and Helen, and through it all, we remained best friends. We always supported each other through better and worse, and through sickness and health.

Through sickness and health.

Enough!

I rose and trudged back to the hospital.

To my consternation, the color of the rectangle had yet to change, showing her still in surgery.

What's taking so long?

I stormed the reception desk.

"I'm sorry, Mr. Higgins. The app froze in the past hour. I made an announcement, but you must have been out. I'll check for you now." She picked up the phone and tapped a few numbers while I stared at the screen, expecting her call would cause the color to change. After a moment, she glanced up and smiled. "You wife is on her way to recovery."

Five minutes later, the surgeon appeared, still in her operating room scrubs, and spoke the magic words: "Clear margins, lymph node negative."

Now, as I waited in a hospital once again for news, this time about the boy we'd dug out of the rubble, I pondered all that had transpired since I lit the candle and awoke my guide. I came to this world to discover the cause of despair. What had I learned? That lessons present themselves throughout life if you pay attention. The latest lesson: even the darkest of times come with a glimmer of light.

As I waited, a stream of less injured children entered the room to be reunited with friends or relatives, most with bandages or crutches, and some in wheelchairs, and each accompanied by a nurse or doctor. The faces of the medical people showed a mix of caring and strain. The earthquake had caused more injuries than usual, but they cared for the sick and wounded every day. It was more than a job, because they knew the stakes.

I'd wasted my one-time wish to pursue a vain quest to find the source of despair, conjuring up a demon I could defeat. These people fought despair every day.

Until every child is well.

I'd been focused on a fantasy, hoping to end all misery with one swing of an enchanted sword, but if no demon was the cause, no sword could be the cure. A stirring arose from within my soul, a hunger for something more. I felt like a man lost on a darkened road in the rain, who spotted a light in the distance, a candle flickering in a cottage window.

I no longer wished to find the source of despair—for I now understood there were many—but rather I longed to find its antidote. My mind scraped and clawed, stretching out toward that distant glimmer, a light I could almost name.

At last, a doctor in green scrubs and a sterile mask emerged with the orphan boy, now awake and alert in a wheelchair. Without querying the receptionist, he wheeled the boy to me.

"This one belongs with you, "he said. Even muffled by the mask, his voice sounded familiar.

When I stood, open-mouthed and stuttering, he lowered the mask, revealing the Mona Lisa smile.

"But how?" I said.

"I warned you of the complexity of your quest, and now, it's reached a dead-end. The chronicler of despair has given up, leaving you more confused than before. The universe may have rules but is not without compassion, so rather than cast you back into a sea of uncertainty, I've been authorized to grant you a second wish, a chance for resolution. But it's your choice. You may end your quest now and go home, or choose a new one."

End my quest.

I could return to Betty and go back to be with Helen for the birth of her child, but also to return to the empty house, to worry about Betty's health and Helen's baby—to a world where despair lurks everywhere, and to where I'd be helpless to make a difference.

And what of my unfulfilled promise to bring Matthias back to his family?

I'd lit the candle to plug a hole in my life, and followed the guide to fill a need, goals I'd yet to achieve. I crumpled my brow. What was I searching for, and might I yet find it in this world?

Sensing my discomfort, he gestured toward the waiting room door. "Perhaps some sunlight might help you decide. Follow me."

I pushed the wheelchair down the green-tiled corridor beneath the glow of fluorescent lights, marching in a surreal parade—a guide who'd materialized from a candle, an injured boy I hardly knew, and a confused old man in a bathrobe and slippers.

As we exited through the double doors, the first beam of sunlight struck my cheeks. I tipped my head back, neckbones cracking in protest, until I viewed the peak of the hospital high above and read the words engraved in the granite.

I turned back to my guide. "I want to go where every child is well."

"No such world exists."

"Or a place where everyone strives to make it so."

"Alas, I know of no such place."

"Then a place where I may yet use magic to do some good."

He tilted his head to one side and eyed me across his nose. "Hmmm... a place where you can make magic of your own." After a moment, he broke into the kind of expression children show when they want to say: *I know something you don't know.* "Yes, I can take you there... if you're certain you want to go."

I glanced up to the words at the top of the building, and down to the face of the injured boy, who regarded me like Hannah when she'd begged me to save Matthias.

I was not ready to return home. "Yes, I'm certain. Show me the way."

"Very well. Once I'm gone, a path will appear. Follow it to the next portal and, beyond it, seek the granite and glass, a place familiar to you. But first observe my exit, a new one I've been working on, and I'll meet you on the other side."

He placed his hands in front of his chest, pressed the tips of both forefingers and thumbs together, and made the symbol for infinity.

My guide, who'd once been a wax candle, now became a statue made of sand. Around us, the dusk deepened, and a fog rose so thick that the peak of the hospital vanished in the mist. A mighty gust blew, dissipating the grains of the statue into a whirlwind. The wind roared like the sound of the earth groaning in the quake, and the grains of sand stung my face, forcing me to cover my eyes.

When the wind settled, I opened my eyes to a different scene.

Gone were the emergency vehicles clustered in rows; gone were the medical people in scrubs; gone was the parking lot itself and the hospital building with it; and gone was the city still grieving from the quake.

Now I stood in the midst of a sylvan glade, at the edge of a dense forest with no apparent exit.

What now?

Before I could get my bearings and concoct a plan, I was startled by a cry from behind.

"Wizard!"

I spun around to find the wheelchair gone, and a different boy racing toward me. As I reached out to greet him, a new strength flowed through my arms, and in place of the pain in my hip, I felt the heft of an enchanted sword.

And the boy....

Both of us had been restored, me to the wizard and the boy to Matthias.

Chapter 18 – The Green Rider

I dropped to one knee and swept Matthias up in my arms. Through moistened eyes, I beamed at him and thanked a source of magic I'd never understand.

I did it. I rescued the boy as I promised his mother and sister.

But where were Elizabeth and Hannah?

I'd left them standing in the throne room of the chronicler of despair, but now, as I glanced about, I found neither the chamber with the vaulted ceiling nor the stairway leading up to the cliff. Instead, Matthias and I stood on a moss-covered mound surrounded by vegetation so dense as to deny passage to a chipmunk.

Behind us, at the crest of the mound, loomed a stone arch made of three boulders tossed together as if built by the children of giants. Two uprights teetered at odd angles to each other, standing at least six feet thick and rising to twice my height. A third balanced at their top, held in place by nothing more than its own weight, forming a rough arch. From where I stood, the arrangement seemed a useless structure lying in the midst of an impenetrable woods, an entrance to nowhere.

Searching for a way out, I circled to the far side of the arch. From that vantage, the forest no longer showed. Instead, an opaque liquid filled the opening, a fluid so illusory as to make me wonder if I could trust my eyes... until I recognized the familiar light filtering through.

A portal.

I clutched Matthias by the wrist and told him to clasp mine, so our arms interlocked. With a firm grip, I drew him to the brink of the portal, but paused before touching the maelstrom, letting the boy adjust to the scene. His eyes widened but stayed locked on me.

He trusts me. Please let me not betray that trust.

"You're a brave boy," I said, "and what you've experienced, I can only imagine. Now I need you to be braver still. Whatever happens, do not let go of my hand."

He flashed a smile more adult than before and nodded. His journey with the wolf-headed man had changed him as well.

I sucked in a final breath of temperate air and slipped through the portal.

On the far side, a fog swirled though no wind blew. Yet unlike the other portals I'd encountered, terrifying images danced on that fog, playing out like on a movie screen—fantastic creatures big and small; lizards spouting fire; a sea battle with ships ablaze; an executioner with axe raised, hovering over a girl bound to a block in a village square; a crowd of innocents fleeing a gunman; buildings toppling in a quake; a hundred-year storm, sending floodwaters raging down a street.

And swept away in that flood... Betty, Michael, and Helen.

I ground my teeth and trudged on, for I now understood from whence these visions came—from the darker corners of my own heart, bought to life by the chronicler of despair. Once we passed through, his gloom would no longer hold sway.

Time has no meaning in portals. Our passage may have taken an eternity or no time at all, but at last the twilight brightened, and an emerging dawn beckoned ahead —our way to the promised quest.

Matthias and I burst through, breathless and with hearts racing, and found ourselves at the start of a dirt road. Behind us, the portal had vanished. In its place nestled a village not so different from his home, but this village teemed with the laughter of children, and tulips and daffodils lined the way.

Ahead, the road led uphill to a familiar structure, less forbidding than the one that loomed over Graymoor on Nox. No blackened turrets marred it, and no soot or ash soiled the air. It appeared instead to be a modern office building made of granite and glass, the kind I'd visited so often during my business trips in years past.

'Find the granite and glass, a place familiar to you.'

Matthias pointed up the hill. "What's that?"

"Where we're meant to go."

As we shuffled up the road with a wary stride, our boots kicking up dust, my thoughts dwelled on the choice I'd made.

As we neared the entrance, the glass doors slid open on their own—magic to Matthias, but mundane technology to me. Inside, a gleaming atrium rose three stories high, with potted plants lining the sides. To my surprise, an oversized replica of the faded tapestry from my study hung on the rear wall, complete with castle and moat, and knight on armored horse trotting across the drawbridge.

A young receptionist sat at a desk in front of the tapestry. When she heard us enter, she glanced up from her work and smiled. "Ah, Mr. Higgins. You're a bit early for your appointment. I'll let Mr. Guide know you're here." Her fingers flew across a keyboard on her desktop. "He'll be available in a few minutes. In the meantime, someone's waiting for you."

She gestured to her left, where a single goose-necked lamp cast light on a sterile alcove with two padded chairs on either side of a coffee table, and a couch behind. Two people rested on the couch, their faces hidden in shadow. I stepped closer, squinting to focus, but as my vision sharpened, my mind refused to accept what my eyes presented.

Matthias had no such hesitation. He let out a whoop and raced inside, leaving me straggling behind. Before me, Elizabeth slumped on the sofa, eyes closed and head laid back on a cushion, with Hannah asleep in her lap.

Matthias's cry woke them. Hannah sat up and gaped, while her mother stared dumbstruck, the two of them a tableau frozen in time.

But only for an instant.

Hannah screamed, "Matty!" and rushed toward him.

Tears flowed, including my own, and all embraced.

When our joy at the reunion had abated, Elizabeth sat back on the couch, with one arm around her daughter and the other around her newfound son, squeezing so as to never let go again.

She let out a satisfied sigh. "I'm so grateful, wizard, but where have you been?"

"Too hard to explain," I said, since I failed to understand it myself. "But how did *you* get here?"

"We waited for as long as we dared, alone in that dreary chamber, until my stomach growled and Hannah complained of thirst. With no idea how long you'd be away... or if you'd ever return... I determined to wait in the market below, intending to buy food and drink, and camp out at the base of the stairs until my coins—or my hope—ran out.

"But when we exited the tunnel, Grim Harbor was gone, and this chamber appeared in its stead. That kind lady—" She gestured toward the reception desk. "—exchanged one of my gold coins for twenty pieces of silver with an eagle embossed on each, and showed us those metal boxes. When we dropped the pieces into the slot, the boxes provided us with sustenance until now."

She pointed to the far wall of the alcove, where two vending machines stood, one with drinks and the other with junk food snacks.

Hannah dug into her pocket and pulled out a bag of chips. "I have some left." She offered the snack to her brother and turned to me. "What happens now, wizard? Do we go home?"

I opened my mouth to respond, wise wizard that I was, but though I managed to save Matthias, I had no answer now. The three of them gaped at me as I scanned the atrium, hoping my guide would appear.

The receptionist saved me. "Mr. Higgins."

I turned and approached the desk. "Yes."

"I almost forgot. Mr. Guide asked me to give you this."

She handed me a package, giftwrapped in shiny paper with images of horses galloping across it.

With trembling hands, I unwrapped the package and discovered what appeared to be a children's book inside. I flipped skeptically to the first page.

A cartoon drawing showed a man with an enchanted sword and a hint of a purple vial shining through his tunic pocket, standing in an atrium similar to this. The caption beneath it read:

Walk through the castle gate
And bring your charges along.

Mr. Guide's message, for sure—obscure and dramatic, as always. I was tired of his games and longed to toss the book away, but what then?

I approached the receptionist, cleared my throat, and waited for her to acknowledge me.

"May I help you?"

I showed her the picture. "Do you know what this means?"

"It's all in the book. Just turn the page." Then she went back to typing.

The next page featured a fanciful illustration of a wizard, a woman, and a boy and girl crossing a castle moat.

"But there's no castle here."

The receptionist wrinkled her nose, a mark of impatience, and without looking up from her work, gestured behind her.

The tapestry.

My guide and I had walked through the locked door of my study, so.... why not pass through a tapestry hanging on a wall?

I gathered Elizabeth and her children and led them like the family in the picture to the back of the chamber.

"Where are we going?" Hannah said.

"Through the castle gate."

"But that's just a picture."

"Hush," her mother said. "Trust the wizard's magic."

We edged closer with hands outstretched. As our fingertips brushed the fabric, the material transformed into a diaphanous veil, thin enough to pass through. Beyond it lay a tunnel made of overarching vines. While our first steps landed on a tile floor, the next settled on a dirt path.

Twenty paces later, the tunnel ended, and we stood in a clearing with a fifty-foot-high obelisk at its center and roads diverging around it. I counted seven in all.

I spun around, unsure where to go. The unmarked paths branching out in all directions gave no hint of which to choose. With nothing left to do, I flipped to the next page of the book, which showed a drawing of the crossroads. A blue dot blinked at its center, next to the scrawled words: *You are here.*

I cursed my guide and turned to the last page. On it, the same seven paths beckoned, but this time, in place of the blue dot, a tiny image of a horse appeared on the third road from the left, and it seemed to be moving toward us.

I closed the book and glanced up, counting the roads. One. Two. Three.

From deep within that road, the thud of hoofs sounded, and out of the mist a lone horseman appeared, a rider clad in forest green: green pants tucked into green leather boots, a green blouse made of silk, a green cape that unfurled as he rode. Everything was green but for a red cap with the familiar purple plume. As he emerged from the trees, the first rays of sunlight caught his face, showing a glint in his eye and skin as smooth as wax.

Elizabeth turned toward the sound and pointed. No apparition here. She could hear him. She could see him.

The horse skidded to a stop in front of the delighted children, and the rider dismounted with a flourish.

As Hannah and Matthias gawked, he reached into his saddlebags, pulled out a pair of shiny red apples, and held them out to the children. With a tip of his head, he motioned toward his mount.

As the children grabbed the apples and jostled with each other to be first to feed the horse, the rider turned to me.

"Do you approve of my new outfit, Master Higgins."

"Better than the silver fish," I said. "And you still wear the purple plume."

He flashed his Mona Lisa smile. "I like this plume."

Then, despite his otherworldly demeanor, I came close and embraced him.

PART THREE

TRAVELER TOWARD THE DAWN

"'I wish it need not have happened in my time,' said Frodo.
'So do I,' said Gandalf, 'and so do all who live to see such times.
But that is not for them to decide. All we have to decide is
what to do with the time that is given us.'"
J.R.R. Tolkien

Chapter 19 – The Road to Where

We set out down the road from where the green rider had come. Hannah and Matthias took turns with him in the saddle, while Elizabeth and I meandered behind. The way, though narrow, was well marked and easy to traverse, a single-lane track of packed earth broken only by parallel ruts formed by wheels bearing loads. I wondered, should a wagon approach from the far side, how we would manage to pass. I needn't have worried. For the rest of the day, we saw neither wagon nor soul.

After a time, the children tired of the horse's novelty, dismounted, and lagged behind, more interested in picking blueberries from bushes at the edge of the road than accompanying the adults. Their search left Elizabeth and me to walk alone.

She turned to me. "Where are we going?"

I shrugged. "We follow our guide and wait to see. Oftentimes, the magic takes time to reveal itself."

She glanced at the rider, his soft umbra visible only to me, and slowed her stride. When convinced he rode far enough ahead to be out of earshot, she spoke in a whisper. "You've been so kind to me. Why do you do it?"

"Do what?"

"Indulge us with your wizardry to ease our sorrows. They say wizards may travel wherever they wish, even between worlds. You must know of happier places than this. Why pick here?"

"I came to seek the source of despair, to use the magic of this world to perhaps end it once and for all."

"And what did you find?"

"That despair is more complicated, that it dwells side by side with hope, the two forever linked with each other."

"I could have told you that if you'd asked. After my husband died, despair overwhelmed me, and I struggled to get out of bed in the morning."

"How did you overcome it?"

"I didn't. It dwells within me still... but from that despair sprung a well of hope, that the next day would dawn and my children needed me."

"What about when Matthias was taken?"

"Then you gave me hope, and now you've justified my faith in you. I'm in your debt and will follow wherever you lead."

I glanced ahead to the green rider, head cocked to one side and whistling a tune, loping along without a care. "You understand why I'm confused? How can I decide a way forward if hope and despair exist side by side? How will I choose?"

She stopped and faced me, brows arched so her eyes rounded. "You choose hope, of course."

"Why?"

"Because in the time that's given us, it's better to dwell in the light of hope than in the gloom of despair."

I nodded, slowly at first and then with more conviction, like a slow student who finally comprehends his master's teaching, at last grasping that the answer may be simpler than he supposed.

I reached out for her hand, and she took mine. We held on.

When Matthias and I passed through the twilight portal, time had lost its meaning. The gloaming offered no hint of morning or evening, no sense of day or night. Now, I realized the dim light filtering through the portal's exit had been the dawn. We walked all morning at a leisurely pace, with a cooling breeze tempering the heat of the sun, stopping only for an occasional drink from the bubbling brook running along the road.

By noon, the breeze had died down, and the sun rose high enough to bypass the shade from the branches overhead, transforming the morning's warmth into sweltering heat. The change arrived unexpectedly, like that first hot day in New England when spring turns to summer in a matter of hours, and the thermometer explodes from a pleasant sixty-five to an oppressive ninety-nine. Our mood changed as well. Whereas before we had sauntered, taking in the scenery and speculating on where our guide might lead us, now we trudged, wary of what lay ahead.

Despite the heat, our guide allowed only a brief respite for lunch, insisting we needed to push on if we hoped to reach our evening's campsite before dark.

The children minded the heat less than the grownups, dashing ahead to explore, and racing back to tell us what they'd found. Whenever they grew tired, they hopped on the green rider's horse for a rest.

Elizabeth and I slogged along, ignoring the heat not by exploring ahead, but by telling stories from our pasts. The more we spoke, the more her stride matched mine, so our shoulders brushed with each step.

Since reuniting, something had changed between us. Yes, she was grateful for my saving her son, but a different sentiment prevailed, the kind of surprise two lonely people feel when they find each other. For me, that feeling spanned two worlds, adding to my confusion.

When the sun sank below the tops of the trees, bestowing a much-needed shade, the green rider tethered his horse to a branch situated so the animal could munch sweet grass on the one side and quench his thirst in the stream on the other. After removing the bridle and the saddlebags from the horse's flank, he led us down a side trail formed by spring runoff from the brook as it entered the woods. We walked single file for several minutes, swatting low-lying branches from our faces, until the path opened into a modest clearing at the base of a hill. Here the brook disappeared through the cracks of a rock outcropping into the earth, but not before creating a pool of water so clear you could count the pebbles at its bottom.

The rider spread out a blanket on the ground beneath the canopy of a sprawling beech, and set out sacks of salted pork and dried apples. The children poked around the surrounding bushes and discovered fresh strawberries to supplement our meal.

After eating, the four of us scattered to the corners of the clearing and collected kindling for a fire, to take the chill from the night air. Then, we laid out the contents of our packs and gathered pine needles to soften our beds. Only after finishing these chores did we give in to the children, who after a hot day on the trail had nagged us to let them go for a swim.

Matthias and Hannah stripped to their underwear and ran screaming to the pond, elbowing each other as they went to keep the other from jumping in first. Finally, Matthias deferred to his little sister. She jumped in with a splash, and her brother followed before the ripple from her dive had settled.

Elizabeth put aside the cleanup from our meal, and joined me at the edge of the pool to revel in the children's joy.

Perhaps it was the moon that set me off. After waxing all week, it blossomed now into a golden orb climbing up the eastern sky and creating a path of gilded glass on the still surface of the water. On either side of this path, the twilight painted a sunset scene with reflected colors from the sky.

As the children frolicked, causing ripples in the scene, the light of the new moon bathed their wet bodies in a shade of childhood wonder and reminded me of a time long ago, off a different trail but with a pond as clear.

"Remember that time," I said to Elizabeth without taking my eyes off the children. "When we hiked in New Hampshire on a hot day like this and discovered a pond off the trail. The water showed as clear, and the children's joy sounded much the same as now."

I turned to her, expecting a glint of recognition, but instead she furrowed her brow.

Her eyes drooped at the corners, though they caused no wrinkle. "Forgive me, master wizard, but I don't know of what you speak. What is this New Hampshire?"

Icy reason rose up within me and overcame my less rational senses. Even in the dimming light, no wisdom lines clustered around her eyes, nor loose skin around her neck. This was not my life partner who wore her years so well. Despite my new body, the woman beside me was impossibly young, too young to remember the day of which I spoke.

"Ah yes," I said. "I'm mistaken. I was recalling another place, another time."

She brushed my arm with her fingertips. "I understand. Common wisdom claims wizards live many lives. Perhaps you mistook this for some prior life."

As the laughter of the children mingled with the splash of water and the caw of a crow flying off to its resting place for the night, I sighed.

"Some prior life, indeed."

Chapter 20 – The Cave

I awoke the next morning in a grumpy mood. Low-lying clouds foretold a dreary day and, despite my badgering, the green rider still refused to disclose our destination.

By mid-afternoon, the puffs of white that had obscured the sun lumbered off westward, fleeing before a more forbidding phalanx of silver-gray. We quickened our pace but the front overtook us, following along the trail and letting loose a shower steady enough to drench our clothing and muddy the road.

But the weather was not done. A rumble of clouds dotted the horizon behind us, and soon silver gray turned to purple—not the iridescent purple of my vial, but an angry purple, malevolent and foreboding.

The storm sped up its pursuit, a mass of thunderheads intent on catching us. We broke into a trot, and when little Hannah slipped and fell on a slick tree root, I swept her up in my arms and raced on. Ahead, through the trees, I spotted a mound built into the hillside, covered in moss and so obscured by vegetation as to be barely visible. As we came closer, the mound transformed into a stone structure with a round shape too well-formed to be other than manmade—a place that might offer shelter.

We broke through the vines draped across the entrance, and ducked in just as the storm struck with a flash of lightning and a boom that shook the leaves from the trees. Then the rains came.

As we huddled in the middle of the shelter, each bolt of lightning revealed more details. The vines that had blocked our way snaked down from the domed ceiling, obstructing the archways on three sides and obscuring a fourth in the back, a black hole leading into the hillside.

A jagged bolt flared nearby, followed by a resounding crack. A tree where we'd stood only seconds before split in half and fell, its shattered trunk still smoldering. A violent wind arose, driving the rain sideways, so the cramped space offered little protection. Reluctantly, I herded my charges into the rear archway that I now realized formed the mouth of a cave.

I hesitated before stepping through. In my haste, I'd lost sight of the rider. Now I beheld him, with his soft umbra highlighting him in the darkness. As he sat high in the saddle, unconcerned by the lightning, he appeared ensconced in a gap in the rain.

When our eyes met, I cast him a questioning glance, but he turned away and stared off into the distance, stone-faced except for the hint of a smile—a look I knew too well. His task was to guide me here, but the rules of the universe kept him from interfering.

My latest challenge. The magic is forcing me into the cave.

No more than three steps inside, all light faded. I unsheathed my enchanted sword, but a greater power overwhelmed the glow from its blade, so we shuffled along in a darkness so deep that my eyeballs ached. The path felt smooth underfoot, but I urged the others to keep as much as possible in my footsteps.

A whimper came from behind—Hannah too afraid to go on. I reached out, urging her to grasp my hand, but with her fist too small to squeeze mine, she clutched my last three fingers instead.

Elizabeth followed with Matthias in tow.

Though the ground lacked slope, our breathing sounded unnaturally loud in the silence, as if an army of ghosts accompanied us.

Something in my hip pocket burned. I reached inside and pulled out the forgotten vial. The purple liquid within, which always emitted a faint glimmer, now pulsed with a luminescence bright enough to light our way. I squeezed it between thumb and forefinger and held it up like a beacon before us.

A hundred yards in, I stopped at a second archway, this one decorated with carvings of fantastic creatures: unicorns and dragons, serpents with fangs, and winged stallions. The familiar opaque haze rippled across its opening.

"What's that?" Hannah said.

Before I could respond, Matthias answered. "It's a portal like the one the wizard and I took to find you. The passage is scary, so you might want to take my hand."

Hannah eyed the portal, and then looked from me to her brother. "Where does it lead?"

The boy grinned with the false confidence of one who has experienced something once and assumed the next time would be the same. "You have to enter to find out."

I fingered the hilt of my sword, raised the vial, and stepped through, but when I beckoned the others to follow, something wicked blocked their way.

Curse the green rider and his quest. I won't leave them behind again.

But when I tried to go back, the same force stopped me from rejoining them. As with my expedition with the chronicler of despair, I was meant to go alone.

I motioned to the family to wait there until my return.

With a last parting glance—and a blind faith that the magic would once again reunite us--I headed deeper inside. As I trudged along, the vial in my hand became so hot I had to remove my tunic to insulate its base with the cloth. Soon, I caught muffled voices echoing off the walls ahead. I followed their sound until the path ended in an ornate chamber with a rounded ceiling, painted black with flecks of white to look like stars in the night sky. At its front, amber-colored curtains framed a darkened stage, forming a proscenium arch—a theater of sorts—but where the audience would normally sit lay an empty space... all except for a lone armchair in the center. I circled the chamber twice, searching for other options. Finding none, I settled in the chair as clearly intended—an audience of one.

With my footsteps hushed and my movement stilled, I focused on the voices coming from the stage. My mind took a moment to comprehend what my eyes presented. In the dim light, shapes and shadows pranced about, though I could make out no faces. It seemed a gathering of sorts, a ghostly cocktail party. On a hunch, I aimed the vial at the stage.

A purple beam sprung forth, serving as a spotlight. As I swung the vial around, unaccustomed to its use, it highlighted multiple scenes: friends and family from home, some from my present, some from my past, some still alive—I hoped—and some gone. In the midst of each, I stood among them, my old self in bathrobe and slippers, and hair beginning to gray.

I steadied the vial with both hands and focused on the nearest group.

Colleagues from work, system engineers all, huddled around a white board with a flowchart scribbled upon it, trying to fix a design flaw. My bathrobe-clad avatar toiled among them, gesturing to the board, grabbing the marker and altering the diagram, as I'd done so often in my career, eager to demonstrate my competence and impress others.

The next group sat around a dining room table, spread with a turkey dinner and all the fixings. At the center lay a harvest decoration, featuring gourdes and dried Indian corn, acorns and pine cones, and an assortment of autumn leaves, all embellishing a bouquet of dahlias, strawflowers, and forget-me-nots—the kind of Thanksgiving centerpiece Betty made each year to bring to my parents. My father sat at the head of the table, carving the turkey, while my mother fussed with young Michael and Helen, no more than eight and six years old. Next to me, my wife beamed at our children while clasping my hand beneath the table.

I swung the beam to the left, and its light revealed a different scene—Helen's wedding. The sound changed as well—music this time, the song Helen chose for the dance with her father. She approached me, sitting next to Betty at a table, and reached out a hand. I rose—still in bathrobe and slippers—and accompanied her to the floor, where father and daughter danced alone. In the light of the purple vial, the cheeks of my avatar shone wet with tears.

Another scene: another meal, this time in the dining room of our Lexington home. Helen and John sat at the table, adults now, with Helen bursting with child, and behind her Betty with one arm wrapped around our daughter. My beautiful Betty, her hair streaked with gray and crow's feet blossoming around her eyes as she smiled, still with the same spark I'd noted the day we first met on the train.

But something was amiss. Unlike the other scenes, I was nowhere to be found. My customary seat lay empty.

I rose from my theater chair and approached the stage, reaching out a hand to touch my dear wife, wanting to apologize for rushing off on this strange adventure, but when I came too close, the vial rebelled, bursting into a blinding flash and going dark.

After a few seconds, the spark rekindled, revealing a different scene.

This time, the faces came from the new world: Elizabeth and her children, the chronicler of despair, the wolf-headed boatman, the couple from Crix Haven, and others I failed to recall. In their midst stood my young self, a wizard tall and bronzed, more athletic than ever in my youth. In my hand, I brandished the enchanted sword, drawn and glowing.

I grasped the vial with both hands and tired to focus the beam on Elizabeth and her children, but as I gazed upon them, they became translucent, less substantial than my family back home.

Of course.

These people were not made of whole cloth, but conjured from my imagination, for that's the nature of magic. Without prior experiences, they could not exist, for I would have no conception of them.

Then it settled upon me, that moment when sounds silence and time stands still, that instant of clarity when you believe you can almost comprehend the universe.

What if the purpose of what we call life is to accumulate experiences, to gather memories sufficient to enhance our imagination, so that when we enter the forever dream, we've gathered enough to stitch together a tapestry more fascinating than reality?

The moment passed, and the scenes on the stage vanished. The vial blinked three times and grew dim.

With barely enough light remaining for me to find my way back, I cast a longing glance at the stage before retracing my steps to the portal.

After the storm ran its course, we left the shelter and rejoined our guide to search out a resting place for the night. The visions from the cave gnawed at me, and I breathed easier when the domed structure faded from sight.

As before, the green rider led us to the perfect campsite, this time a sylvan glade steps off the road, but hidden from view by a row of hedges so dense as to have been planted with the intent to conceal. The place offered all the necessities—a stream running alongside, plentiful kindling for a fire, a carpet of pine needles for bedding, and a canopy of leaves to protect us from all but the heaviest rain.

Only one anomaly made the campsite odd. In the exact center of the clearing, the pine needles had been swept aside and replaced by a sweet-smelling circle of rose petals, too small and impractical as bedding for mere mortals. Before me lay the kind of setting I might find in my novels, a place where mystical beings had gathered the night before.

Hannah approached without hesitation, though she stopped with her toes not quite touching the edge.

"A fairy circle," she cried.

I looked to Elizabeth to explain.

She smiled. "A story their father used to tell, a place where fairies slept. When surrounded by evil, he taught them a fairy circle would always protect them."

As dusk crept in, the stars broke through the clouds, casting their pale light on the clearing and contrasting with the gloomy cave. We ate our meal in silence, each of us digesting the events of the day and contemplating what lay ahead.

After we finished, the green rider allowed the children to feed one apple to his horse, their traveling companion these many miles, and then urged them to sleep.

The children set their bedding close to the fairy circle. With their daytime energy spent and surrounded by the scent of the flowers, their eyelids drifted closed, and they dozed off, safe and secure as only children can be.

Elizabeth and I hovered over them, watching until their breathing settled into its nighttime rhythm. We adults needed more time to quiet our minds. We plopped down on the soft ground, shoulders touching, and stared into the embers of the dwindling fire.

Elizabeth broke the silence first. "You haven't spoken a word since you emerged from the cave. What was it you found there?"

"Visions of people I used to know. People from this world, people from the other. Some I still care deeply about."

She grabbed a stick and poked at the fire, causing a branch supporting the pyramid to collapse, sending a stream of embers into the dark. We both followed them until they vanished into the night.

She turned to face me, her eyes reflecting the flame. "Were you ever married?"

"Yes... to the woman I saw in the cave."

"What happened?"

"She lives in another world."

"Do you miss her?"

I took the stick from her, stoked the fire to make it flare, and tossed it into the flame. "Yes... I do." A hint of a tear seeped into my wizard's voice. "Every moment of every day."

A night breeze blew through the glade, forcing us to rub our arms with our hands, but we drew no closer. Soon after, we retreated to our respective places on the pine needle floor, Elizabeth nearer her children, and me guarding the entrance to the clearing.

After she fell asleep, I rose, unable to join her slumber, and wandered off to find my guide. The horse remained tethered to a bramble bush, and I scanned the road for its rider. In the deepening shadows, I found him resting on a rock and whittling, nearly invisible in his dark green but for the umbra only I could see.

When he noticed me, he stopped his whittling and glanced up. "Are you pleased with your quest so far?"

"No. You promised me magic I might use to conquer evil. All you've shown me are visions that muddle my mind. Where's the villain for me to face, the enemy for me to vanquish?"

He sighed. "You may be my biggest challenge since the chronicler of despair."

The blood rushed to my face, and my fists tightened. "I? Like him? That poor spirit, drowning in misery? How am I like him?"

He held his wood carving up to the starlight. It appeared to be the head of a horse. Then he sheathed his knife and gave me his full attention. "Like you, he sought the source of suffering. Failing that, he asked to conquer evil. Only later did he settle for a better understanding of the causes of despair."

I pictured the hoary face, the mask of unending sorrow. "Why does he stay?"

"Because the longer you remain in this world, the harder it is to leave. I pray you don't stay as long."

I glanced back at the clearing where mother and children slept, a family that had come to believe in the wizard—a fantasy if there ever was one. "I pray for that as well... but I'm not ready to return. I want to make magic first. I want to use magic for good."

He strode up to the horse, who chewed away on the sweet grass with no concern for the problems of men. As he patted his mane, he craned his neck and gazed up at the stars, communing with whatever mystical authority set the rules for his magic.

After what seemed like forever, he turned back to me with a hint of worry clouding his features. "Very well. Get some rest. Tomorrow, I'll grant your wish, and we'll see how grateful you'll be."

Chapter 21 – Ambush

The next morning, I awoke to the twittering of birds welcoming the dawn. During my working years, I'd wake to a more jarring sound, the beeping of a digital clock. In response, I'd squeeze my eyes shut and fight a losing battle to ignore the alarm. Then, before confronting the day, I'd play a mind game—trying to remember whether I slept alone in some nondescript hotel or at home beside Betty.

Since retiring, my routine had improved. With no alarm set, I took my time before waking, to fix the night's dream in my memory so I might replay it throughout the day. But with the events in the cave unsettling me, I'd tossed and turned that night before drifting off into a dreamless sleep.

Now, with the chirping of birds in my ears, I wondered which world they sang in.

The whisper of children gave my location away. Michael and Helen were grown and off on their own, and due to the snow, Betty remained stuck at school. In my home world, I'd awaken alone.

I opened my eyes to find the others scurrying about, preparing to leave. Embarrassed, I scrambled to my feet, buckled on my sword and hurried to fill my pack. Minutes later, our small party joined the green rider on the road.

All traces of the prior day's storm had fled, leaving a blue sky and a trailing breeze that lent cheer to our journey. Wherever the rider might lead us, and whatever trial awaited, I could at least expect a pleasant day.

The pleasantness lasted less than ten minutes. Soon after the sun cleared the treetops, a rogue cloud ambled in from the north and blotted it out, casting shade on the trail. From nowhere, a gust blew in our face, sending dried leaves skittering toward us on the path, and a cacophony arose in the trees, crows cawing in alarm. Their cries were answered by other birds farther along, and again by those farther still, sentries warning of our approach. From what had appeared to be a still linden, a flock of blackbirds rose in a cloud and whirled away, fleeing a danger unseen.

I slowed my pace and eyed the way forward, with my right hand resting on the pommel of my sword.

No more than a few hundred yards ahead, the road bent to take advantage of a notch in a hill. The green rider trotted to the bend to scout out the way, but as he rounded it, his horse rose up on its hind legs and emitted a high-pitched whine—a cry of fear rather than a whinny. The rider tugged on the reins to regain control, whirled his mount around, and galloped back toward us, kicking up dust. But instead of stopping where we stood, he kept going, the animal's flank coming so close it grazed my shoulder and nearly knocked me down.

As he passed, he hissed in a voice too soft for the others to hear. "You asked to fight evil. Now's your chance."

The next trial.

I motioned Elizabeth and the children to fall in behind me, and strode toward the bend in the road, tightening my grip on the hilt of my sword. Though I believed this a fantasy realm where nothing could harm me, my heart pounded. As I turned the corner, facing due east, the rays of the morning sun streamed through the notch in the hill and mingled with the dust kicked up by the horse, blurring my vision.

I cupped a hand over my eyes and squinted, straining to see what had spooked the animal.

A man stood in the middle of the road, tall and so broad of shoulder, his feet straddled the wagon ruts on either side. The glare obscured his expression, but from his bearing, he seemed intent on blocking our way.

As I edged forward, the dust settled, and my adversary came into focus—a stout man, bare-chested and well muscled, but unarmed. Yet more alarming, he bore the head of a bull, complete with horns—not a mask like the wolf man, but with the head of a beast joined seamlessly with his torso.

I exhaled a long stream of air and assumed the posture of the minuteman.

He let out a roar, lowered his horns, and rushed at me, but when I unsheathed my sword, he pulled up and eyed me anew.

My magic is equal to his, my courage greater. I will prevail.

A sound like a buzz saw started up from deep within his belly and poured out from his snout, so loud the leaves on the trees quaked.

A gasp came from behind. I chanced a glance back to catch Hannah's hand fly to her mouth and her eyes dart from side to side as she pointed past the bull-man.

The hills on either side of the notch had begun to darken with shadowy shapes flowing down toward the road, similar to the gloom that filled the children's buckets. Yet this gloom was alive and obeyed the will of the bull-man—a shadow army.

If this world is an illusion like all of reality, why does the tip of my sword tremble?

I stood my ground as the river of gloom sped toward me, but wary of my blade, it bypassed me, flowing around my legs. Before I could sense relief, I realized my charges had no such protection.

"Run," I cried.

I fell back to give them cover, but the gloom flowed faster than Hannah could flee. I grasped her in my free arm and took off with Elizabeth and her son.

Behind us, the bull-man roared, not like a mindless animal, but more like a general commanding an army. The gloom spread around us as dark tentacles raced ahead, blocking our retreat down the road.

I set Hannah down. No choice now but to confront the demon.

Before I engaged, Hannah tugged at my elbow. "No need to fight. Come this way, back to the fairy ring."

To my left, the path to the campsite lay open, still free from the shadow. We turned and raced down it, not pausing until we stood at the center of the perfectly formed circle lined with rose petals.

Not a moment too soon, for within seconds, the shadows caught up and surrounded the ring. Bubbling and boiling around us, they emitted a sound like the moans of the damned, but true to the tales told by the children's father, they refrained from crossing the perimeter of the circle.

We waited all day under the protection of the fairies, held captive by the gloom. As darkness fell, images joined the moans, playing out like videos against the night. Rather than ghoulish scenes of torment in hell, they appeared as distortions of my own memories, an evil alternate reality. I viewed the waiting room in the hospital after Betty's surgery, but this time the doctor told me the cancer had spread. Matthias once again fell into the clutches of the wolfman, but this time Hannah was taken as well, and rather than suffer in silence, the two cried out for help. I rummaged through the rubble of the earthquake as before, but this time I found a broken body with a bloodied hand scratching at the air. Helen screamed in the throes of labor, crying out for me. Each of these apparitions begged me to grasp their outstretched hands, but always they lay out of reach, beyond the boundary of the circle.

We stayed all night trapped in the ring of flowers. While the children slept, Elizabeth and I stood arm in arm, not to ward off evil, but because the circle offered too little ground for adults to lie down.

Morning brought no respite. The taunting images vanished, but the shadow army remained, with their master waiting patiently at the edge of the clearing.

In the haste of our flight, we'd abandoned our provisions, including the water skins. Now, as the sun rose higher in the sky, I struggled to bring moisture to my lips. The blood grew hot in my veins at the thought of the children suffering from thirst. Back home, I'd heard too many stories of sorrow, from relatives and friends, from my parents and Betty with her cancer. Back home, the earth shuddered and people died. Back home, the news showed the evil men do every day. *Every day!* And what could I do about it? Could I protect Betty from the onset of some new disease, or shield Michael and Helen from harm? Could I ensure the health of Helen's unborn baby?

Like my own world, this place offered horrors as well, but in this young body and with my enchanted sword, I could shelter those I cared about from the storm. Here, when monsters appeared, I had magic to fight back. Here, I might battle the sources of despair and defeat them. Isn't that why I left the comfort of my study with its shelves of fantasy books? Isn't that why I asked my guide for this quest?

Time to act.

I drew my sword and stepped outside the circle. As before, the shadows spread before me, clearing a path between me and their master.

He glared at me with bloodshot eyes, but neither of us rushed to attack, approaching instead with a wary stride until we stood two paces apart.

A cry rose from behind. Elizabeth. "Hannah, come back!"

I kept my shoulders squared to the demon but turned my head to catch them out of the corner of my eye. Hannah had left the protection of the circle in an attempt to help, and the shadows, sensing a vulnerable victim, had slithered toward her, so close a single tentacle rose serpent-like to within an inch of her ankle.

Her mother snatched her back to safety before the shadow could strike.

The bull-man, detecting my distraction, lowered his head and charged. I tightened my grip on the hilt of my sword, my left hand joining the right. The blade burst into a flame brighter than ever, and with both hands, I swung.

The bull-man roared in agony. He flailed, clawing at his chest, and began to disintegrate— not like my guide, as sand scattered in the wind, but as a flash of golden light spread through the clearing. Wherever the light touched, the gloom disappeared.

After the cries of the beast quieted, and the glow from my blade faded, I scrambled to the top of a waist-high boulder to survey the scene. The calm had returned; The shadow army had fled. My head swam, giddy with the thrill of victory. I'd done it. I'd used magic to vanquish evil, but which exhilaration brought a flush to my cheeks and made my heart beat faster—defeating the demon, or protecting those I cared about most in this world?

Isn't this why I came?

A cry from behind shattered my triumph—Matthias screaming, "Wizard!"

Back in the fairy circle, the children knelt by the limp body of their mother. Hannah stroked her arm in a futile attempt to awaken her, while Matthias cradled her head in his lap and begged her not to leave like their father.

Tears streamed down Hannah's cheeks. "My fault. I only wanted to help. We almost made it back to the circle, but a shadow caught the tip of her finger. And now this."

I looked at where she pointed. Elizabeth's right hand had turned gray, like the hem of my bathrobe when touched by the shadow in my study. As I watched, the gloom spread past her wrist to her forearm.

I lifted her into my arms and carried her to the stream, where I tried to wash away the gray as if it were a muddy stain. I tore off a strip of cloth from my tunic, dipped it in the cooling water, and tied it around her arm, a finger's width above the gray.

The progress slowed, but the gray remained.

I spun around, heel to toe, making small circles, wanting to scream at the surrounding hills.

How has my quest come to this?

I walked back in my mind the path I'd traveled: the gloom factory, the village, the castle, the dark spirit. Where was my guide, who had advised me at every turn? Might he now show me the way once more?

I found him at the bend in the road where the bull-man had first appeared, sitting astride his horse and staring into the distance. He neither flinched nor met my gaze until I grasped his waxen arm.

"Don't you care what happened here?"

He yanked his arm away and pulled on the reins, turning the horse to face me. "This is your quest, and I'm only your guide. If you need help, ask, and I'll do what I can."

No way could he cure this woman. He was a guide, not an actor in this world. Yet he might empower me if I posed the right question.

"Do I... possess the ability to heal her?"

"You requested magic to fight evil, not to heal."

"But there must be something I can do. You have to help."

He closed his eyes, communing with the powers that ruled the universe. When he roused, he swung off his mount and stared a long moment at the road ahead. At last, his shoulders heaved, the motion of a sigh without sound. "Very well. Hoist her onto the horse and follow me."

With the help of the children, we draped Elizabeth across the saddle.

As he led her away, I asked, "To where?"

A grimace overtook his smile, and he uttered these words: "To the House of Mercy, where the power to heal abounds."

Chapter 22 – Borderland

We trudged along at a sadder pace. Hannah and Matthias no longer frolicked about but slogged instead, as if bearing their buckets of gloom. With the two of them lagging behind, and Elizabeth unconscious, I traveled alone with my taciturn guide as he led his horse by the reins. Neither of us spoke a word.

We walked until Hannah and Matthias could walk no more, and though I longed to keep going for Elizabeth's sake, the children needed to rest. While the others drank from the water skins and munched dried pork from the saddlebags, I settled on a rock by the side of the road and buried my face in my hands. When my guide approached to offer a drink, I declined.

He hovered over me, not content to leave me alone. "Are you not pleased?"

I glanced up, my facing burning hot. "Pleased? How can I be pleased when the mother of these children struggles to find her next breath?"

He scrunched his brow, though it caused no wrinkles in his skin. "But... I provided what you asked for since your quest began, an evil demon and the magic to defeat him. You're finally the hero of your novels, a force for good. Why are you so unsettled?"

I formed my words like a parent explaining a complex concept to a child. "Is your magic so narrow, it can only defeat evil but not help those in need?"

"It's not *my* magic. The magic belongs to the universe. I channel it for your benefit, but you decide its use."

"Then, dammit, channel me some magic to help this poor woman."

He swept clean a space on the rock beside me and sat down. "You play frivolously with the rules. Magic is like a flame—powerful, but not to be trifled with. Every use comes with a cost. You think moving between worlds is simple? Each such move causes a ripple in the fabric of the universe. Too many transfers cause a storm, forcing the universe to protect itself at your expense. Do you understand?"

Now I scrunched my brow. Even in this young body, I could feel that the gesture caused furrows in my forehead. "No, I don't. Unlike you, I'm not an expert in the ways of the universe. Please explain in terms I can understand."

He withdrew his dagger and commenced to draw the sign of infinity over and over in the dirt at his feet. "I'm one of a few dozen guides, created by the universe to keep life from becoming... predictable. Only guides may move freely between worlds. We've been granted the power to bring those like you along, a way of expanding your perspective, but this business of moving between worlds is unnatural for those who quest, and cannot be sustained for long. That's why you feel a sense of displacement, of not knowing where you belong. That feeling grows over time, until you're forced to choose."

He kept drawing his marks on the ground until I reached down and stayed his hand. "Where *do* I belong?"

"That's for you to decide, but know this: the longer you dwell in this world, the harder it will be to return."

I counted the marks, now grown to sixteen. "Can I save this woman first?"

"Perhaps, but I make no promises beyond that."

I glanced back at Elizabeth's listless body. Matthias dripped water from his skin onto his mother's cracked lips, while Hannah rubbed the wounded arm with what appeared to be a sprig of white flowers. Despite the children's efforts and my poor excuse for a tourniquet, the gray had spread above the elbow.

My guide followed my stare. "The gloom grows worse. If you want to help her, you need to decide now. Do you want to proceed?"

A thought struck me, more like a skip of my heartbeat. "Before I say yes, may I visit my home?"

He replaced the dagger in its sheath and hovered over me. "Your muddled requests have diminished your allotment of magic. You have little left, but I can let you observe unseen using a lesser enchantment, much as you observed events with the chronicler of despair. I can let you view the other world for a few instants without becoming a part of it."

He waved a hand, and the kitchen of my Lexington home appeared. Betty sat at the table, sipping a cup of tea. Helen stood beside her, still full with child, resting a comforting hand on her mother's shoulder. Their eyes showed swollen and red.

My eyes welled up as well, and I shuffled closer and cleared my throat, but neither looked up. I waited a moment before speaking, but when I spoke, neither heard. I reached out to brush their cheeks, but neither felt my touch.

Hannah interrupted and the vision vanished. She held up the sprig in her tiny hand, a circle woven from the branches of a nearby tree. Its white flowers gave off an intoxicating scent.

"It's a dogwood necklace," she said, her voice cracked with tears. "My father taught me it has curing powers. He said it may heal any ill, but only if we wish hard enough. I tried, but my magic's not very strong, so I asked him to help."

"But your father's gone," I said.

"Oh, no... my mother told me angels dwell unseen in this world, and my father has joined them and watches over us. I'm sure he's watching now, but even with his power added, my necklace proved lacking. What we need is a wizard. Will you try too?"

She drew me to where her mother lay and offered the necklace to me.

To please the child, I accepted the totem, squeezed my eyes shut and pretended to wish.

Sadly, in this world, as in my own, wishing was not enough. Her mother never stirred, and the pallor on her skin remained.

An exhausted Hannah limped along with one arm draped around her brother's shoulder, but she refused to stop.

"How much farther?" I said to my guide.

"Not far. You'll spot the access at the crossroads ahead."

He pointed to where the road forked—the main path proceeded to the right, while a secondary trail branched off to the left, the latter's entrance marked by a statue of an angel praying over a fallen child.

True to his word, less than a hundred paces down, a building loomed, but some enchantment confounded my view. Like a mirage in the desert, light flickered around its edges, hiding its actual form. I squinted, trying to focus, and the scene steadied, but only for an instant before changing again. The vision resembled the prizes I found in Cracker Jack boxes as a child, the ones I called wiggle pictures—images that wavered and changed as you wiggled the card or altered your point of view. These prizes tickled my fancy, creating the illusion of motion with the slightest tilt of the head. *Flip*—a stationary eagle flapped its wings. *Flip*—a dragon opened its mouth and breathed fire. I suspected somewhere hidden in my attic lay a shoebox full of them.

This illusion was different, life-size and real. One instant, I'd behold a glass and steel building with sliding doors at its entrance—the look of a hospital back home. Ambulances jammed the canopied driveway, each marked with a cross, and nurses in green scrubs bustled about, triaging the patients and transporting them on white-sheeted gurneys. Then, with the slightest tilt of my head, the picture flipped into an older structure made of roughhewn stone, more like a Tibetan monastery. Here, ox carts bore the sick and lame, and hooded monks rolled them away in wheelbarrows.

The children perceived the latter.

"Healers!" Matthias cried.

"Healers?" I said. "How do you know?"

He pointed to the nearest monk, who wore an extravagant string of jewels around his neck. "He wears the healer's amulet."

His words made me re-examine the monk, knowing I had much to learn about this world. The necklace held smaller stones on either side—amber and quartz, with red rubies and green emeralds closer in, but most striking, alone at the center, hung a teardrop-shaped amethyst. When the healer bent to touch a patient, the purple light from the stone pulsed like the vial in my pocket.

Hannah rushed forward and tugged at the healer's robe. "Please, sir, help my mother."

The monk approached the horse, studied the sickly gray on Elizabeth's arm, and called for two aides, who placed her limp form on a barrow.

As they wheeled her away, I turned to watch. *Flip.* The barrow turned to a gurney, the monks to paramedics.

I followed them inside, querying my guide as I went. "What is it I'm seeing?"

"This place straddles all worlds, for the magic of mercy is universal. How you perceive it depends on where you're from."

Now I understood. Here lay a borderland, an intersection between worlds. But a borderland between where? This world and my home? Fantasy and reality? Or hope and despair?

We followed the paramedics/healers into a four-story high atrium, with potted palms embellishing its edges and glass elevators rising and falling. In the center, a woman played a harp, music to calm the concerns of the loved ones seated around her.

I closed my eyes to let the music calm me as well.

Hannah tugged at my tunic. "What are you doing?"

"Listening to the music."

As I turned, the harp silenced and the scene flipped. In place of the harp, a man stood at the center of an audience, sawing away at a crude instrument similar to a fiddle. He played a haunting melody, much like a Scottish reel, while the children danced to the tune. Young girls in frocks locked arms with boys in pantaloons, and they spun around three times before switching to the next partner.

Two worlds coexisted in this borderland. I wondered which one's magic would be stronger, and whether either would be enough to heal Elizabeth.

Hannah grabbed me by the thumb and pulled. "No time to dawdle. They're taking mother this way."

We followed the monks as they wheeled their patient down a candlelit corridor—the children, lacking the ability to view both worlds, perceived only their own.

At the corridor's end, a guard in leather armor stood before a wooden gate and blocked the children's way. "No young'uns allowed."

I glanced back at my guide and nodded.

He nodded back; no words needed.

I rested a hand on each of the children's shoulders, and knelt low so our eyes met. "Go with the green rider and listen to the music. I'll watch out for your mother."

No sooner did we pass through the gate than *flip*—the monks turned into paramedics. Fluorescent lights flickered overhead as they wheeled Elizabeth down a sterile corridor to an examining room and attached the appropriate devices to monitor her vital signs. A screen behind the bed displayed a rapid heartbeat and a respiration rate too fast.

A nurse pressed a digital thermometer to Elizabeth's temple until it beeped. "Hmmm...."

I took one step forward. "What's wrong?"

"Temperature—a hundred and three point five. I'll fetch the doctor."

A young doctor in a white lab coat bustled in and perused her chart before removing the sheet used to cover the injured arm. To my shock, in place of the gray gloom, a gaping wound appeared oozing puss.

"Sepsis," the doctor said, spinning around to the nurse. "IV antibiotics, stat!"

Moments later, an IV team hustled in, inserted a needle to the back of their patient's hand, and secured it with tape—applying a more familiar magic from my home world. As the liquid hanging from a metal pole began its drip, the nurse handed me the call button and left us alone.

I stared at the monitor and at Elizabeth's chest rising and falling, trying to match her breathing to the blips on the screen.

After a few minutes, she stirred. Her lids fluttered, her eyes opened, and she gaped at something behind me. "Dear husband," she said, with little breath to her words, "and mother and father too. But where are the children?"

A shudder ran through me as I recalled a different place and time.

My mother had a fear of dying in a hospital, so Betty and I did everything possible to keep her at home, staying with her during the day, buying groceries, fetching medicines from the pharmacy, and making meals. Over time, her condition worsened, and we had to bring in hospice.

As she neared the end, I stayed with her overnight, unwilling to leave her alone when she passed. Despite our urging, she'd stopped eating three days before. The day she died, I was sitting on a sofa in her living room, reading one of my fantasy novels, when her silver bell rang, the one she used to call me.

"Can you bring me some water, please?" The voice of the woman who had raised me now sounded more like a little girl.

"Would you like something to eat as well?"

She shook her head.

When I returned with a half glass of warm water, the way she liked it, she took two sips and her eyes widened at something over my shoulder, a look so compelling I had to turn as well.

Nothing there.

"Can't you see them?" she said.

"See who?"

"Your father and your baby sister."

My sister died of rheumatic fever at only two years old. I was five at the time, old enough to remember, but not to understand.

When I turned back, a chill passed over me, as if the air conditioning had kicked on. A half-smile crossed my mother's lips. She took two shallow breaths, whispered goodbye, and was gone.

Perhaps she'd encountered a guide like mine and had traveled to another realm. Perhaps she dwelled there still, battling dragons, or more likely casting healing spells like those practiced at this House of Mercy. And by using so much magic, like the chronicler of despair, she'd lost her ability to return.

Elizabeth's eyes rolled up into her lids, and her head collapsed back on the pillow. Knowing the dangers of a high fever, I pressed the call button. When the nurse returned, I demanded to see the doctor at once.

The same young resident sauntered in, looking annoyed.

"She awoke briefly but sounded delirious," I said.

"It's the fever. The medicine needs time to work."

"But will it heal her?"

He fumbled with her chart, a way to avoid eye contact. "I hope so. Her sepsis was far along when you brought her in. The antibiotic is usually effective, but there's no guarantee. We're not magicians."

I whirled on the doctor, trying to make him face me, and the scene flipped.

Now, a healer stood before me, hood lowered, revealing wizened features and eyes filled with compassion, a more comforting presence than the young resident. The purple gem in his amulet pulsed. "Can I heal her? Perhaps, but our magic is imperfect. If you wish to try, the magic will be stronger if performed by a loved one. Did you bring your amulet?"

"Can't I use yours?"

One eyebrow raised, and he eyed me curiously. "Surely, a wizard knows such charms are attuned to the person."

"Ah, yes," I lied. "In the strain of the moment, I forgot."

"Then you should fetch your amulet at once, and together we'll pray for your greater magic to work."

What could I do? Deny my wizardhood? I dashed back to the atrium to locate my guide, wondering which world he'd be in.

I found him standing with a handful of adults, watching the children frolic to the fiddler's tune. He bobbed his head to the rhythm, such that the feather in his cap swung to and fro.

I grabbed his elbow and pulled him aside, away from the others. "They say I need an amulet to heal her, but I possess no such charm. What am I to do?"

"Ah, a healer's amulet."

"Do you have one?

"Of course not, but I can show you where to find one."

He spun on his heel and stepped out at a brisk pace. Visions of my sword springing forth from the waves danced in my mind, but the ocean was far away, and we had no time to search for a jetty.

I called after him. "I hope this trek's not too long."

We raced through endless corridors, dashing from ward to ward, our passage made more disconcerting by the constant flipping between worlds. Here, a thoracic unit with oxygen tanks lining the walls. There, gaunt men and women suffering from the plague, with teams of monks chanting over them as they swung censers, sending clouds of incense wafting through the air. The vapors may have possessed healing properties, but they further muddled my mind.

Then we came to a broad archway with a bright light shining around its edges, almost like a portal. The view as we passed was difficult to describe. Here, the scene never changed—no flickering, no flipping between worlds. Instead, all existed at once in a corridor that was at the same time narrow and broad enough to hold all living things. Here, I encountered those not just from my home and my adopted world, but thousands of others, creatures great and small, dressed in the simplest and most exotic attire.

Moments later, the corridor opened into a vast chamber, much greater than that of the chronicler of despair. At its rear, a crowd had gathered, facing what appeared to be a glass wall.

With a hand to the small of my back, my guide nudged me forward.

I shifted sideways and slipped through, apologizing as I went. As I neared the front, I understood why we'd come, for no greater magic exists in the universe.

Before me lay an ocean of mercy, a sea of hope. Row after row stretched out as far as I could see, of plastic containers, wicker cribs, and baskets woven of straw. Each contained a new life born into this world, an infant who'd not yet learned despair.

Back home, I always yearned to find magic—the reason I rummaged around in eclectic shops and out-of-the-way alleys. But here, in this House of Mercy, babies entered the world in the usual way. Viewing them now, how had I ignored the magic? How had I denied the miracle?

A vision of Helen filled my mind, her belly ripe with child. When I left the comfort of my home for this quest, her due date was less than two weeks away. I tried to count the sunsets spent in this world, until I recalled the words of my guide. Two weeks may have passed back home... or no time at all. Helen might have born her baby, or the child might have grown to an age greater than mine. Or perhaps Betty, Helen, and their entire world had ceased to exist when I passed through that wooden door.

The murmuring that filled the hall silenced, and I realized the crowd had cleared before me, revealing a more classic portal into the place where the infants lay.

By its side stood a cowled figure in a black robe, the same monk who'd ministered to Elizabeth. He beckoned to me.

Together, we crossed through the portal. The usual weakening at the knees overwhelmed me, forcing me to spread my arms to my sides for balance. I closed my eyes and waited, inhaling through my nose and blowing out air through my pursed lips until the dizziness passed. When I opened my eyes, the infants had vanished, and I stood at the crest of a moss-covered hill, at the peak of which lay a single bassinette. A piece of paper tape stuck to its front bore these handwritten words: Baby Higgins. Inside rested not an infant, but an amulet like the one the monk wore, but with an amethyst twice the size.

I reached for the charm, eager to test its healing powers, but the monk stayed my hand. "You must first yield your sword."

"But—"

He shook his head. "Mercy may not coexist with weapons of war."

I fingered the hilt, recalling my pride when I'd vanquished the bull-man. Without a weapon, I'd be helpless when the next challenge came. Yet my heart filled with longing, not to vanquish another dark lord, but to help the ones I loved... in this world or the other.

I unbuckled my scabbard and let the sword clatter to the ground. Then I reached into the basket and retrieved the amulet, a weapon not of strength and pride, but of mercy and love.

Time not to fight but to heal.

I prayed this new kind of magic would lighten my load in this world... and show me the way home.

Chapter 23 – Homecoming

With trembling hands, I secured the latch, binding the amulet around my neck. Despite its apparent heft, the glowing amethyst barely tickled the hairs on my chest. No time to admire it. I took off at a sprint to the ward where Elizabeth lay.

The charm had a secondary effect—grounding me more in this world. The flickering diminished. Green tile gave way to stone-lined corridors, fluorescent lights to torches in sconces on the walls. By the time I reached Elizabeth's room, the world of my old life had vanished, but my heart skipped a beat when I peered inside.

Six monks surrounded her bed, chanting in unison, with a seventh swinging a censer.

My eyes began to tear, not from the incense but from the near-lifeless patient within.

The gloom had spread up one arm and down the other, and so far across her breast that the skin of her neck had turned translucent. The barest spark showed through the slits of half-closed eyes, and her face bore the color of chalk.

I shoved past the monks.

My sword vanquished the bull-man. My amulet will heal the gloom.

The chanting stopped, leaving only Elizabeth's labored breathing.

As I stood over her, the worlds flickered once more. In place of Elizabeth lay Betty, as she had on that Christmas Day following her final chemo.

Christmas that year fell on the eleventh day of her three-week cycle, the low point for her white blood count. Over the course of the infusions, she'd lost weight, so the skin around her cheeks sagged, making her eyes big like a child's.

During her treatment, I supported her as best I could, holding her hand through each four-hour session, cheering her up when she was down, and carrying her to bed when she could no longer walk. She became so frail that I had to steel my courage when I entered her room, fearing I'd show my concern and add to her worry. Always before, when despair dragged me down, she'd been the one to lift me up. Now she needed me, and I was determined to raise her from the depths.

That Christmas was a homecoming of sorts. Michael had taken to skipping holidays, a way of asserting his independence, but on this day, he came home to visit his ailing mother. Helen had gone off for her freshman year, and the holiday marked her fist time back.

Betty sat at the table, gripping the arms of her chair and putting on a brave face for the children, but she managed the facade only through the first serving of turkey. Before she collapsed, I carried her to bed.

Michael and Helen stayed at the table, hoping to maintain their holiday cheer.

After a while, I stormed out of the bedroom and insisted they bring their chairs and meals to join their mother. There, the three of us sang carols—Silent Night and Jingle Bells—in our well-intentioned but tone-deaf way. When we attempted one beyond our talent, we broke into laughter.

Angels we have heard on high....

Betty rolled onto her side, facing us.

Sweetly singing o'er the plains....

When we butchered the chorus, her expression changed.

Glo-oo-oo-ri – a....

She smiled.

I smiled too at the memory of that day, but only for an instant. The scene flipped, and Elizabeth lay before me once more.

I gathered my will, as I'd watched Hannah do with her totems, then clutched the amulet and closed my eyes. I envisioned not old Burt Higgins, but a powerful wizard who had overwhelmed the chronicler of despair with hope, rescued Matthias, and defeated the bull-man with his enchanted sword.

Now I will defeat despair once more, using the power to heal.

After a dozen breaths, I opened my eyes.

Elizabeth never stirred, and the gray remained.

I squeezed the amethyst harder, not only to enhance its magic but to threaten its existence.

Heal this woman or I'll crush you to dust!

Nothing changed.

I squeezed until my knuckles turned white and my fingers throbbed, and then let go lest my trembling rip the amulet from my neck.

Magic be damned.

I gazed down at this woman I'd come to care for, and pictured her children, robbed of their father before his time, and soon their mother as well. I leaned in and kissed her forehead. Her skin felt cold and dank, a precursor to death. Helpless, I lifted her limp body into my arms, hugged her to my chest, and wept, more than mere tears streaming down my cheeks, but full sobs that racked my frame.

There came a sharp intake of air too strong to ignore. The limp body convulsed, and Elizabeth began to breathe.

I lay her back down on the bed and fell back a step, no longer a wizard impressed by his power, but a fool in awe of a miracle.

The next day, the monks transferred Elizabeth to a more comfortable part of the complex, a section we'd call rehab back home. Here, the setting was less intense, and the children were allowed to stay with their mother.

They showered her with affection and brought so much food and drink she was forced to say, "Thank you, but please, no more."

The green rider joined us as well. I wondered, given all those he'd guided over so many lifetimes, did he take some pleasure in the turn of events? Was it possible he could feel?

By late afternoon, Elizabeth, still weak from her ordeal, begged us to let her rest.

Matthias and Hannah raced off to the entrance hall to cavort with the other children while a lady dressed in a gossamer gown played what sounded like a harpsicord.

The green rider and I settled on a bench, outside the patient's room.

I placed a hand on his shoulder and turned him to face me. "This time, I *am* pleased. You showed me hope and courage, and now you taught me the power of love. Thank you."

"Then why do your brows droop, and why does that wrinkle form on the bridge of your nose?"

I pulled away, surprised at his question, but when I searched my heart, a different image flitted through my mind. I glanced over his shoulder to a place far away. "Can you tell me, in the scene in the cave, why did no place setting grace my seat at the table?"

"Because you're no longer of that world."

"I don't exist there?"

He sighed. "Existence is such a complex concept. Even I struggle to understand it. What you saw was a vision of a possible reality, what will happen if the lines of time continue on their current course."

"Then I can still change it?"

"Yes, for now."

I grasped the jewel, which had healed Elizabeth, and stared into the purple stone, trying to pierce to its core. "If I return to my home world, can I bring this amulet with me?"

He stood and made three small circles before stopping to face me. "Always with you, the solution is magic, but my ability to channel magic for you is running out. Time for you to find magic on your own."

I spread my arms palms outward. "But how? Help me understand."

"Very well. Give the woman two days to regain her strength, and we'll travel again to a place where understanding abounds. We'll go to the House of Wisdom."

Then it struck me. I'd found courage and hope, but confusion still reigned. The next leg of my journey required wisdom.

Chapter 24 – The Grove

Two days later, the blush returned to Elizabeth's cheeks, but she remained too weak to walk, so we hoisted her onto the saddle—sitting this time—and set off with the green rider leading his mount by the reins. After one night's sleep in the fresh air, she grew strong enough to travel a bit on her own. While she was appreciative of the House of Mercy and the monks who'd cared for her, the chance to stroll outside energized her.

As she sauntered along, she beamed at the world around her. "I've been touched by death, and now I'm showered with wonder. The smell of the flowers, the green of the trees, the sun on my face, and being here with the children and you—all of these make me grateful to be alive."

By late afternoon, our guide ended our march for the day, though he implied our destination lay within reach. "Better to stop early and be well rested when you arrive tomorrow. You'll need all your strength for the trial ahead."

He loved to tease me with dire warnings, but I took his advice to heart, lying down for the night while the sun still shone, comforted that my companions slept safely nearby.

The next morning, with the sun not quite a glimmer on the horizon, he awoke me with a poke from the toe of his boot. "Time to rise. This is no day to dawdle."

During Betty's chemo, each day had dawned like a kick to the gut. At night, I'd escape to my dreams, flying on a winged horse through cotton-like clouds, or questing like a hero in a fantasy adventure. Then morning would come and shatter those dreams in a blast of reality: *Betty has cancer and needs me.*

Despite my guide's grim greeting, this dawn broke with a lighter touch. I'd been living the adventure, had faced a nightmare of trials and prevailed, and though my next challenge loomed, I sprung awake, eager to confront the day.

When all had washed and stowed their provisions, the green rider joined Elizabeth on his horse and set off at a trot, forcing the children and I to jog to keep up. To my relief, he pulled up after no more than fifteen minutes and lowered his passenger to the ground.

We caught up at a stone pillar marking a fork in the road. This impressive column rose to a polished point several feet above my head, but offered no indication of where the two trails led. The only hint seemed to be a crow perched on top facing the leftmost path, but no sooner did I read its intent than it hopped around and faced the other way. Then, as if to confuse me further, the bird turned head on, no longer favoring either trail, and glared at me with that one strange eye on the side of its head. At last, deeming me of no import, it squawked and flew off to who-knows-where.

I edged closer to study the two paths. The left one descended into a grassy vale nestled beneath the shade of a row of elms—an inviting place to travel. The other, more rugged, climbed steeply and angled into a notch between boulders, obscuring what lay beyond.

I turned to my guide for direction. "Where do they go?"

"They converge at the same spot but the approach differs. The low path is easy, a passage for the content, for those blessed with innocence and concerned only with the way things are. The high path is more... challenging."

"Why would anyone choose the harder one?"

"Because that path provides the answers you seek."

I glanced back at my adopted family. "May they accompany me this time?"

"Not on the high path. That's for the discontented like you, for those who insist on imagining the way things ought to be."

I cast a glance at Elizabeth, loath to leave her and the children behind, but reluctant to cause her more pain.

My guide answered my unspoken doubts. "They may not come with you. The high road is for those on a quest, not those who accept their place in the universe. For them, such a journey would be a curse."

"Why?"

"To reach the House of Wisdom, you must pass through the grove. Within, you'll encounter the four levels of understanding: the simple, accepting the world as it is; the complex, the struggle to discern the primal cause; the hint, wherein lies the meaning behind all things; and the secret, which you may comprehend but never put into words. You can rejoin the woman and her children if you make it through to the other side."

A shudder rippled across my spine. "*If* I make it through?"

"Some become lost in the grove. Some go mad. The fortunate ones who pass through take heed from what they've learned but vow never to return."

I eyed the high path. It appeared a challenging hike, but no more treacherous than some I'd taken with the children on a summer weekend. Yes, I hadn't attempted such a climb in more than a decade, but in this youthful body, I was certain to thrive. Yet I hadn't considered the risk to my mind. What if the high path confounded me and I lost my way? What if what I found drove me mad? I stared until my eyes watered, but learned no more.

Behind me, the children shuffled their feet and whispered to their mother, "Which way will the wizard choose?"

I turned to my guide. "Will they be in any danger?"

"No. As with most of your kind, they'll keep to the path they've been on their whole lives, a walk through the woods, and I'll stay with them to show the way."

I gazed up the high road, calibrating the change in elevation. "How long will it take?"

"For them, a morning's stroll. For you, time will not matter."

I kissed each of the children on the forehead and hugged Elizabeth, a lingering embrace. Our arms intertwined and held fast.

"Go with the green rider," I said, "and I'll meet you on the far side."

I started my trek as I had so often when hiking through New Hampshire's White Mountains. My assessment of the climb proved to be true, a trail cluttered with rocks and roots, and a slope that challenged the breathing, but no more difficult than the bridle path up to the Mt. Lafayette hut. I set a slow but steady pace, grateful for my newly acquired youth.

After about an hour, the trail plateaued. Rocks gave way to a grassy plain, and I paused to reassess the terrain. Ahead, the flat area ended at what looked like a wall of thunderheads, but these floated too close the ground to be clouds. As the scene came into focus, my heart raced—not storm clouds, but trees so dense, they appeared more black than green.

The grove lay farther away than expected, but with little slope and reliable footing I soon stood at its entrance. Before me, a shadowy path cut through the woods, forming a tunnel beneath a canopy of willows. Through the arched branches, an icy headwind blew, making me shiver.

Though I felt exposed without my sword, I raised my chin and stiffened my back.

No malevolence here. Just an ordinary trail chilled by the absence of sunlight.

I drew in a breath and stepped inside.

At first, I found little amiss. The branches overhead let through splashes of light that dappled the path, marking my way. The headwind stilled, further easing my discomfort, though in the ensuing silence, no birds sang.

Soon, the splashes of light diminished, leaving me shuffling my feet and stretching out my toes to feel the way. Despite the darkness, the swish of my boots through the pine needles soothed my mind, triggering a memory that made me glance up. Above me, the tangle of branches changed, now showing black and silky, like Betty's hair the day I met her on the train. The leaves gave off a familiar scent, and a sense of calm settled over me, a contentment I'd rarely known. The willows whispered that everything in the universe had a place, and it had been so since the beginning of time. All was created such that the pieces—both the good and the bad—fit together according to a plan.

As I proceeded, daylight dimmed further and vanished, leaving me in total darkness. Still, the contentment lingered, the change in lighting sinister only in that the branches of the willows had intertwined, letting no light through.

Then, a light from some unknown source illuminated the canopy as if an unseen hand had snapped on a projector. What had appeared like locks of Betty's hair floated to the forest floor, as they had that day she shaved her head before chemo. Scenes from my life unfolded on the remaining branches. At first, they were benign: Michael blowing out candles on his second birthday cake; Helen riding her bicycle for the first time without training wheels; or me taking the children to their first Red Sox game. Later, they matched the darkness of this place, displaying gloomier images: Betty's cancer; my parents' deaths; the wolfman snatching Matthias away; the gray creeping up Elizabeth's arm; lonely old Burt in his bathrobe glued to the TV as an anchor barked out the bad news. The chatter from the trees changed as well, more strident now, commenting on the gloomy collage: *the universe is a complex place, and contentment is for fools, those who squeeze their eyes shut and deny reality.*

My guide's warning echoed in my mind: the simple first, then the complex... the struggle to understand. My guard went up as the willows began to glow like a Fourth of July fireworks display. Each branch transformed into a filament of light expanding outward, forming a gleaming chrysanthemum. As they spread, the voices changed from chatter to screech, screaming a single word: *why?*

I tried to follow all of the petals at once, believing—hoping—they would lead to an answer.

No answer came.

The universe owed me no answer because I was too insignificant to understand. The whistles turned to chants, like the crowd at a sporting event, urging me on: go farther; go to where you never dared go before.

I tried, stretching my thoughts to their limits, like the dying strands of the fireworks. As their light spread wide and thinned, I thinned as well, becoming like a wraith—without substance.

At the edge of rational thought lay the answer, so near but impossible to comprehend, for existence is a complex thing, and to understand it, one must be willing to cease to exist.

The voices faded away like the dying embers of the flares. In their last breath, now little more than an echo, they urged me to release, to let go. *Only the universe matters.*

And therein lay the secret: *to continue to exist means to never understand; to cease to exist means to no longer care—the ultimate contentment.*

"Should I take the leap?" I asked aloud, as if hearing my own voice might help with the decision.

My mind recoiled. If I followed the flares to their end, I would belong to no world. I'd found the antidote to despair—oblivion—but as the flares faded into the darkness, I projected a light of my own. Faces on the branches above appeared, Elizabeth and Betty, Hannah and Helen and Michael and Matthias, and in the blurred background a child I'd yet to know.

I shook my fist at the trees. "No!"

The flares died out and the shadows brightened, revealing a path through the woods. At its end rose a gleaming structure, a double half-pyramid perhaps twenty stories high, with the bottom broad at the base and the top inverted, forming a narrow waist. Gleaming glass and silver steel formed its walls, constructed in a matrix of diamond-shaped windows.

I quickened my stride, eager to leave the grove behind, convinced I'd find a grand entrance around the next bend—marble stairs perhaps, guarded by statues of dragons or unicorns—but no such entrance appeared.

What if I've found a dead end?

At once, a gust kicked up, making the leaves in the surrounding trees rustle, and with the wind came another sound, windchimes trilling in the breeze. I followed the sound and there, half-hidden by an ancient growth of ivy, lay a door too humble for the structure, wide enough for no more than a single person to pass through, and visible only as a break in the diamond-shaped pattern.

I approached skeptically, since neither knob nor latch marred its surface, but as I extended my index finger, some unseen sentry spotted me.

The door slid open on its own, hardly making a sound.

Chapter 25 – House of Wisdom

Beyond the door lay a concrete tunnel with glossy red paint coating every surface—walls, ceiling, and floor. As I took my first halting steps, a ghostly reflection followed me on all sides. The glare of lights off the floor made it difficult to distinguish up from down.

Lights?

I glanced up. The solid ceiling was as unbroken by light fixtures as the floor. I scanned both walls. Neither held torches. Somehow this enclosed tunnel remained lit, not by the electricity of my home world or the flames of my adopted one, but by a new form of magic. I recalled the trek through the grove. Where the House of Mercy straddled all worlds, perhaps the House of Wisdom straddled none. Perhaps it belonged to the universe.

I passed through two oaken doors to a broader corridor, sporting a gothic arch overhead. Mounted on pedestals on either side sat a veritable menagerie of stuffed animals: crows and eagles, hawks and owls; racoons, weasels, and foxes; larger animals like bears and tigers, as well as some I failed to identify. The curator—if one existed—had sorted them by category to show off his skill in zoology, and positioned each so its eyes seemed to follow me. As I shuffled along, glancing from side to side, the flickering light from the unseen source reflected off their glassy stares and made them appear alive.

At the end of the exhibit, I rounded a corner and the corridor burst into a breathtaking view. I craned my neck like a child entering a circus tent for the first time, spinning heel to toe to take in the glass and steel soaring overhead. My twenty-story estimate seemed laughable now, for the bottom half-pyramid alone rose to at least that height. Crisscrossing through the center lay a network of switchbacks floating in the air, with no visible sign of support. At the top of each stood a landing bracketed by shelves of books.

I proceeded warily across the massive chamber, taking care to mind my footing rather than be distracted by the wonders above. The floor consisted of metallic squares one pace to a side, with black rivets at the corners. Once again, a ghostly reflection stared back at me from the shiny surface.

Do these panels reflect some illumination from high above, or are they themselves the source of light?

I settled my right boot on the lowest slat of the first floating switchback, and the platform never budged—steady, as if supported by granite rather than air. Convinced the stairs would support me, I began my ascent. Unlike the House of Mercy, which bustled with activity, no footsteps but mine echoed here. This library—if that's what is was—contained no librarians, no students... not so much as a weary traveler come inside to rest. My sole companions were row upon row of books, so many they might chronicle the accumulated knowledge of many worlds. At the head of each row hung a metal sign designating the stack's category: science and philosophy; music and art; gardening and quilting; humor and poetry.

Yet none offered the answers I sought.

As I shuffled between stacks, gawking like a pilgrim in a cathedral, the air laid so still, the millions of pages around me failed to muffle my footsteps.

Halfway up, I spotted a section marked history. I turned in to browse, thinking this a proper place to start. What in the past had transpired in this world? What had brought it to its present state?

The books disappointed. Along each spine, faded lettering announced the life of certain ogres and wizards, or the reign of kings with names too complex to pronounce, but at the end of the row, I found at last what I'd been searching for. On a teak shelf, newly polished and free of dust, stood a single volume, its cover facing outward. This leather-bound tome, its title blazed in raised gold letters, beckoned to me: *A Brief History of Our World, or How It Came to Be.*

I spun around, searching for a place to sit and read. Finding none, I resolved to stand, but no sooner did I take the book from the shelf than the space around me transformed. Walls appeared where none had been, along with an overstuffed chair covered with hide. On either side, massive fireplaces blazed with a fire more than twice my height. The flames cast shadows that tickled my imagination, reflecting red and making the floor below me ripple like lava—a setting I'd relish as a study back home.

I settled on the chair and flipped through the pages, reading of battles of old. I learned of demons who terrorized the people, and pure-hearted heroes who defeated them—fantasies of the sort that had long been my way to fill the empty spaces in my life. I discovered how the original dark lord had built the castle at Grim Harbor, and issued the proclamation ordering the wolf-headed boatmen to steal the children for war.

My ponderings were cut short when I turned the page to the final chapter. I blinked twice at the title: "The Legend of Albert, the Wizard."

I read aloud, tracing each word with the tip of my finger as my grandfather, new to the English language, might have done. The words recounted in flowery prose tales I already knew: my mysterious appearance in this world; the wolf-headed boatman snatching Matthias away; the journey downriver; my discovery of the enchanted sword; my encounter with the chronicler of despair; my victory over the bull-headed demon and his minions; my finding the magic amulet to heal Elizabeth; and the hints of a budding romance I had hitherto failed to appreciate.

My fingers trembled as I neared the chapter's end. Soon, I'd discover my fate.

When I turned to the last page, a white sheet glared back at me, revealing nothing but the reflection of the firelight.

My fate is yet to be written.

As I closed the book, a weariness overcame me. My guide claimed time had no meaning in this place, and now I understood why.

How long have I sat here and read?

I slumped back against the padded chair, my head too heavy for my neck, and soon fell into a deep sleep.

At first, I dreamed of wizards and dragons, and heroes and demons, like in the book, but soon my dreams became muddled and dark. Unlike my recent battle, this time the bull-man chased me and Elizabeth down an ever-narrowing canyon with sheer cliffs on either side. Soon, we needed to run single file, so I sent her fleeing ahead while I trailed behind, a rearguard with a drawn sword.

A fog streamed through the canyon, clouding my vision. I stared into the haze until my eyes watered, worrying my enemy would be upon me before I could react. For lack of sight, I held my breath and listened, hoping to detect the scuffle of his steps on the gravel. Nothing. Even the wind had calmed, leaving only a nameless fear.

When I awoke, I squeezed my eyes shut in hopes of letting the dream play out, but its ending eluded me, lurking like a phantom beyond my peripheral vision, just out of reach, there yet not there.

What if this dream is my true reality, my family gone, and me alone in a narrow canyon with insurmountable walls, forced to face my demons at last?

I pried my eyes open to find the fireplace flames burned low, now each a pitiful ember, shedding little more light than my dream. Both fire and dream had diminished to shadows that taunted my imagination, nothing more.

I struggled to my feet and resumed my search through the stacks.

Nearer the top, I found a section labeled fantasy, back home my favored genre. To my surprise, fantasy here referred to familiar books from my home world: Churchill's histories of the two world wars; *The Rise and Fall of the Third Reich*; Plutarch's *Lives*; Plato's *Republic*; the wisdom of Immanuel Kant. The list read like a syllabus for a dual major in history and philosophy. Perhaps, some weary librarian had mislabeled the stack.

Deeper in, topics were arranged by geography, and within these, progressing forward in time. I located the shelf for my home country and devoured book after book, a compulsion driving me on. What did the fiction writers of *this* world have to say about what I always believed to be history?

According to these authors, the Green Mountain boys' assault on Fort Ticonderoga was an act of magic, and Daniel Webster's speech in a remote Vermont field a fairy tale. The battle of Lexington with its shot heard round the world became an epic battle between good and evil.

And my town's twentieth century transition from farms to an incubator of technology—what some called the Massachusetts Miracle—became an actual miracle, propagated by an Olympian god.

The tragedy of 9/11 transformed into the machinations of a dark lord, an attack by the forces of evil. No villain in my novels had perpetrated such cold-blooded harm.

9/11!

I recalled what I still believed to be the real event.

My workplace had closed, and the school had sent the children home. They, like everyone else, were glued to the TV for the rest of the day, trying to make sense of what had happened. My son watched as if unable to distinguish between the news and a disaster movie, but Helen, always the more sensitive, sat cross-legged on the floor before the TV and sobbed. I urged her to join me on the couch and wrapped a comforting arm around her.

"No one will hurt you," I said. "You're safe here with me at home."

"That's not why I'm crying. I'm not afraid."

"Then why?"

"Because I never believed people could do such things. We read about wars in history class, but I thought we'd grown past that. Now I know what we're capable of."

A wolfman snatching innocent children; a bull-man with a shadow army whose touch can kill; terrorists opening fire on young revelers at a night club; fanatics flying planes into buildings.... Which of these was real and which fantasy?

What if all I believed to be real turned out to be fiction, and the here and now was reality? What if all I'd studied in school turned out to be fantasy, and the stories in my books were real?

At this moment, I had only one thing to cling to, the people in either life whom I'd touched.

I tore my eyes away from the book, fearing where the next pages might lead, and gazed up at the steel and glass soaring overhead. More than what I found in the grove, would what I read next turn me mad?

I'm trapped between worlds, with no guide for help. Perhaps I'm already mad.

I flipped the pages to near the end, discovering, as expected, a chapter about a simple man named Albert Higgins. It chronicled my family, the birth of my children, my marriage and career, Betty's cancer and her quest for an MFA, and the upcoming birth of Helen's baby.

Then, on a snowy day, as I awaited a call from Betty, telling me the results of her biopsy, I received a call from Helen instead. "Mom called and won't be here until tomorrow."

According to the book, old Burt held the phone from his ear for a second or more before replying. "Why didn't she call me?"

"She tried, but she couldn't get through."

"But I've been here all day."

The narrative went on about how old Burt's mind flashed back to the cancer. "Eighty-three percent survival at five years," the oncologist said.

But what happens after five years?

The book continued. With the weather too severe to venture outdoors, Old Burt headed into his study to lose himself in fantasy.

With trembling fingers, I turned the page.

> *After shutting the door, I cleared the clutter from the surface of the desk to make room for my elbows. Before cracking open the book, I leaned in to admire the shelf above the desk containing my favorite souvenirs – my collection of candles.*
>
> *I fingered the candles one at a time: the tall one from Jerusalem with the blue and white braided wax, used to mark Sabbath's end; the elephant from Dehli with the wick sticking up*

from his rump; an Irish rose with the wick nestled between its petals; the tacky Stratford on Avon skull I couldn't resist buying – poor Yorick, etc.; a winged cherub from Rome bearing an urn upon its shoulder; two parakeets nuzzling; and my favorite, the one molded in the shape of a boy.

I picked up the last and fingered its wax surface, recalling how I'd found it in a dusty shop off an alley in the old city of Prague. The shopkeeper had urged me to handle it with care.

"A unique candle," he said. "It will provide light when nothing else can dispel the gloom."

I suppressed a grin. I liked the look of the candle but found the storekeeper odd. "Are you suggesting this candle is magic*?"*

The man drew closer. "Magic indeed."

"Will it grant my every wish?" I asked, playing along. The sandalwood incense pervading the shop must have dulled my skepticism.

He chortled, an unnerving sound. "Not wishes. It's not a genie in a bottle."

"Then will it provide answers to my hardest questions?"

His magnified eyes glistened through coke-bottle glasses as he whispered these words. "Not wishes, not answers, but this candle will light your way so you may find the answers you seek. Of course, its success depends on the questions you ask."

I struggled to maintain my manners, though a part of me wanted to believe – the reason I searched in these alleyways.

As I groped in my pocket to pay, he gripped my arm and squeezed until he commanded my attention. "A warning: don't light it frivolously."

I pulled out a twenty euro note and extended it to him, but he withdrew the candle.

"Not enough?" I said.

"I cannot sell this boy alone."

I smirked. These tourist shops were all the same. "How much more?"

"Nothing, but a second piece must accompany it."

"But wait, *there's more," I mumbled under my breath, parroting a thousand commercials I'd seen on TV.*

The shopkeeper released my arm and shuffled behind the counter. From beneath it, he pulled out something concealed in the palm of his hand. As he extended it to me, his fingers spread, revealing a thumb-sized vial, which glowed with a purple iridescence, though it was unclear whether the color came from the glass or the liquid inside. The vial was capped by a black cork.

"Take this as well. No charge."

"Is this potion magic too?"

The shopkeeper's lip curled, a slight wrinkle, but less than a smile. "The candle will light your way, but in the moment of choosing, this will bring you peace."

I closed the book and fingered the purple vial, still warm in my pocket. No need to continue reading. The remaining pages would recount the appearance of my guide, and my passing through the portal to this world, no more.

The book would never reveal my fate, because my future lay clouded in scrim. Yet here in the House of Wisdom, I'd learned what I'd come for. None of us belong to a world, but instead we choose our own reality.

The end of my quest was clear—the moment of choosing—though I had no clue how to get there.

I scrambled down the book-lined ramps of the House of Wisdom to an exit at the rear. Outside, I blinked three times at what I saw—the sun hung at the same position in the sky as when I'd entered. Had no time passed as I scanned the volumes searching for answers? Or was I viewing a new day? In my long hours of reading, I'd suffered neither thirst nor want of food, but now a different hunger drove me on—to find my guide and query him about what I'd learned.

Ahead, a gentler slope marked the way back, and I loped down a mossy path much like the one the others had taken. After an easier jaunt than the trail leading up to the House of Wisdom, I spotted the horse grazing ahead, and a few paces behind him, my family.

The children raced up to hug me, and Elizabeth embraced me as well.

"We've only just arrived," she said. "Such magic to allow our paths to converge at the same instant."

Magic indeed.

Though I longed to hold the embrace, I released her and sought out my guide. I found him by an apple tree, picking fruit for his horse.

He showed no reaction to my return.

My breath came in short bursts, more from excitement than from the effort of the trek downhill. "I'm ready. Will you lead me to the moment of choosing?"

He gaped at me with that infuriating smile. "The moment of choosing is not a place but a time. If you were indeed ready, you would already be there."

I crumpled my brow, a recurring gesture whenever he tried to explain the universe to me. "Very well, a time not a place.... Can you help me get there?"

"No."

My voice rose in pitch. "Why not?"

"The answer is complicated. It's not for nothing we guides apprentice for six hundred years. We're limited in our duties by two rules. The first, I told you: a guide may not use magic to change the nature of the universe. And the second: we may in no way influence the choice of the one we guide."

"The choice?"

"All journeys end in a choice."

"And what will be my choice?"

"Ah, to tell you would be to influence it."

I glanced back at the family, worried what my choice would mean for them.

Perhaps a different approach. "Where does the moment of choosing take place?"

"At the mountain of choosing."

Progress, at last. "And where *is* the mountain of choosing?"

He shuffled over to his horse and offered a ripe apple to the eager animal. "It doesn't exist yet."

Again with existence. "When *will* it exist?"

I guessed the answer before finishing the question, and we responded as one: "At the moment of choosing."

I threw up my hands and sighed. "I give up. You're the guide. Show me where to go next."

He rubbed his chin as if scratching stubble, though his waxen skin lay smooth as a babe's. After a moment, he slipped a boot into the stirrup and, in a single motion, vaulted onto his horse. "Perhaps you're right. Not ready yet, but soon. First, you need to find perspective."

I gaped at him as he trotted off, and after gathering up the others, we followed.

Chapter 26 – The Room at the Top of the Tower

The next six days painted a collage of alternating moods. On odd days, sunlight streamed through gaps in the leaves, highlighting a path more moss than stone, a passage that reminded me of the Minuteman Park in Concord. That park was a place devoid of danger, where the most excitement would be to run into a neighbor who would smile and offer a cheery good morning though the time was well past noon.

On even days, clouds shadowed the trail, making it hard to distinguish a dip in the road from a rock. Roots the width of my wrist thrust up from the ground in unexpected places, threatening to trip us. Where the vegetation lay thickest, nearly invisible filaments from old spider webs cluttered the way and stuck to the sweat on my cheeks. On these days, I slogged rather than strolled, scanning for obstacles, worried a root might come to life and transform into a snake.

On the seventh morning, the gloom from the day before persisted. Had my guide been toying with me, biding his time while I searched for the elusive perspective?

Since the moment he appeared in my study, I'd trusted him. He introduced me to the village where I met Elizabeth and her family; he transformed me into a young wizard so I might rescue Matthias; he helped steer our tub down the river to Grim Harbor, tossed me the enchanted sword from the sea, and launched a journey where hope marched alongside despair; he humored my longing for heroism, providing both villain and victory; he brought Elizabeth to the House of Mercy, where I acquired the healing amulet and learned the power of love; and he set me on the path to the House of Wisdom to gain insight. Always before, he hinted at a purpose for each trial, explaining as much as my mortal mind could absorb.

Now, he'd gone silent.

At every stop, I begged him to tell me more, pleading for him to reveal how much longer until the moment of choosing.

His Mona Lisa smile twitched, no more than a curl at the edges, but all he said was, "That's up to you."

By that afternoon, when the odd day's pleasant weather had refused to return, a dread crept over me, a feeling I experienced as a boy each fall when the weeks of October dwindled. As the leaves fell and the days turned colder, an autumnal gloom would sneak in, bringing with it a steel gray sky portending the bleak winter ahead. I sensed it now, the southerly breeze shifting to the northeast, and I tugged my collar to my chin.

A squawking from behind spun me around—a flock of geese in chevron flight, but flying to where? To a warmer clime or to the place I missed more than ever? How I wished I had wings like them, or that these muddied boots had the power of ruby slippers to whisk me back home.

As the geese flew away, I tracked them until their honking faded in the breeze and they disappeared over the horizon, leaving nothing but a longing in my chest.

Once they'd vanished from sight, I lowered my gaze and rubbed my eyes at what I saw. A mere hundred paces ahead stood a massive, shrouded tower. Even lost in my ruminations, how could I have missed such an imposing structure? Had it appeared from the ether, as my guide had once appeared from the smoky glow of a candle? Yet this was no moment of choosing. Though the phantom loomed high, it was no mountain.

My guide reined in his horse and stared down at me. With a tilt of his head, he gestured toward the tower.

He sees it too. The phantom is no mirage.

Before he spoke, I blurted out what he was about to say. "My next trial, and I suppose you expect me to go alone. Can't they for once—"

He shook his head no.

I glanced back at my companions, who'd done too many farewells already. Elizabeth and Matthias nodded, resigned, but Hannah insisted on a parting hug.

When she released me, I slipped past her, forcing myself not to look back.

Moments later, I stood at the entrance to the tower. Its builder had constructed the base of rough-hewn blocks an arm's length wide, impenetrable but for a single archway so small that I needed to duck to enter.

The stone stairs inside lay rutted and uneven, as if worn down by an army of questers before me. Unlike the House of Wisdom, torches on the walls lit the way up, spaced so far apart that shadows danced on the steps between them. I trod with care, wary of what a slip might mean to one such as me—a wanderer of unknown age straddling worlds.

Twenty stairs in, I encountered the first of many chambers, each reminiscent of the exhibits at the Minuteman Museum, doorways blocked by a plexiglass panel, rooms to be viewed but not entered. But in place of a tranquil scene of Native Americans around a campfire, or colonial villagers at a tavern in town, these displayed images from my past.

The first showed a family vacation in Switzerland, with a younger replica of me posing on the pastured slope of a mountain along with Michael and Helen, ages nine and eleven. The three of us pointed to a cow while a laughing Betty aimed her camera and positioned us for the perfect picture. Each of us appeared lifelike, with every aspect of the wax figures—if that's what they were—displaying extraordinary detail: Michael's pre-teen disdain, Helen's eagerness to please her mother, and Betty's beaming face, more proud parent than photographer.

A dozen steps later, a different tableau appeared, this time a scene at the corner of our street on an early September morning—Michael waiting to board the bus for his first day of school. He cocked his head and mugged for the camera, hiding his apprehension from his friends. Little sister Helen clung to her mother's hip, clutching a stuffed bear. Even in wax, her lower lip seemed to quiver at the thought of her brother going off without her to who-knows-where. I stood arm in arm with Betty, the two of us smiling at the children, though with a trace of a tear in our eyes, a harbinger of the empty nest yet to come.

More steps brought more memories, reminders of the life I'd left behind. Only at the seventh landing did a scene from the new world appear, showing old Burt in his bathrobe at the village fountain, with one arm draped around Matthias and the other around Hannah. In this tableau, the figures were made by an artisan of lesser skill. The children's features were sculpted less sharply, and viewed through a smudged window, their eyes lacked spark.

Other scenes followed. A knight on horseback crossed a moat like on the tapestry hanging in my study, but again the image was blurred. The hooves of the horse lay cloaked in dust, and the lines of the knight's armor merged with the castle walls. Higher up, a darker memory appeared—a faded version of the wolfman snatching Matthias. Elizabeth's face was so poorly depicted, I struggled to distinguish anguish from joy.

Next came a room nestled in the shadows between torches. This one showed sharper than the others, an image etched in my brain. My wife lay in our bed, with her eyes open in slits and her face the color of chalk. I recognized the scene at once—Betty after her final chemo, her strength sapped and the joy sucked out of her by the poison the doctors had pumped into her veins. But who sat next to her? A man I hardly recognized.

That's me, old Burt in my bathrobe, holding her hand.

How haggard I looked. How helpless, loving her so much but lacking the magic to heal her. At the time, I prayed never to feel that helpless again.

I forced myself to turn away, and took the next flight two stairs at a time, arriving at what should have been my most joyous moment in *this* world—returning the rescued Matthias to his mother—but as before, shoddy artwork tempered the joy. The boy's mouth drooped at the corners, making it difficult to tell grin from grimace, and as he rushed to his mother's arms, the path he took was off. Had this wax figure continued in motion, he would have missed her and smacked into a nearby tree.

I began to understand why. Though the images from this world were fresh in my mind, their representations appeared less crisp, like the difference between how we recall a scene read in a novel and a scene lived. The memories from my home were curated by time, fixed and immutable. These others were artifacts of my imagination.

This world is less real.

I trudged on, not from exhaustion—my young body had energy to spare —but from weariness, as each successive scene tore at my heart. I lost count of how many I viewed, or the number of stairs I climbed. This tower, like The House of Wisdom, seemed unbound by space or time.

Yet the stairway *did* end. After a dozen more torches and double that many scenes, the final landing loomed, fronting the entrance to the ultimate room. This one differed from the others, with no plexiglass barrier barring the way, but rather a solid door with a latch.

What now? Could this be the source of despair, the one I might yet defeat to the benefit of all?

I fingered the amulet, and prayed for courage while cursing the loss of my sword. Then I blew out a stream of air, grasped the latch, and eased the flat of my hand against the door.

It creaked open two fingers' width, and I peeked through the crack. Inside lay a small room, no more than five paces square, with a desk set against the back wall. Dimness cloaked the scene except for the flickering light of a half-spent candle. Slumped over the desk sat a familiar figure in a rumpled bathrobe.

I snuck through.

The figure remained still, unmoved by my arrival. By his hand rested the vial I knew so well... unopened.

What sorcery is this?

I cursed my guide—and his universe—and spun around to leave, but as I did, I felt the brush of silk on my forearm. I glanced up to behold my dearest Betty floating by, wearing the turquoise satin nightgown she favored. I drew in a quick breath, as one does when meeting a ghost, but this was no ghost. I smelled her scent and heard the pad of her bare feet on the stone floor.

She stopped short, scanning the rafters of the room and sniffing the air, as if startled by a sound beyond her hearing. As she turned back, continuing toward the figure slumped over the desk, she passed right through me.

I am the ghost, not her, illusory and insubstantial.

I imagined my adopted family waiting below. From this height, they'd appear so small they might be toys. Then I caught sight of a photograph on a shelf, a picture of young Betty and Burt, resting on a rock ledge after a hike to the top of a mountain. Her head tilted in my direction, and she smiled at me as if to say: *How can you believe I'm not real?*

Perspective! Both worlds bring joy and sorrow, but only one is real.

The day before I lit the candle, Betty had called Helen rather than me. Helen assured me her mother had tried to reach me but couldn't get through, though I'd been around all day. Was she reluctant to share bad news over the phone? The simmering fear in my chest came to a boil.

What if...!

Perspective.

I would return to my world to confront my fate, good or bad, but just in case, I'd demand the healing amulet come with me.

I cast a longing glance at the picture, and at the wraith of my beloved Betty hovering over the slumped form at the desk. Then I turned my back on the scene and fled down the stairs.

Chapter 27 – The Tarralon Sea

As dusk settled over the land, the children's shadows lengthened, stretching out across the road like spidery giants. Before all light faded, the green rider reined in his horse and halted our party by a gnarled tree, its trunk similar to the one where the wolf-headed boatman had landed. In place of a hole, however, a knotty whorl bulged out, resembling the face of a curious man with brows raised and mouth opened in surprise. Behind it lay a narrow path, its entrance obscured by the tree.

The rider dismounted and turned to us. "We go through here. At the end, we'll find lodging and water, a pleasant place to spend the night."

As we shuffled along single-file, surrounded by thick vegetation, the wind stilled and the air became sweet with the scent of lilac and honeysuckle. What we could make out through the leaves above showed a sky so cloudless, it might have been a becalmed lake reflecting the first evening stars and the glow of a rising moon.

We trod the path in the light of that moon. Hovering like a beacon, it bleached the landscape, so as we passed between a stand of birch trees, their branches shimmered like strands of silver.

Eager to explore, the children raced ahead, with their mother chasing after them and calling for them to wait.

I lagged behind with my guide. When he dismounted at a break in the trees to gather grass for his horse, I confronted him. "I found perspective. I'm ready to choose."

He stopped his gathering and faced me with one eye narrowed and the opposite brow raised. "Are you? Then why do I see no mountain before us?"

"I'm ready, I swear. I want to go home... but on one condition. This amulet must come with me."

"Again with the magic. No. You're not ready." With a huff, he turned his back on me and led his horse down the path.

Uncertain of our destination, the others had paused to wait for our guide, and we proceeded together. A hundred paces later and around a bend, the trail opened into a clearing fronting a lake.

Dusk approached and daylight dimmed to its most magical time, casting a calm over the lake, so smooth that the trees on the far side merged with their reflection. Water bugs skimmed over the surface but made hardly a ripple.

When Hannah spotted the lake, her eyes grew large, and she cried, "Is this the Tarralon Sea?"

Elizabeth nestled a loving arm around her daughter's shoulder and smiled. "No, the Tarralon Sea is much bigger and far more beautiful."

Our guide tethered his horse to a nearby bush, and wandered off as usual to spend the night by himself, to commune, I supposed, with the universe. Mere mortals, Elizabeth and I gathered firewood, and began preparing the evening meal and, with some effort, corralled Matthias and Hannah to help.

As soon as we finished eating, the children begged to sit by the water's edge while their mother and I cleaned up.

She agreed, but with a stern warning. "Not too close to the water."

When we completed our chores, she cleared a spot for her family to sleep beneath the branches of a broad linden. As she gathered straw in piles for bedding, she urged me to check on the children.

I found them obeying their mother, but barely. Matthias stood on the shore skipping stones, while his sister squatted nearby, counting the skips aloud, with her boots so near the water that the ripples from his throws lapped her toes.

I headed toward the pond, dragging my feet through the dried leaves, making a swishing noise to alert the children of my approach. When I sat on a log by the water's edge, they paused their game and joined me.

The three of us slowed our breathing and stared as the water settled. With no hint of a breeze, the surrounding trees reflected off the surface like an upside-down painting.

After a moment, Matthias turned to me. "They say a wizard may take many forms and live in many worlds. How long will you stay with us? I asked the green rider, but he never answers my questions."

I laughed. "Mine either."

Hannah rested her tiny hand on my cheek and pressed until I faced her. Her dark eyes widened in that way she had when making up one of her stories. "But you must know. You're a great wizard who studied in the House of Wisdom. If you won't answer Matty's question, at least share with us what you learned. If you can't say how long you'll stay, tell us what will become of us when you're gone."

I stretched out an arm to either side and beckoned until they snuggled in close. "Well, here's one thing I learned. What happens to you will depend on your spark."

"Our spark?" Matthias said.

"Yes. Each of us is born with a spark inside, which flares and dims based on the events in our lives."

"Like what?"

"Like how well you skip a rock across a pond."

He hopped off the log and bounced on the balls of his feet. "Or my escape from the boatman?"

Not to be outdone, Hannah turned me back to her. "Or defeating the shadow army?"

Matthias squeezed my arm to regain my attention. "Or healing my mother's gloom?"

Hannah's gaze slipped from mine to the ground, where the heel of her boot was digging a hole in the earth. "Or my father's leaving?"

I nodded. "Yes, all of those and more."

Later that evening, after the children fell asleep, Elizabeth and I sat on the same log, bracketed on either side by a waist-high clump of seagrass. The moon had cleared the trees now and laid out a gilded pathway across the water, almost inviting us to follow. The warm night air hung thick and still, and in the distance, a mourning dove cooed for her mate to join her.

"What is the Tarralon Sea?" I said.

She laughed, slightly embarrassed. "Their father was prone to flights of fancy and would make up stories to please the children. His favorite tale was about the Tarralon Sea." She lowered her voice in an attempt to mimic her husband. "As a young man, I went off to fight a war against the evil lord. We finally prevailed, but at the battle's end, I'd become an empty shell and needed time to heal. I built a small boat carved out of an oak tree's trunk, made a mast of bed sheeting, and sailed off into the Tarralon Sea.

"After weeks of being tossed about at the whim of the waves, I came upon a tiny island—a miracle my small vessel found it in such a broad expanse of ocean. I understood then that the winds had steered me to that spot for a purpose. On that island, I met a beautiful girl, and we fell in love."

Her voice returned to its normal girlish lilt. "Both children would listen with eyes wide, no matter how many times they heard the story. Every time, at its finish, Hannah would ask, 'And where is that girl now?' He would pause for effect, keeping them waiting, before pointing to our little home and announcing, 'Why she's right here, in that cottage, your mother.'"

As she beamed at her sleeping children, the rising moon highlighted her profile with a soft glow. In its light, she became almost ageless, like Betty of today merged with the girl on the train.

She turned and met my gaze with an odd look, as if viewing a man who was at the same time a wizard and the ghost of her dead husband. "When I first saw you, I thought you appeared as my husband would have, if he'd lived into our elder years. I feared you chose such an appearance to tempt me, for it's well known that wizards may take on any form, but over time I viewed your arrival more as an act of kindness, the gift of remembrance. For my husband is gone, never to return, and the Tarralon Sea is but a story."

She stared out at the lake as if expecting to find her husband's image gliding across its surface.

When the silence grew long, I turned her back to me. "How *did* you meet your husband?"

"He came from a nearby village, having left his parents to prove he could be on his own. He was a quiet man, but proud. With the few coins he'd saved, he bought a cottage, with two goats and a few chickens. We met when I was fetching water from the fountain for my family. Soon it became a routine. We timed our trips so we'd meet each day, to sit on the stone wall and talk. Over time, we decided to combine our lives, and the result has been Matthias and Hannah.

The moonlight shifted and the gilded path now lay before out feet, framing our reflections in the water, a man and a woman, not young but not old either. As I stared, I recognized my younger self, full of dreams, and beside me a woman not so different from Betty. In the pale light, her hair took on an older hue, no longer raven as when I'd first met her, but with a hint of gray brought on by the passage of time. For in this world, as back home, the time that's given marches on like any other.

The words of Betty's song echoed in my mind:

Let us be lovers and marry our fortunes together.

After Elizabeth retreated to lie beside her children, I remained on the log, craning my neck to gaze at the moon now rising overhead. With no breeze, the seagrass stayed so still it appeared more portrait than plant, forcing me to reach out and confirm it was real. The blades of grass quivered under my touch, substantial and responding as things in the physical world should be, but I remained unconvinced.

Wiser men than I claimed reality is subjective, that we each view the world through our own lens. What if reality is more than subjective? What if that which we refer to as reality has no independent existence, but coincides with our consciousness, and once that consciousness ends, reality winks out like a dream? What if my guide possessed no magic at all, but merely allowed me to view my reality anew? Is that why the question of whether my home still exists was so difficult to answer? My home and this new world may be nothing more than creations of my mind, their existence dependent on how I perceive the universe.

If so, the existence of this woman who so recently warmed my side would rely on my continuing to dream, and that of my dear Betty would depend on my desire to return home.

Will I have the will to destroy the one to save the other when the time of choosing comes?

I had not met Betty on the Tarralon Sea, nor by a fountain at the center of a shire-like village. We met on a train in New Jersey, and after we married our modest fortunes together, we bought a small cape in a

Boston suburb on a street called Vagabond Way—the only lyrical aspect of our young lives. We were far from vagabonds, with no quests or magical guides, and with no demons to fight with enchanted swords, yet we fashioned a magic of our own. And I vowed to stay with her... through sickness and in health.

As I lay in my bed of pine needles staring up at the stars, the breathing of my fellow travelers quieted and the chirp of crickets arose, along with the occasional croak of a frog. Alone now in this confusing universe, my mind raced, pondering all I'd learned. I tracked the moon from its apogee to the horizon before my own breathing eased, and I fell into a deep sleep.

I dreamed I was back at the fountain in Graymoor on Nox, at twilight with the whole village gathering. When all had assembled, we marched to the river, somber and silent. As before, a torch appeared upriver, a glimmer in the dark growing brighter as the boat approached. As before, the wolf-headed man disembarked and waded toward the hole in the tree, but this time he called not for Matthias, but for me.

I edged toward the river fingering my enchanted sword, wary but unafraid. When I reached the bank, I realized in the torchlight that two boats bobbed in the water, one facing upriver toward the source, and the other out to the sea.

The wolfman pointed a bony finger at me and uttered a single word: "Choose."

"But where will they take me?"

He glared with unblinking eyes and snarled. "I'm forbidden to influence your choice." When I remained silent, he hissed his command once more: "Choose!"

Chapter 28 – The Cost of Magic

The next morning, as the first beam of sunlight struck my eye, I rolled onto one elbow and cast a glance around the campsite. Elizabeth snored softly beneath the linden, and my guide, as usual, was nowhere to be found, but the piles of straw where the children had slept lay empty. Concerned, I scrambled to my feet and scanned my surroundings. Through the path to the pond, I caught sight of the boy's slight form.

My sudden stirrings awoke Elizabeth, who sprung up as well and glanced at me with pleading eyes. "The children...?"

I pointed to the pond. "Matthias... and I assume Hannah as well."

A ground mist snaked about our ankles as we rushed to the water. To our relief, we found the boy searching for flat rocks, with his sister crouched nearby, hidden behind the seagrass.

The air lay still, with no hint of movement, as if the world held its breath. The rays of the rising sun lit up the pond, painting a trail of light more vibrant than the night before.

When the children saw their mother, they rushed toward her, the two of them speaking at once.

"We stayed out of the water as you told us...."

"...but couldn't we please go in?"

"The day's getting hot...."

"...and we've been traveling so long."

"Just for a little to wash off...."

"...the dust of the road."

"Couldn't we please?"

"Couldn't we please?"

Elizabeth sighed and relented, but only partway. "Very well, you may go into the water, but no deeper than your knees."

The children squatted by the shore, removed their shoes and socks, and waded in. As they broke the water's surface, the reflection of the trees splintered like shards of a stained-glass window, but reformed after they passed.

"Can they swim?" I said.

"Like fish. In the summer, they spend hours in the river Nox, with a current far more treacherous than this."

"Then why?"

Despite the warming air, she wrapped her arms around herself and rubbed. Her eyes took on a distant stare, as if remembering the gloom creeping up her limbs. "So much strange has happened since you arrived, forces at work beyond knowing. Better to take no chance."

We settled on the log and reveled in the children's laughter as they splashed around, although with the steep drop-off, they'd waded in only a few paces. Their play made ripples strong enough to slap against our seat, making a sloshing noise like waves against a boat in mooring.

When the sun's rays transformed the warmth to heat, the impatient children returned to their mother, the skin of their legs gleaming wet.

"Up to our knees doesn't go very far," Matthias said. "Why can't we go in all the way?"

Hannah gazed up at her mother from beneath her eyelids. "Our clothes will dry in the sun. Please let us show how we swim."

Elizabeth glanced at me, seeking approval.

The children's joy overcame my judgement, and I nodded.

As they plunged in deeper, their mother called after them. "Not so far."

Quickly, the water reached over their heads, but the pond's depth provided no challenge. The two swam with a confident stroke, proving their mother's boast.

As they dove into the murky water and resurfaced, teasing and taunting each other in their children's game, Elizabeth marveled at them. "I always said they swim as angels fly."

I grasped her hand and squeezed until she shifted closer on the log. "Hannah told me you believed in angels in this world. I need to know... after all you've witnessed, do you still believe?"

"No, I never believed. It was just a story to comfort a seven-year-old." She threaded her fingers through mine, all but the index finger, whose tip made gentle circles on the back of my hand. "But what of you? You said you came here to find the demon who causes despair. Do you still believe in demons?"

"No, not anymore. Perhaps I never did. It was more a simplistic wish than a belief, the result of reading too many fantasy novels. Now I'm not sure what I believe."

"Well, master wizard, who may dwell in many worlds and live many lives, here's what *I* believe. Though my one life has offered much joy and much pain, none has been visited upon me by demons or angels. The demons and angels exist within each of us. The demons prod us to despair, and the angels preach hope. The great choice is to determine which voice to listen to."

"And which voice would you choose?"

She glanced up to the trees and beyond to the heavens, brightening with the morning light. "That of the angels, of course." Her eyes drifted downward until they fixed on mine, and she squeezed my arm with a strength of certainty that surprised me. "When are you planning to leave us, wizard, and when will you tell the children?"

My mouth opened and closed, but no answer emerged. I swallowed and tried again. "I've made... no such... decision."

She let go and slid farther away. "But you will leave soon, because wizards always leave, once they've changed our lives."

"Hopefully, I've changed your life for the better."

"The better for sure, but have we changed yours?"

I fingered the amulet hanging around my neck. If I returned home, this charm would be the most important change. No longer would I rely on the magicians of my day, the doctors and nurses who knew less than they claimed. I would bring back magic of my own to heal the ones I loved.

I longed to assure her I'd changed for the better, but before I formed the words, we were interrupted by a scream.

In a rush of words, Matthias explained that a shiny object at the bottom had caught Hannah's eye, but when she dived under to fetch it, something went wrong. Her garment had snagged on a sliver of a shattered tree lurking beneath the surface. She fought to get free, but the more she struggled, the more the branch pulled her under. With each attempt, she surfaced for a briefer time, until she was gasping for air.

I raced into the water and dove in, grasped her around the chest, and swam for daylight, but every time I burst through and managed a breath, some sinister force dragged me back down.

Why can't I do this? In this youthful body, I should be strong enough to pull up the branch and the child.

Then I realized what held me back, a weight tugging at my neck. In the water, the amulet had begun to throb and grow heavier. The magic that had saved the mother now threatened to let the daughter drown.

I tried once more, kicking and stroking with my free arm, but to no avail. The child's life force was failing, and she would survive but one more try.

As we sank back down, I reached behind my neck, fumbled for the latch, and released the amulet. Now, with less weight, I swam upward again, child in my tight embrace as I kept track of the glowing charm sinking to the bottom.

I tried to mark the spot as it buried itself in the muck. *I tried.*

With no time to spare, I kicked furiously, pulling Hannah to the surface and dragging her to the shallows. Elizabeth and Matthias waded into the would-be Tarralon Sea and helped carry her to the shore, where she lay motionless on the sand. I propped her to a sitting position, pried open her mouth with my thumb and forefinger, and pounded on her back once, twice, three times, until a trickle of water dribbled out. The tiny shoulders shuddered, and with a gasp of air, she breathed.

The child's eyes opened, and I saw in them the meaning of hope.

Assured of her safety, I plunged back in, diving to the bottom and sifting through the muck. No sign of the amulet. Perhaps, in the perversity of magic, it had buried itself beyond reach.

When I staggered to the shore, my head hanging low from more than exhaustion, I found my guide standing there, still with that infuriating smile.

"Why so glum?" he said.

"I lost the sword, and now the amulet as well. For all my questing, I have no magic to show for my efforts."

"And yet you saved the child. Is that not magic enough?"

I gawked at him, and opened my mouth to answer, but before I could utter a response, Matthias cried out. His eyes rounded as he pointed at something over my shoulder. An unbelieving grin spread across his face, and his eyes took on the glow of someone witnessing a miracle.

I spun around to see what he had seen, and my eyes rounded as well. Where before only a flat plain stretched out beyond the edge of the forest, now a striking mountain rose in the distance, terrain too dramatic to have missed before.

The boy from the candle, my ethereal guide, edged closer, his usually unchanging smile broadening and almost causing a crease on his waxen skin. His fingertips brushed my arm, as human a gesture as an immortal could manage. "You're right at last. I do believe you're ready."

Magic or no, the moment of choosing had come. I'd go home to Betty, and if her cancer had returned, I'd do my best for her... for whatever the time that's given.

Chapter 29 – The Gathering

The view of the mountain lasted only a short while. Once we entered the woods, the horizon vanished, hidden beneath the branches of oak, maple, and poplar. Their foliage hung thick overhead, obscuring what was to come, but for now at least, a pleasant path lay before us. A blanket of green cushioned the ground, adorned here and there with yellow and purple flowers. The green rider's horse padded ahead, making a sound more like slippers than hooves, and we four pilgrims shuffled behind, our footsteps muffled by the spongy moss. Our whole party floated between the trees like wraiths, so insubstantial as to barely be part of this world.

After a time, gaps in the canopy opened to reveal patches of sky... and with them a glimpse of our destination. When we at last emerged from the woods, the rider reined in his horse, not to rest but to let us take in the view.

At the end of a grassy plain, the mountain loomed sharp and distinct. A treed slope girded its base, scarred on all sides by landslides past. Each of these scars pointed up to its source, a sheer rock cliff with a flat summit. White snow frosted the upper third, and in the glare of the afternoon sun, the tips of columns showed, appearing like the ruins of a Greek temple. A bonfire glowed at its center, giving the impression, from this vantage, not of a mountain, but of a massive cake with a candle on top.

I turned to my guide. "Is that where I'm supposed to go?"

The rider swiveled in his saddle and nodded.

"It looks insurmountable."

"You've overcome worse. From here, the cliff appears sheer, but on closer inspection, you'll find a series of switchbacks cut into its side, a moderate trail worn smooth by more seekers than I can recall."

I licked my lips and swallowed to moisten my throat. "Tell me, you who has guided so many. Am I the biggest fool?"

"That's not for me to judge. My role is to satisfy the longings of the one who lights the candle, so long as the quest stays within the bounds of the universe. No, you are not the first to question the foundation of that universe, but the answer is elusive. In the end, I neither approve nor condemn. The seeker must find his way."

He dug his heels into the horse's flank and clucked, setting the horse off at a canter. The rest of us followed at a slower pace, but in the open terrain, we never lost sight of the rider. Soon enough, we caught up and joined him at the base of the mountain.

I craned my neck, searching for the way to the top. "How long will it take?"

"A half a day, no more."

I glanced back at Elizabeth and the children, catching their breath from the dash across the plain. The blood coloring their cheeks drained as they eyed me and the mountain.

A hollow formed in the pit of my stomach, and I confronted my guide. "Give me a few minutes to make my farewell. Then I promise I'll follow you as I have since the start of this quest, all the way to its end."

His eyes softened, and his unblinking gaze met mine. "You have no need for a guide anymore. The path is well marked, and you know better than I where it leads."

I lowered my chin to my chest and rubbed my forehead. "I don't understand. I'm to make this final journey... alone?"

"No. For this last time, the others may come with you."

A grim smile crossed my face, and I turned back to the family who'd accompanied me through so many trials. My eyes misted.

"Thank you," I whispered.

Before rider and horse took their leave, Elizabeth grabbed some provisions from the saddlebags and stuffed them into her pack, as if we were going for a holiday stroll through the woods. Once she added warmer clothing for the children, the four of us gathered at the trailhead.

As I'd done so many times before, I stared up the mountain, assessing the trail. Concern over the difficulty of the hike mingled with anticipation of what lay at the top.

As we set off, daylight dwindled and the temperature dropped. Halfway up the treed part of the climb, a light snow began to fall, enough to dust the vegetation without making the footing slick. Elizabeth paused to dig through her pack and pull out jackets, while Hannah and Matthias spun about trying to catch flakes on their tongues. The snow enhanced what had become a surreal scene—a festive mood masking a somber affair.

As the children reveled, our pace quickened, and faster than expected, we traversed the gentler slope that formed the approach. Trees turned to scrub and scrub to scree, until nothing but rock remained. This close to the sheer face, the way forward revealed itself.

I traced the remaining trail, envisioning every switchback, though the summit itself had become shrouded in fog. As I took my first steps, a climb from long ago flitted across my mind.

When I was a boy of no more than six, my father took our family out to the Ponkapoag reservation, a recreational area at the foot of the Blue Hills southwest of Boston. Along with dozens of other families, we joined in the mid-summer ritual, cooking hot dogs and hamburgers on the grill, and enjoying our meal around a wooden picnic table.

By tradition, after a proper interval to digest, we children would go off to the bathhouse to change into our suits and go for a swim in the pond. On that day, however, a chilling breeze blew in, making the air too cold.

My mother broke out a deck of cards to keep us entertained, but my father had no patience for games. Instead, he shifted on the bench and rested a hand on my shoulder. "Well, Burt, how'd you like to come with me to explore?"

Why had he singled me out? I was the middle child, with a younger brother and an older sister. Nothing about me stood out. My father worked long hours six days a week, and on Sundays, he was often too tired to spend time with me, so going off alone with him was a dream come true. No way would I turn him down.

We wandered across a grassy field where people tossed frisbees and played fetch with their dogs, until the rest of the family shrunk in the distance. At the tree line, I expected him to turn back, but he kept going to a marker announcing the Skyline trail and one-point-two miles to the top of Big Blue. A shadowy path behind it beckoned, bracketed by a dense growth of spruce and pine.

My father was a practical man, not prone to whimsy, but the passage behind the sign seemed magical to a child. The trail stayed flat for no more than a dozen steps before rising and bending to the right, obscuring what lay beyond.

"Where does it go?" I said, sounding like Hannah confronting the portal in the cave.

His lips parted into a toothy smile, unusual for him, and he winked. "To find out, we have to climb."

We set off. Though the start of the trail presented a moderate grade, my heart pounded from excitement rather than strain—my first quest.

As with most mountains—though Big Blue was more hill than mountain—the summit forewarns you. Trees turn to scrub and more rock appears, until you burst out into the open and a magnificent view.

When we reached the top, that six-year-old thought he'd entered a fantasy realm, and since then, deep where that child still lived, I believed travel to such worlds was possible.

Now, as the last rays of the sun turned the cliff bright red, time slowed, and I viewed this trek like that hike with my father. When I sensed the top, I leaned into the hill and quickened my pace, breathing so hard I had to check my hands to see if I'd reverted to old Burt again. Elizabeth and the children trailed farther behind.

By the time I burst into the clearing, night had fallen, but the bonfire shed enough light to illuminate the scene. I hesitated at the edge, unsure of what my eyes presented. Before me stood a throng of people waiting in a spiral queue snaking around the fire. They appeared as all manner of beings—rich and poor, young and old, of all shapes and sizes, dressed in the familiar garb of my home and in the costumes of cultures unknown. As I gazed upon these fellow travelers, each shifted from one form to another: a Samurai warrior flickered into a middle-aged man in a business suit; a princess with a sword slung across her back transformed into a woman dressed in warmups as if headed to Yoga; a Mongol horseman with battle axe on his shoulder became a boy in jeans fresh off a sandlot baseball game; and a Chinese emperor bedecked in silken robes morphed into a lesser man who oddly resembled my landscaper back home.

All so different, but with one thing in common: each clutched a purple vial identical to mine.

The pilgrim at the back of the queue sported a scraggy beard and, with his right leg missing from below the knee, one of those new, computer-aided prosthetics. When the light flickered, he became a pirate with a wooden limb and a patch over one eye. A more impressive beard took the place of his sparse whiskers, long enough to reach to mid-chest had he not forked it into halves and tied off the ends with beads. His good eye caught me staring, and he beckoned for me to join him.

Drawn by his gesture, and the utter magic before me, I started forward, but pulled up short when I recalled my companions.

Not yet.

I held up a hand, signaling for him to wait, and turned to find Elizabeth and her children.

They huddled together at the edge of the clearing, looking more like a tableau in a wax museum than a living family. Their hands extended as they groped like mimes along an invisible barrier, searching for a way through.

As I crossed that barrier, they re-animated, and in the reflection of the firelight, I noted Elizabeth's cheeks had moistened. When I drew my fingertip from her temple to her cheek and wiped away a tear, she blinked as if awoken from a dream.

I gathered my will to speak the truth. "I'm sorry I have to leave."

She forced a half-smile. "I don't weep because you're leaving. I weep because...." The rest of her words caught in her throat.

"...because wizards always leave?"

"No. Wizards or mortals, we all eventually go. I weep because I feared you left without giving the children your blessing, and without saying goodbye to me."

I glanced back at the throng awaiting their turn at the bonfire. The pirate still beckoned, but Elizabeth didn't respond.

She doesn't see what I see.

I motioned for the children to come near. Both rushed toward me, buried their heads in my hips and squeezed with the kind of love a child should reserve for their father, an affection I didn't deserve.

"Do you have to go?" Matthias said.

"I'm afraid so, but I left you a gift."

Hannah looked up with glistening eyes. "What is it?"

I pointed to her heart. "The spark that burns within."

She probed at her breast. "I don't feel a spark."

"But you will someday, if you nurture it and let it grow."

I moved on to their mother, and we embraced. We held on for too long, but at last she pulled away. As our arms slid apart, unwilling to break off contact, our fingers intertwined, and we gazed at each other across the gap. I tried once more to pull her close, causing me to slip across the invisible barrier, but this time she came with me. At once, the light around her wavered like a mirage, and she turned translucent, all except for her eyes. As I stared into those eyes, the rest of her took substance, and like those seekers in the queue, she transformed.

I let out a gasp. Before me stood my beloved Betty, here in this fantasy world but seeming so real.

The moment of choosing has come, and I know what I need to do.

I went back to the pilgrims surrounding the fire, and joined the pirate at the end of the queue. As we progressed at this boundary between worlds, I flickered like the others, the change most evident in my hands, which alternated from young to old. My garb changed as well, from that of a wizard to old Burt's robe.

The line moved at a slow but steady pace. More joined behind me, and soon I reached the inner circle of the spiral, with a better view of our goal. As each pilgrim came to the fire, they made a choice: to cast away the unopened vial, or dump out its contents onto the flame. No sooner did they complete the task than their image firmed—one way or the other.

Too soon, those in front had chosen, and all eyes focused on me.

This close to the flame, my cheeks reddened and drops of sweat formed on my brow, but a greater heat burned at my side. I reached into my pocket and withdrew the vial, now throbbing with a life of its own, too hot to cling to for long.

As I inched to the bonfire, the whispers of those behind me silenced, the shuffling of their feet stopped, and I noted how I no longer flickered, a wraith no more, but the warring parts of me all substantial at once.

Finally, at the edge of the flame, I rocked on the balls of my feet and extended my arm, recalling the words of the old shopkeeper in Prague. "Do not open the vial until the moment of choosing."

I pressed my thumb and forefinger around the cork, squeezed, and twisted. When the cork popped free, a pungent odor filled the clearing, making the crowd draw back. I raised the vial over my head and poured.

At first, the bonfire fought the magic, hissing and spitting out sparks, but then it sent forth a purple flare... and everything winked out.

Everything.

Fire.

Flame.

People.

Mountain.

World.

And I floated alone in the dark.

Chapter 30 – A Fantasy World

As I stirred to the click of a door unlatching, my left hip throbbed, the result of old bones kept in an awkward position too long. Uncertain of what I might find, I stayed still, like the revelers during the nightclub attack, trying to survive by playing dead.

The door creaked. "Oh my. Are you all right?"

I opened one eye to find my forehead nestled in my arms on the surface of my desk. As light from the doorway drove away the darkness, I sat up, blinked, and eased my chair around.

Helen filled the door frame, full with child, her face pale and brows curved down in a lingering anguish. But for the expected concern for me, I might have thought she was about to deliver my grandchild on the spot.

"We've been so worried," she said. "I tried to call. Mom too, but we couldn't reach you. They cancelled her flight, but she was desperate to come home, so she took the eight-hour Amtrak from Ithica. I would have come sooner, but the train was delayed, and I didn't want her waiting at the station in the cold."

My knees cracked as I struggled to my feet. She offered me her arm, but I declined. "Just stiff. Been sitting too long."

I staggered to the kitchen where, to my delight, I found Betty at the table, hands wrapped around a mug of hot chocolate.

She glanced up, and her eyes brightened, though the rims remained red. "Burt! I...."

I stood over her and pressed my hand to her cheek. Its warmth brought a flush to her skin.

She covered my hand with hers. "I was worried."

"Me too."

Helen let out a yelp.

I spun around. "Are you okay?"

"I'm fine, dad. It's the baby. It had gone quiet out in the cold, but now inside, it's kicking like crazy. It's getting so strong."

"May I feel it?"

"Of course."

I rested a hand on her belly, and a rounded bulge responded to my touch.

Life in the making.

As I reveled in the miracle, the light streaming through the window caught my eye. The storm had ended, leaving dripping icicles hanging from the eaves and glazed branches glowing in the sun—a winter wonderland, so much like a fantasy world.

Could it all have been a dream?

I groped for the enchanted sword at my hip and, lacking that, the amulet around my neck.

Nothing.

Then I searched in my bathrobe pocket, where the vial still lay, and pulled it out.

The stopper was gone. The vial was empty.

Epilogue

I sat in the waiting room with Betty. To make the time go by, I asked her about the past month, about school and what kind of art she'd worked on. When she questioned me, I mumbled about my boring routine, how I read books and went for long walks, and how much I missed her.

No need to discuss her health for now. She'd been reluctant to call until the results came back, not wanting to worry me. At last, the news arrived. The biopsy turned out to be benign. Fate, it seemed, would be kind to us for now. We'd stay together and watch our grandchild grow. While I worried how long the calm might last, I'd learned to live in the moment.

The waiting ended when a nurse approached, her smile easing our concern.

"It's a girl," she said. "Mother and daughter are fine."

Betty and I exchanged expressions of relief. After thirty-one years together, no words were needed.

"You can see her now, if you'd like. Follow me."

She led us down a long corridor, lit with fluorescent lights. At the automatic door, wide enough for a gurney to pass through, she paused to push a metal square and the door opened. On the far side of this portal, a faulty overhead light flickered on and off, but Betty and I remained unchanged.

We passed the nurses station, where a nurse glanced up from her paperwork and directed us to room three-thirty-eight.

Three-thirty-eight. Where would that be?

With no one to guide me, I was on my own.

But this was a familiar world. My world.

When we reached the room, I offered Betty my hand, and she took it. We opened the door.

Helen rested in the bed, exhausted, a weak smile on her face, but one hand rose with a white tag on her wrist and gestured across the room.

At the far wall lay a plexiglass basket. As we approached, my eyes misted, and the little being inside transformed—from elfin princess to baby to angel.

Magic at last!

"Hope is the thing with feathers
That perches in the soul
And sings the tune without the words
And never stops at all."
Emily Dickinson

THE END

ACKNOWLEDGEMENTS

From start to finish, any novel worth its salt is an enormous amount of effort and would not be possible without a lot of help. Thanks to the team at Evolved Publishing, especially my editor, Lane Diamond, and my cover artist, Cindy Fan. But this book, written during one of the most difficult periods of my life, required much more. It would not have happened without the encouragement and love of my wonderful family and friends, too many to mention. Finally, I want to acknowledge my dear readers, who are, after all, the reason I write.

ABOUT THE AUTHOR

The urge to write first struck David at age sixteen when working on a newsletter at a youth encampment in the woods of northern Maine. It may have been the wild night when lightning flashed at sunset, followed by the northern lights rippling after dark, or maybe it was the newsletter's editor, a girl with eyes the color of the ocean, but he was inspired to write about the blurry line between reality and the fantastic.

Using two fingers and lots of white-out, he religiously typed five pages a day throughout college and well into his twenties. Then life intervened. When he found time again to daydream, the urge to write returned.

David now lives in the Great Northwest and anywhere else that catches his fancy. He no longer limits himself to five pages a day, and is thankful every keystroke for the invention of the word processor.

For more, please follow David Litwack online at:
Author Website: www.DavidLitwack.com
Publisher Website: www.EvolvedPub.com/david-litwacks-books/
Goodreads: www.goodreads.com/author/show/6439448.David_Litwack
Amazon: www.amazon.com/David-Litwack/e/B008JG79A6/
BookBub: www.bookbub.com/authors/david-litwack
Facebook: www.facebook.com/david.litwack.author
Instagram: www.instagram.com/davidlitwack/
Twitter: @DavidLitwack
LinkedIn: www.linkedin.com/in/davidlitwack/

MORE FROM DAVID LITWACK

David Litwack has produced multiple award-winning books and series across multiple genres, though all of his books carry elements of fantasy and speculative fiction, written in a literary style. Whatever your reading preference, you can always count on David Litwack for entertaining stories loaded with great characters. They might even stretch you a bit and make you think about life, love, loss, purpose....

On the following pages, we'll tell you a little about each of David's 5 other books to date:

1) Along the Watchtower
2) The Daughter of the Sea and the Sky
3) The Seekers #1: The Children of Darkness
4) The Seekers #2: The Stuff of Stars
5) The Seekers #3: The Light of Reason

We know you're going to love them.

ALONG THE WATCHTOWER

A tragic warrior lost in two worlds.... Which one will he choose?

WINNER: Readers' Favorite Book Award - Bronze Medal - Fiction Drama
WINNER: Pinnacle Book Achievement Award - Best Literary Fiction
FINALIST: Beverly Hills Book Awards - Military Fiction
FINALIST: Massachusetts Book Awards - Fiction

The war in Iraq ended for Freddie when an IED explosion left his mind and body shattered. Once a skilled gamer as well as a capable soldier, he's now a broken warrior, emerging from a medically induced coma to discover he's inhabiting two separate realities.

The first is his waking world of pain, family trials, and remorse—and slow rehabilitation through the tender care of Becky, his physical therapist. The second is a dark fantasy realm of quests, demons, and magic, which Freddie enters when he sleeps. The lines soon blur for Freddie, not just caught between two worlds, but lost within himself.

Is he Lieutenant Freddie Williams, a leader of men, a proud officer in the US Army who has suffered such egregious injury and loss? Or is he Frederick, Prince of Stormwind, who must make sense of his horrific visions in order to save his embattled kingdom from the monstrous Horde, his only solace the beautiful gardener, Rebecca, whose gentle words calm the storms in his soul.

In the conscious world, the severely wounded vet faces a strangely similar and equally perilous mission to that of the prince—a journey along a dark road, haunted by demons of guilt and memory. Can he let patient, loving Becky into his damaged and shuttered heart? It may be his only way back from Hell.

"This is a book that deserves to be read." ~ ***Awesome Indies Reviews***

THE DAUGHTER OF THE SEA AND THE SKY

A thought-provoking look at the line between faith and fantasy, fanatics and followers, and religion and reason.

WINNER: Pinnacle Book Achievement Award - Best Fantasy
WINNER: Awesome Indies Seal of Excellence
WINNER: FAPA Gold Medal - Adult Fiction: General

Children of the Republic, Helena and Jason were inseparable in their youth, until fate sent them down different paths. Grief and duty sidetracked Helena's plans, and Jason came to detest the hollowness of his ambitions.

These two damaged souls are reunited when a tiny boat from the Blessed Lands crashes onto the rocks near Helena's home after an impossible journey across the forbidden ocean. On board is a single passenger, a nine-year-old girl named Kailani, who calls herself The Daughter of the Sea and the Sky. A new and perilous purpose binds Jason and Helena together again, as they vow to protect the lost innocent from the wrath of the authorities, no matter the risk to their future and freedom.

But is the mysterious child simply a troubled little girl longing to return home? Or is she a powerful prophet sent to unravel the fabric of a godless Republic, as the outlaw leader of an illegal religious sect would have them believe? Whatever the answer, it will change them all forever... and perhaps their world as well.

"Author David Litwack gracefully weaves together his message with alternating threads of the fantastic and the realistic.... The reader will find wisdom and grace in this beautifully written story."
~ ***San Francisco Book Review***

THE CHILDREN OF DARKNESS
(The Seekers – Book 1)

A thousand years ago the Darkness came – a terrible time of violence, fear, and social collapse when technology ran rampant.

WINNER: Pinnacle Book Achievement Award - Best Sci-Fi
WINNER: Feathered Quill - Gold Medal - Sci-Fi/Fantasy

"But what are we without dreams?"

The vicars of the Temple of Light brought peace, ushering in an era of blessed simplicity. For ten centuries they have kept the madness at bay with "temple magic," and by eliminating forever the rush of progress that nearly caused the destruction of everything.

Childhood friends, Orah, Nathaniel, and Thomas have always lived in the tiny village of Little Pond, longing for more from life but unwilling to challenge the rigid status quo. When they're cast into the prisons of Temple City, they discover a terrible secret that launches the three on a journey to find the forbidden keep, placing their lives in jeopardy, for a truth from the past awaits that threatens the foundation of the Temple. If they reveal that truth, they might once again release the potential of their people.

Yet they would also incur the Temple's wrath, as it is written: "If there comes among you a prophet saying, 'Let us return to the darkness,' you shall stone him, because he has sought to thrust you away from the Light."

"The plot unfolds easily, swiftly, and never lets the readers' attention wane... After reading this one, it will be a real hardship to have to wait to see what happens next." ~ ***Feathered Quill Book Awards (Gold Medal in Science Fiction & Fantasy)***

THE STUFF OF STARS
(The Seekers – Book 2)

If the Seekers fail this time, they risk not a stoning, but losing themselves in the twilight of a never-ending dream.

WINNER: Pinnacle Book Achievement Award - Best Sci-Fi
WINNER: Feathered Quill - Gold Medal - Sci-Fi/Fantasy
WINNER: Readers' Favorite Book Awards - Siver Medal - YA Sci-Fi

Against all odds, Orah and Nathaniel have found the keep and revealed the truth about the darkness, initiating what they hoped would be a new age of enlightenment. But the people were more set in their ways than anticipated, and a faction of vicars whispered in their ears, urging a return to traditional ways.

Desperate to keep their movement alive, Orah and Nathaniel cross the ocean to seek the living descendants of the keepmasters' kin. Those they find on the distant shore are both more and less advanced than expected.

The seekers become caught between the two sides, and face the challenge of bringing them together to make a better world. The prize: a chance to bring home miracles and a more promising future for their people. The cost of failure: unimaginable.

"In this YA sci-fi sequel, Litwack pushes his characters into new physical, mental, and emotional realms as they encounter an unusual, tech-based society. A grand, revelatory saga that continues to unfold." ~ ***Kirkus Reviews***

THE LIGHT OF REASON
(The Seekers – Book 3)

Orah and Nathaniel return home with miracles from across the sea, hoping to bring a better life for their people. Instead, they find the world they left in chaos.

WINNER: Pinnacle Book Achievement Award - Best Sci-Fi
WINNER: Feathered Quill - Gold Medal - Sci-Fi/Fantasy
WINNER: Readers' Favorite Book Awards - Bronze Medal - Dystopian

A new grand vicar, known as the usurper, has taken over the keep and is using its knowledge to reinforce his hold on power.

Despite their good intentions, the seekers find themselves leading an army, and for the first time in a millennium, their world experiences the horror of war.

But the keepmasters' science is no match for the dreamers, leaving Orah and Nathaniel their cruelest choice—face bloody defeat and the death of their enlightenment, or use the genius of the dreamers to tread the slippery slope back to the darkness.

"In this third installment, Litwack gives fans a plot both action-driven and cerebral. All around, a superbly crafted adventure. An enthralling finish to a thoughtful, uplifting sci-fi series." ~ ***Kirkus Reviews***

MORE FROM EVOLVED PUBLISHING

CPSIA information can be obtained
at www.ICGtesting.com
Printed in the USA
LVHW111004181119
637667LV00005BA/316/P

9 781622 534425